Volume One of

The Muse of Mischief

Trella

Cover image by
Derrick Briscoe Photography, LLC
www.derrickbriscoe.com

Published by
Catrina Briscoe Photography, LLC
www.catrinabriscoe.com

Have no friends not equal to yourself

~Confucius

THE EMPEROR BY THE SEA

"I swear! You look just like him! You even sound like him. Luckily though, you don't have his hair." The Muse of Mischief enjoyed teasing her old friend.

"Bah!" Emperor Bartala said waving his hand toward M, "You are only telling me this because you want me to return home, to distract me from the fun! I could not possibly look and sound like an Earthling theatre star. Wait, what's wrong with his hair?"

The Muse of Mischief laughed, she was having fun. Emperor Bartala, M's oldest friend, was a fun loving jokester from Ploosnar. He was someone who was actually able to understand and enjoy her mischievous side. They had known each other since they were children.

"I'll tell you what my dear Bartala. We will show you an image of Londo Mollari, and if you honestly don't think you look like him at all, I will enter the portal of your choice, and race you back here. BUT! If you concur, that there is a resemblance, you will return home to Ploosnar. Deal?"

Bartala lifted his fifth or sixth glass of Nekmid and tossed it back like it was a shot of Tequila. Nekmid was his drink of choice. It is a colorless alcohol that tastes something like spicy teriyaki sauce. It is awful, but somehow the taste of it grows on you. M guessed it was at least twice as strong as the spirits of Earth. Agent Brzko and M had been here for several hours, trying to convince Bartala that it was time to go home, back to Ploosnar. But he was having none of it. This was not the first time they'd been in this situation with the Emperor. The three had done a little planet hopping together before he ascended to the throne of Ploosnar. Bartala's wife, Empress Nalau, had asked for their help. Bartala is a betting man and he seems to have created the ultimate game here on the Planet of Portals.

They were in a small establishment in the community of Vassbr, seated outside on the shore of the Vassbr Sea. The weather was a perfect temperature, a light breeze blowing in from the water. The Vassbr Sea is a green the shade of emeralds. Bartala was being incredibly stubborn today, but M and Brzko were not in a hurry, this place was just too lovely. The Planet of Portals has three suns; two of them are very small and hang just below the main sun. They were slowly progressing toward the horizon over the sea. Their color was just beginning to reflect off of the water, it was stunning. After growing up on a planet with only one sun, seeing the reflections of three on the water still seems odd to M and Brzko.

The Portals here, in Vassbr, lead to random places, they are a little dangerous. A traveler could step through a portal and end up on the Black Sea Planet. If you couldn't swim, you'd be in real trouble. Or you could end up on Chyke 2C95, and that might be a little too hot for most travelers, considering the planet is pretty much covered with active volcanoes and Haplogawas. The inhabitants live underground in old lava caves.

There are tamer places on the Planet of Portals, for example Unilond where all of the portals lead to a habitable place in the Glion Galaxy. But a traveler has to pay a small sum to access these portals. There are even portals that lead to different times. The random portals here in Vassbr were free, and dangerous.

Bartala had started a betting game with weary travelers, but unfortunately for them, the game took much longer than they usually anticipated. Bartala would bet them that if they walked through the same portal together, he could return to this spot faster than they could. Whoever made it back first would collect the money or item of value that the game players had agreed to leave in escrow with the owner of this establishment.

"Hey wait a minute, how much Nekmid do you think I've had?" Bartala said, hitting the table with his open palm, doing his best to sound perturbed. "That bet means nothing from you two, because you are able to open your own apertures, travel through space *and* time, and return here immediately. But I do like your wit my friends."

As Emperor of Ploosnar, Bartala commanded the entire fleet of ships, unfortunate for the travelers he toyed with. Most of his unsuspecting prey had come to the Planet of Portals because they couldn't afford to travel any other way, and those that traveled via the random portals of Vassbr were often desperate, criminals on the run. Space travel for the masses was still quite slow compared to the immediacy provided by portals. But the portals were one way, so these unsuspecting betters had little chance of returning before Bartala. He only had to contact his fleet and await their arrival. It was still dangerous, but not nearly as dangerous as it was for the common traveler.

"All right then, show me this image of the Great Londo from Babylon 5 and I will consider returning to Ploosnar."

Brzko took his tablet out of his inside jacket pocket, unfolded it, and sat it on the table. He opened the database app, scrolled through the list and found Babylon 5, he scrolled through the character images until he found one of Emperor Londo Mollari, of Centauri Prime. He lifted the tablet and turned it toward Bartala.

Bartala jumped from his seat, knocking his chair over. He began stomping his feet, both of his hands flew up to cover his mouth, a feeble attempt at stifling his excitement. He emitted something like a scream. Brzko thought his squeal sounded just like that of a twelve year old Earth girl at a boy-band concert. Bartala started bouncing up and down.

"OK, you win, you win, you win! I cannot believe this. Tell me the truth you have altered an image of me, no? Oh I do not care this is priceless. This Londo even dresses as I do - beautiful coat with a jeweled medallion. And I want that hair! We have to go. I must return to Ploosnar and find a coiffeur. I need this image, please print me a copy."

"Of course Bartala, in fact we'll just take you back to Ploosnar with us."

"Brzko, you are just as witty as the Muse of Mischief! I do not need an escort back to Ploosnar. But I cannot resist the immediacy of your style of travel. I will contact my ship and tell them to return without me."

Brzko settled the bill with the keeper while Bartala contacted his ship. The trio walked a short distance from the bar, Agent Brzko and the Muse of Mischief had learned long ago that most beings were not comfortable observing the immediacy of their travel. Either of them could transport a willing being with them, they just needed to maintain physical contact.

The Muse of Mischief took Bartala's arm as though he were her escort, "Ready Bartala?"

The trio vanished.

~~~

The palace courtyard on Ploosnar is like no other. It is a tiered garden space, from the bottom step it looks like a vast mountain of marble stairs with a large landing every twenty steps or so. The main stairs are lined with trees that look sort of like palms, except they are blue, as are all plants on Ploosnar. The roinad on Ploosnar continuously regenerates which, given its value, is lucky for the Ploosnarians. They trade the valuable element throughout the Universe, distributing the profit amongst the citizens. Agent Brzko and the Muse of Mischief aren't sure what all of its uses are but it seems to be the key ingredient in everything from atmospheric filters to fabrics. The mining process is considered to be sustainable, done in a way that doesn't damage the planet or atmosphere. Something about the chemical composition of roinad and the attributes of the Ploosnar sun, cause the flora to be blue.

Brzko and M looked around, trying to take it all in. They never tired of Ploosnar. "I'm far too old to climb all these stairs." The Emperor said, sounding winded.

"Ha! We're the same age Bartala; perhaps it's the nekmid that interferes with your ability to ascend the stairs?" M fired back.

"It's so beautiful I don't even notice the climb." Commented Brzko as he drank in the beauty of the landscape.

"Uh-oh, here comes Empress Nalau, I'm going to be scolded." Bartala turned to face his wife as she walked toward him, holding out his arms to embrace her. "Hello my love, I have returned, will you forgive me?"

"My dear Bartala, why must you worry me this way?" Always demonstrating the class of an Empress, Nalau embraced her husband with grace, even though she was no doubt frustrated with him. They had officially joined many years ago, when Bartala ascended to the throne. But sometimes he still acted as though he were young and free.

Ploosnarians are one of the many species that look very much like humans. They all have disturbingly bright blue eyes. If you look closely you can tell that their necks are a little longer, as are their fingers and toes. They eat the same types of foods - with the exception of those derived from animals, Ploosnarians do not consume them - and breath the same type of atmosphere but they live more than twice as long. Maybe it had to do with them having three small hearts evenly distributed along their torsos.

"Friends, welcome to Ploosnar. Please stay, I would like a chance to properly thank you for bringing my husband home." Nalau left Bartala's embrace and now stood near Brzko and the Muse of Mischief. Brzko reached for her hand, removed his hat, and bent as he kissed her hand in the fashion of a proper Victorian greeting.

"It would be our pleasure Empress." Nalau giggled like a schoolgirl at Brzko's irresistible charm.

~~~

"I always forget how comfortable these rooms are, the purple is fantastic!" Brzko exclaimed.

The Muse of Mischief and Emperor Bartala had known each other since they were both adolescents. When he took the throne he made an official declaration that the purple guest rooms were reserved for the Muse of Mischief and Agent Brzko. This ensured that regardless of his location, as long as he was the Emperor, the pleasurable accommodations of the Ploosnar Palace were available to them. The entire palace looks like it has been carved from a giant slab of marble. The purple room is a large circular room with very high ceilings. The top of the room is domed, with windows on the sides of the dome let in wonderful natural light. Large flowing tapestries of purple, trimmed in gold, hang from the peak of the dome. They slowly billow, creating a dreamy effect. There is a large bed in the center of the room, round of course, with a luxurious looking purple quilt. Gold and purple pillows placed in the center of the circular bed. There is a side table along the wall opposite the door, curved to exactly match the curve of the wall. It looks like it has been made of the same type of stone or marble that the palace is made of. There is always a decanter with nekmid and two glasses on a crystal tray. Today there is also another platter with lusimis and what look like blue carrots. They even taste similar to carrots.

"Maybe we should retire here, I'm sure Bartala would be fine with us living here on Ploosnar."

"Retire, ha ha! I just don't see that happening. Resting maybe…. Besides, some day Bartala will surrender the palace to the next Emperor, hopefully his heir."

"To good rest." Brzko and M toasted and tossed back their nekmid. There was a knock at the door.

"Come on in." Brzko called.

"I'm sorry to intrude but I want to thank you, to thank you for bringing Bartala home again."

M stepped forward, making a small curtsey, and addressed the Empress "It's our pleasure Empress Nalau."

"You and Agent Brzko have been a great help to us on several occasions, and we need your help again. Our mining team discovered something odd out in the barren land and we'd like you to see it while you're here. After you've rested we'd like to take you there."

"I always enjoy a tour on Ploosnar; we'll be ready in a few minutes." Brzko said with enthusiasm.

"Wonderful, we shall meet you on the palace steps in a few minutes." Nalau turned toward the door to leave. "Wait, one more thing… who is Londo and why does my husband want his hair?"

Brzko and M both cracked up. "Show her the image Brzko." He was already ahead of her, taking his tablet from his pocket and unfolding it.

Empress Nalau showed almost the same excitement as Emperor Bartala when she saw the image of Londo from the Earth sci-fi series Babylon 5, bouncing up and down and waving her hands. The reaction was very unlike her.

"It looks so much like my husband! Now I see why he wants that hair, it's like nothing I've ever seen. But I like it. This is from some kind of Earth entertainment?"

"Yes, it's a science fiction show about a space station called Babylon 5."

"Well that's ironic, an infantile planet that does not yet know of the Universe creating a show with a character that looks like my husband! I will never understand why advanced beings like the two of you were hidden on such an archaic planet." Nalau said.

With that, Empress Nalau turned and left, leaving the Muse of Mischief and Agent Brzko to wonder is she knew anything else about their origins.

~~~

A short time later, the Muse of Mischief and Agent Brzko headed to the palace entrance. At the top of the stairs, just outside the front entrance there was a small crowd. As they approached the group Emperor Bartala jumped out and exclaimed "Do you like it my friends?!"

He had changed his hair; he now looked almost identical to the character Londo Mollari. If he didn't have the bright blue eyes and the Ploosnarian accent he could have passed for Londo.

"Well hello Londo," teased Brzko, "where is your sidekick Vir:"

"You watch this is going to become a trend. Every male on Ploosnar will want this hair, some of the females too I suspect. I owe it all to you, the only friend that can hold her nekmid."

"You're welcome Bartala, I enjoy having a worthy nekmid partner. Poor Brzko here usually has to keep up with me."

M and Brzko were having so much fun with Bartala that they hadn't heard the aircoaches approach. They look a little bit like Earth cars but they don't have wheels, they hover a few inches above the ground. Each one of the convertibles had three bench seats that went all the way across, there didn't seem to be a "driver's" seat. Instead there was a control panel accessible from the front bench seat.

Emperor Bartala and Empress Nalau made their way to the front vehicle, as Nalau climbed into the front seat. Bartala opened the second door and motioned to M and Brzko. They slid into the seat behind their hosts. Two of the palace guards took the seat behind them. Nalau had been working the control panel, entering the coordinates for their outing.

"I hope you enjoy the scenery. We're going to the barren lands where most of our roinad is mined." Explained Bartala.

The aircoaches departed from the palace. It didn't take long before they were in the midst of a dense blue forest. "I haven't been out this far in a long time Bartala. It's lovely, the blue is amazing…" M trailed off. She was struck by the beauty of the blue forest. The forest is a buffer between the city and the open land, or barren lands, as Bartala called it. Once they were past the forest, the aircoach was gliding above the blue sands with seemingly no effort. It seemed like they were in a convertible but there must have been a force field in place, there was no wind.

They were passing a large structure, far off to the right. Brzko leaned forward to address Bartala, "Is that part of the mining operation?"

"Yes, this is where we package unprocessed roinad for interstellar shipping."

As they neared the structure, lines of shuttle transports became visible. It looked a lot like an Earth trucking operation, except these were small space ships rather than semi-trucks.

Off to the left, still far in the distance, something was coming into view. "There it is" Nalau pointed.

It looks like a variety of junk spread around in a loose pile. The aircoach circled around the debris before landing. The remaining two aircoaches took defensive positions on either side of the landing party. Everyone on Ploosnar was well cared for and generally happy, but when you are an Emperor and Empress personal security is a requirement. The debris is spread over an area about the size of a football field. As M and Brzko slid out of the car they were speechless. They had no doubt that all of this debris was from Earth. The most intriguing artifact was a wooden sign partially buried in the blue sand. It was made of old weathered wood, and the text had been crudely burnt into it. The sign read "*Scorchbrooke Oregon, Est. 1857, Population 2*".

"What is this place, a dumping ground?" asked Brzko.

"That's what I thought at first," answered Emperor Bartala, "but I couldn't imagine how, or why, someone would transport such a variety of "junk" from Earth to Ploosnar. So I had security begin monitoring the site. It seems that these items just appear from time to time. My nanny told me stories of such space traps. But it was about the sending side, not the receiving side. The stories are folklore meant to frighten a young child into behaving."

Empress Nalau turned to M "This must be quite shocking. We are hoping that you will help us figure out what has created this place and why. It has not always been here, we don't know when it started, but we do know that it was not here in the last planetary imaging survey, that was done around 10 Ploosnar cycles ago."

"Of course, Brzko and I will help you figure this out. It's weird. Can you tell if everything is from Earth?"

"It looks to us as if all of it is from Earth, but we have had much less exposure to that planet then you two..." Empress Nalau trailed off as she slowly spun in a circle looking at the debris.

"We will need a little time to sort through the pile and look for clues as to the origin. The suns will be setting soon. If it's alright with you Brzko and I can return in the morning and start looking for clues."

"Yes, yes, that sounds fine. Let's return to the palace, I hope you will stay with us tonight. I want to prepare for a grand entrance at tonight's dinner. My "Londo Style" hair will be making its debut!"

The old friends shared a good laugh about Bartala's new hair, and then returned to the palace.

~~~

"Oh that's just sick!"

"What, what did you find?"Agent Brzko asked heading over to see what the Muse of Mischief had found in the debris pile.

"It's a naked Barbie Doll with a G.I. Joe head!" They both cracked up as she tossed it aside. Everything in the pile was from Earth. There was an odd mix of items, like the Scorchbrooke Oregon population sign, a Kitchen Aid mixer, a Toro lawn mower, a rusty infant swing, a set of army men, a few garden tools, and a dog collar. There were even a few folding chairs half buried in the blue sand.

"OK, so let's figure this out. Everything here is from Earth, right?" Brzko asked resting his foot up on the rusty lawnmower.

"Yes, it looks like everything is from Earth. Although not necessarily from the same time, everything could be from the same place. Emperor Bartala's security team has been watching for any movement in the area and no one seems to be traveling here, by aperture or ship. The junk just appears."

"Let's ask Bartala for the surveillance files when we return to the palace. If we look at them in say three hour intervals (a Day on Ploosnar was about 37 hours) we should be able to figure out if there is a pattern for the arrival times."

"We should start researching Scorchbrooke Oregon. I've never heard of it but there is something creepy about that sign. What kind of town has a population of two and why haven't we ever heard of Scorchbrooke. We need to find the place, it seems like the portal must be there."

"I'm a step ahead of you M; while you were playing with Barbies I had Lelelu start gathering information about Scorchbrooke."

"Then I guess you'll have plenty of time for playing with the army men Brzko."

"Ha ha, smart ass. Let's head back to the palace. I want to catch Bartala before he's had too much nekmid and I'm hungry again."

The Muse of Mischief and Brzko walked over the where they had left the Bisporks tethered.

Bisporks are four legged, semi-intelligent creatures kept as working pets on Ploosnar. They stand well over 10 ft tall and sort of resemble a dinosaur with fur. The humps in their backs make a perfect seat for a rider. They run incredibly fast and smooth, and they love to run. Because they have some intelligence and a vocabulary the rider "asks" them to take them where they want to go. They seem to enjoy having a rider to serve.

As M approached the Bispork she had ridden out from the palace it bent down and put its head right next to hers. "Hello my friend" she said as she rubbed forehead.

"Ahhhhhhhhh" M took the happy sound as a positive greeting.

"Will you please take me back to the palace?"

"Yeeeessssssssssss" the Bispork said in its grunting way. It lowered itself even further so she could climb on. M turned to see if Brzko was ready to go but he was having issues. His Bispork was shaking its head.

"What's wrong Brzko?"

"My friend here is a jokester. He says I need a code word!" Both Bisporks seemed to find this hilarious and let out a series of snot spraying grunts that were surely laughter.

"OK, nuf, go." Brzko's Bispork said and lowered itself so he could climb on. I guess he had gotten enough of a laugh at Brzko's expense.

They took off for the palace, racing across the open blue sands of Ploosnar. When they neared the city a few minutes later, the Bisporks slowed down a bit as they entered the forested region. That was just fine with M and Brzko because blue forests are not a common sight. Most of the plants look tropical, with large leaves and flowers.

With the Bisporks turned in at the stable they set out to find Emperor Bartala.

"You know you could have taken an aircoach instead of bisporks," Emperor Bartala said as they entered Bartala's sitting room "they can be quite unpredictable. Let's have a drink and you can tell me what you found today." Bartala was still sporting his Londo hair style; and because he favored the same style of clothing, it was actually a little disturbing.

"A drink sounds great, I thought you'd never ask my friend." as M was saying this as a member of the palace staff entered the room. He also had a Londo hairstyle. Evidently this was going to become a trend on Ploosnar. M considered the implications of showing them an image of the female Centauri characters from Babylon 5. Except for a long ponytail, they were bald. She decided to leave well enough alone.

SCORCHBROOKE, OREGON – POPULATION 1

Emperor Bartala had agreed that it would be a good idea to station a Gaznzulian surveillance team to watch the area, at least until they could figure out what or who was causing items to randomly appear on Ploosnar. The Muse of Mischief contacted Zri as soon as she and Agent Brzko returned to their home in Lincoln City, Oregon. Zri has been looking out for the Muse of Mischief since she was an adolescent.

Gaznzul is a small planet with a population of agamic beings. They provide security throughout the Universe. Gaznzulians are known to have the highest integrity, loyalty, and intelligence. Their technology is second to none. That, combined with their physical prowess, makes them the ultimate protectors. Gaznzulians project their appearance; when they are near humans, they look human when they are on Cazoova they looked like Cazoovians, hooves and all! Brzko once saw a Gaznzulian dead lift a Bispork after it fell on its rider. Considering how much a Bisporks weighs, that is an amazing feat. Gaznzulian security is expensive and worth every penny. Except... they aren't paid in pennies.

It is always easier for M and Brzko to work from their home base in Lincoln City. Reviewing the satellite images of the Scorchbrooke junkyard on Ploosnar, did not identify any pattern to the times of appearance. Both the timing and the items seemed to be random. The only item that had provided a clue to its origins was the sign from Scorchbrooke, Oregon.

M and Brzko were seated in front of their main communications portal. They were engaged in an interstellar communication session with Lelelu. "I've never heard of Scorchbrooke Lelelu, what have you learned so far?" asked M.

"I think Scorchbrooke is near the now semi-ghost town, Hardman, Oregon. There was a lot of activity in the area around 1870. Scorchbrooke was never an official town. Locals have heard stories about it, but it doesn't exist in any official records from Marrow County. It's said to have been in the mountains outside of Hardman, near a rocky outcropping that lies between Lucky Spring and Midway Spring. But if you cross Alder Creek, you've gone too far. The only written "record" I've been able to find is this letter that a man named Billson Blythe found with his grandfather's personal records. Billson lives in Pendleton now but after his grandfather passed away he came across the letter while he was cleaning out his grandfather's place in Hardman. It was written by his great-grandfather, also named Billson. I guess it was a family tradition for the first born son." Lelelu sent an electronic image of the aged letter to both Brzko and M's tables so they could read it for themselves. The paper had yellowed over the years, and the edges were mostly frayed. But the ink was still clear enough to read.

"My Dearest June,

I hope this finds you well. Things here is just fine, although I find being away from you very diffcult my darling. Our house is almost finished, we managed to get the roof on yesterday. Even though the winds was fierce. I still plan to come to Portland and get you from yer mother's house round early in May.

You gonna like Hardman, it is very quiet. Most folk round here are very hardworking and keep to themselves. There are a few other wives here so you won't be alone while I'm tending the fields or hunting. I hear tell they are opening a school down the way in Rawdog, we even have a saloon and two stores. I know you gonna be happy raising our family here.

Now I know you do not approve of time spent in a saloon. But a man can get a hot meal and good drink after a hard day working, so sometimes I admit I do frequent the saloon. I sure God gonna forgive me long as the house be done on time.

Yesterday I seened the strangest man I have ever seened sitting down the bar from me. His hair twas as white as snow and his eyes was black. He was hunched over the bar with a drink in his hand and my, his fingers was LONG. His clothes seemed normal nuff. He didn't speak to no one, just finished his drink and left. When he walked by it felt cold like twas someone dancing on me grave.

I asked Lefty (he's the saloon man) who he was after he left. Lefty told me went by the initials R.G. and that he had a secret place up in the mountains. He said he ain't never seened the place for himself but he hears it be a mine called Scorchbrooke and the only person he ever seen from there is R.G. What they mine he did not now, said R.G. keeps to his self. A few have gone looking for this Scorchbrooke, just curiosity I reckon, the first one was lost for a few days and finally made it back here to Hardman without his horse and unable to member where he been. But the second man never returned. His kin went out searchin for him but dint find him. They dint find Scorchbrooke neither, said they heared and seen weird things out there. So ever since then folk round here stay clear of this R.G. Ain't that somthin? We gots our own mystery man here in in Hardman.

Well darlin, I gotsta get back to work. I has ta finish bulding a house fer me n my famly.

Much love,
Billson

"When do you think this was written Lelelu?" asked Brzko.

"Well the school in Rawdog was opened in 1879, so it had to be just before that."

"It's amazing how much you can find out without even being on this planet Lelelu. You're a great detective."

"Thanks Brzko. Success lies in how you ask the question. I assume you two are taking a road trip, be careful and let me know if you need anything."

"Since modern day items continue to appear on Ploosnar, there must still be someone in Scorchbrooke. We'll keep you updated on what we find. Bye Lelelu." M terminated the communication and turned to Brzko, "Time for a little off roading adventure!"

~~~

The only downside to using apertures to move through space and time is that it's safer to know exactly where you're going, and there are limits to what you can carry. Since the Muse of Mischief and Agent Brzko didn't know exactly where Scorchbrooke, Oregon was, and they wanted to take enough gear to be ready for anything, they decided to travel by Jeep. And let's face it a little off road driving in a couple of Jeep Wranglers is fun. M always enjoyed a good 4x4 trip through the remote areas of Oregon.

Zri was on earcom link and monitoring their positions from orbit. Should he hear or observe anything of a threatening nature he, and his team, would arrive at M or Brzko's location almost instantly.

The Gaznzulian earcom links they wore came in handy whenever they were on a mission and needed to separate. M especially liked the emergency beacon feature. Just like the panic alarm at their house, the emergency beacon would summon Zri and his Gaznzulian security team. And since they always had a few undetectable ships in Earth's orbit, they would arrive within seconds.

Hardman was less than a day from their home in Lincoln City. They arrived in the ghost town early in the morning and just kept going. When they arrived at Anson Wright Park south of Hardman, there was still a chilly morning fog. With their Jeeps parked far from the few campers that were there, they got out to stretch and check the maps.

Taking a deep breath and then exhaling M declared "I just love the smell of these huge pine trees."

"I know, I think the fog makes them smell even better." Brzko took out his tablet, unfolded it, and called up the map of their current location. "Where do you want to start?"

M leaned against the hood of her Jeep facing out toward the forest, seeming to absorb the beauty. "Well I've been thinking about that. The lore of the 1880"s put Scorchbrooke here, at this rocky outcropping. But there are no roads close to that. So I'll approach from the North and park here at the end of Forest Road 033 and you can approach from the South and park here on Forest Road 146. Then if we use the drones to survey the area, we should be able to spot something. Once we get a visual, we can jump to that location and search on foot."

"OK, but I'm not crazy about the idea of splitting up. But I know what you're going to say…. We can cover more ground, and Zri is basically traveling with us." Brzko said.

Zri tried to reassure Brzko, "We're standing by Agent Brzko, and we can be there at a moment's notice."

"Thank you Zri. He turned back to M, "It looks like I have a little further to go but both roads look a little rough, so be careful M."

"You too Brzko stay in touch."

With a plan in place they left the campground, Brzko in the lead as they headed down Sunflower Flat Road. At the first intersection M headed north on Board Creek Road and Brzko headed south on Forest Road 022, until it intersected with Tupper Road.

As M hit Forest Road 033 it got rough. It was more like a trail than a road. Luckily she didn't run into anything the Jeep couldn't handle. There were a few washouts that left her boulder hopping on three tires, and the skid plates did their job a few times, but she was comfortable with all of that. It was a Jeep after all.

Brzko had farther to go but since he didn't encounter any washouts they arrived at their destinations at about the same time. "Hey M are you parked yet?"

"Sure am, I'm running preflight checks right now. How about you?"

"B-Drone is already in the air, I win!"

"Yes, you win Brzko. OK M-Drone is up. Here we go. This forest is just amazing, the trees are thick but I love these open areas."

Brzko and M began a typical search patterns. Both running east to west, back and forth, moving out and toward each other. Their drones were not typical Earth drones. They looked like Yuneec H520 six-rotor drones but they'd been enhanced with Gaznzulian technology. They could sustain a flight time of about 20 Earth hours and the camera was controlled with eye movements behind a pair of glasses. They used a control panel that looked like a normal Yuneec control panel but it had also been enhanced.

"M how close are you to 45.093206 by 119.451589? I found the rocky outcropping and I just saw someone with white hair moving in the rocks."

"I just got there, I missed the white hair but I see the rocks."

"OK, we know where we're going then. Let's pack it up and jump to the clearing just west of the rocks."

"Got it, I'll meet you there."

They packed up their drones and locked them in the Jeeps. They wouldn't need them now, because the remainder of the search was going to be on foot.

~~~

The Muse of Mischief was already in the clearing when Brzko arrived. "Hey there slowpoke, so you saw a person or being of some kind?"

"I had the camera looking straight down in the rocks and I saw the top of someone's head. But only for a second, then it was gone. But that doesn't make sense, there's nowhere for anyone to go, it's an open area."

"Now I'm really curious. Let's go!" She headed east toward to the rocky outcropping.

They were close, so it didn't take long to get to the rocks; they had walked all around each outcropping and hadn't seen any indication of an inhabitant. M and Brzko were able to communicate with looks and hand gestures while searching. They needed to maintain the element of surprise. They began working their way back the way they came.

As they rounded the edge of a large outcropping, something caught Brzko's eye. He stopped short.

"What, what do you see?" M asked quietly as she turned in the direction he was looking.

"Do you see that shimmer? Well not quite a shimmer but that boulder doesn't quite look right. It almost doesn't look solid."

"I see what you mean." M said as they both began to walk toward the boulder.

As soon as they were within ten inches of the surface they could feel air moving toward them. But how could air be rushing out of stone? Stone is a solid surface. It looked like a rocky surface, but at the same time it didn't look solid. Brzko took a tiny step forward and reached toward the stone. His hand passed through the surface, the facade disappeared, they could see into a large cave or room. The back was sloped as if it went deep into the hillside. They were still trying to process what they were currently seeing, as well as no longer seeing, when they heard an awful high pitched screeching sound.

"Heeeeeee!!!!! Heeeeeeeeee!!!!! Heeeeeeeeeee!!!!!"

Suddenly there was someone or something rushing toward them. It was all happening so quickly their reactions were automatic. M dove down in front of the creature, throwing her right shoulder into it as she connected. This knocked the wind out of it at the same time she stopped its movement and toppled it. Brzko was already above the being, holding it in place. Having strength, superior to that of Earthlings allowed him to easily subdue the being while it writhed around flailing. It was moving so quickly they couldn't quite make out what it was. It looked humanoid with white hair and black eyes.

"We aren't going to hurt you. Can you understand me? We will not hurt you. We just want to talk to you." Brzko repeated these phrases a few times, his calm patient voice and energy seemed to calm the being and it stopped struggling. Brzko had learned to project his calming energy to others whenever they were in a sticky situation. It always helped to defuse the situation.

"No hurt." said the being with white hair.

"No, we will not hurt you, I promise. If I let you get up will you stay calm and talk to us?" asked Brzko.

"Yas, yas, calm. Rogsaar calm."

Brzko moved to the side and took a knee next to the being. He took his hand and helped Rogsaar sit up. The Muse of Mischief knelt down beside them, on the other side of their new friend.

"Rogsaar, is that your name?" she asked.

"Yas, Rogsaar."

"I'm the Muse of Mischief and this is Agent Brzko. We just want to talk to you. Are you ok, do you need anything?" asked M.

"No no hurt. Yas, want go home."

"Where is home Rogsaar?" asked Brzko.

"Rogsaar here since small, no remember exactly where from. Think home called Myaad."

"How did you get here?" asked M.

"In that" he said as he pointed to the boulder that wasn't really a boulder.

"Is that a ship?" asked Brzko.

"Yas, yas ship of Rogsaars. The older Rogsaar bring me here when small. We watch funny species called... human." He said with a slight sneer. "The ship broked, cannot control ship to leave so stuck here."

"Was the older Rogsaar your parent?" asked Brzko.

"No, yas, a little, Rogsaars from hive, older ones care for younger ones. All in my group are Rogsaar. Older Rogsaar fell from cliff, slide all the way to bottom, not survive. I try to regenerate in stasis compartment but no work. Come I show you." in a flash Rogsaar was on his feet heading toward the rocky outcropping that wasn't really there.

Brzko and M fell in step behind him. But when they came to what appeared to be the surface of the stone, Rogsaar walked into it and disappeared. M and Brzko both came to a dead stop.

Rogsaar stepped back out and looked them up and down, "Ah, know what is. No, nothing here to hurt you, could lower the facade but no like. What if sky camera take image that minute?"

"Sky camera?" asked Brzko.

"I think he might mean satellites." suggested the Muse of Mischief.

Rogsaar stepped back into the facade, M and Brzko both stepped right up to the edge and leaned the upper half of their bodies past the facade. It was amazing; they were in the doorway of a large ship. The room was a triangular shape with a center structure that went from what seemed to be floor to ceiling. It contained multiple displays, some looked like the LED displays used on Earth, while others were made up of a series of lights and buttons. The lights were different colors, some flashing some solid. There were also several things that looked like switches, and knobs. The center structure was surrounded by a track or groove in the floor. There was something that looked like a stool mounted in the track. M wondered how Rogsaar could possibly reach the upper consoles; even standing on the stool wouldn't make him tall enough to reach them. After taking a few moments to absorb the interior of Rogsaar's ship, both M and Brzko were reasonably comfortable and stepped in.

"Welcome." said Rogsaar. He seemed much more comfortable now that he was sure M and Brzko had not arrived to hurt him. M estimated that Rogsaar was about six feet tall. He had stark white hair and black eyes. He appeared humanoid with the exception of the length of his fingers, and his eyes.

"Thank you Rogsaar. Your ship is quite impressive; we haven't seen a ship like this before. How long ago did you arrive on Earth?"

"Rogsaar small when arrive, here almost 200 rotations of Earth." he answered.

"So you're more than 200 years old?" asked M.

"Yas, yas, Rogsaars live very long time, maybe 300 of Earth rotations."

M continued the casual interrogation "Why did you come to Earth?"

"Myaad send out many Rogsaar ships. Watch planets, look for species can learn from, maybe trade. But humans no ready, still ride horses when Rogsaars arrive. Want desire go home but ship broked, try to repair but older Rogsaar perish. This his ship, not know to repair, try to use flashport for go home but something not work. Send things but not know if things getting to Myaad, not know where they go."

"We might know where the "flashport" is sending things. Tell us about some of the things you have sent." said Brzko.

"Things Rogsaar find in forest, belongings of juvenile human, something called Kitchen Aid, small machine, chair. Why humans bring things and leave piles in forest? It make this planet ugly."

"Yes it does. Some humans seem to like dumping trash far from their homes. We don't understand why they do this. There is a proper place to dispose of unwanted items. And on a planet that thrives on excess, there is much to dispose of." M said, shaking her head in disgust.

"Last item in flashport is sign say "Scorchbrooke", when trapped on this planet, older Rogsaar call this place

Scorchbrooke. Make sign." he said with a shrug. "If I send home maybe they know where to find me."

"Can you show us where the flashport is, how it works?" asked Brzko.

"Yas, what send?" asked Rogsaar as he sat in stool near the center console.

"You can send this." M said as she removed her scarf.

"Place on spot there." said Rogsaar pointing to a slightly darkened area on the floor about six feet from the center console. M followed his instructions and placed the scarf on the dark area of the floor.

The stool that Rogsaar sat on raised at least five feet to allow access to an upper control panel. Then it came down a few feet and slid through the track to the backside of the console. They could hear a humming sound coming from beneath them. A clear tube like structure came out of the floor and surrounded the scarf. The tube protruded from the floor until it met the ceiling. The walls of the tube seemed to be solid but not rigid. It looked like they could form themselves around larger items if needed.

"Ready to flash" said Rogsaar, as his stool moved along the track, returning to the original position. There was a brief flash of light and the scarf was gone. There was an audible beep, beep, beep… signal, as though the scarf were being tracked. Rogsaar was intently watching one of the control panels with flashing lights. The beeping stopped.

Clearly let down, Rogsaar turned to them and said "Another item send don't know where."

"It's OK Rogsaar. We're going to help you get home to Myaad. We just need a little time to work out the details. It could take a few days, will you be OK here? Or would you like to stay with us?" asked Agent Brzko.

"Scorchbrooke my home, here."

"One of us will come back and check on you. You can use this to contact us in an emergency." M said as she handed him an earcom link. "Just place it in your ear so you can hear us, press this button, and speak. We will be able to hear you."

"Yas, yas, press talk."

"Do you need anything? Do you have enough food?" asked Brzko.

"No, no need sustenance. Ship can still make." answered Rogsaar.

"OK, one of us will be back to check on you tomorrow." said M. She and Brzko stepped out of the ship, back into the light of the afternoon.

They walked a short ways from the facade before speaking. "When I get back to the Jeep I'll contact Emperor Bartala and give him an update." said M.

"Zri, have you heard of Myaad?" Brzko asked.

They heard his answer in their earpieces, "I've heard the name but I am not personally familiar with it, I will query our databases."

"Thank you Zri," Brzko said. "I'll contact Lelelu and get her started on researching Myaad. Zri, will you please keep an eye on our new friend? We wouldn't want anything to happen to him before we can get him home."

"Yes, of course Agent Brzko. We've started monitoring the area for any activity."

"I'll see you at home then M."

"OK Brzko, enjoy the drive, I know I will."

BIVOORS, DUMEERS, AND ROGSAARS OH MY

By the time the Muse of Mischief and Agent Brzko returned to their home in Lincoln City, Lelelu had already found a complete history of the planet called Myaad. With the Muse of Mischief at his side, Agent Brzko initiated an interstellar chat session with Lelelu at the main communications portal. Thanks to technology, Lelelu was able to work from her home on the Planet of Portals. She kept her own small ship, and could travel when she needed to. But she had to be careful about visits to Earth and other places with infantile inhabitants. Trelods are bright blue but otherwise look like humanoids. They don't have hair like humans and while that is easy enough to hide with a hat or wig, the bright blue skin is not.

"Hi Lelelu, I hear you've got some information about Myaad." Brzko said.

"Yes, this is really an interesting place. Myaad is a small, completely terrestrial planet in the same sector as Ploosnar. There is no surface water, what water there is can be found under the surface of the planet in aqueducts. It accumulates there after rains. The Myaads are traders. They operate on a sort of CBDR system - common but different responsibilities. They are made up

31

of three groups; Bivoors, Dumeers, and Rogsaars, one of which you've met. The Rogsaars are explorers and scientists, looking for new planets and new species to learn from and barter with. Dumeers handle pretty much everything else; retrieving fresh water from beneath the planet's surface, building and maintaining housing and other structures, growing, harvesting, storing, and preparing sustenance, and making sure there is adequate clothing, medical supplies, and anything else of a non-scientific nature. The Bivoors are the administrators. They kind of oversee things, but at the same time they stay on the same "level" as the Rogsaars and Dumeers."

Lelelu's image was momentarily replaced with an image of all three types of Myaads. The Bivoors, Dumeers, and Rogsaars all looked about the same, the Rogsaars and Dumeers were identical except in size. The Dumeers were taller and more muscular than the Rogsaars. The Bivoors were the smallest group. All three had stark white hair and eyes so dark that they looked black.

Lelelu continued, "They are parthenogenetic breeders, the word they use for their reproductive chambers translates as *hive* but that isn't quite accurate. At least it's not a hive as we would define it."

"OK, I have to ask..." said M "parthenogenetic?"

"Don't feel bad M, I had to look it up" Lelelu said. "It basically means that they can reproduce without fertilization. There are several species on Earth that reproduce this way. Most, but not all, of them produce genetic replicas of the "mother" as Myaads do. They are an asexual species - neither male nor female."

"Wow!" Brzko and M said simultaneously.

Lelelu continued "Almost two hundred Earth years ago the planet went silent. It seems like their trading partners just stopped hearing from them."

"Have you been able to contact anyone on the planet Lelelu?" M asked.

"Yes, I sent a communication portal to the planet via interstellar bot and I've been in touch with one of the Bivoors. We've spoken a few times. Most of the population was wiped out by an illness they have yet to identify. It even infected their hives and they have not been able to reproduce. Because of that, their population has been drastically reduced. The symptoms begin with small lesions on the feet, and then eventually it attacks the respiratory system. It doesn't appear to be contagious, but the survival rate after symptoms appear is 0%. I don't know how many are left on Myaad. Bivoor says that there are well over one hundred Rogsaars stranded throughout the Universe"

"Have you told Bivoor about Rogsaar?"

"Yes and Bivoor is anxious to have Rogsaar back home. But they don't have the resources to help. They have not been able to maintain the exploration fleet, and with maintenance neglected for so long they are no longer able to contact the explorers that were on assignment when the illness hit. Much of their infrastructure has fallen into disarray, which wasn't a big deal with such a drastic reduction in population, except their off planet communication system ceased to function. Which is why Rogsaar, well all Rogsaars, have been left to fend for themselves for so long. They shut down all flashports on Myaad in order to make sure they didn't add to the illness, they don't know where it originated. Bivoor said that they have adequate scanning, quarantine, and detoxification protocols, meeting the standards of most interstellar traveler's." Lelelu explained.

"So they have no idea what the illness is, or where it originated?"

"They don't have any enemies. The Myaads are thoughtful in their exploration. They tend to stay away from warring species but since they have had contact with so many I suppose it is possible that someone wanted to harm them. But the general feeling is that this was a naturally occurring illness. Even though their quarantine meets the universal standard, it's still possible that some biological contaminant made it through." explained Lelelu.

"Has Bivoor asked us, or anyone, for help Lelelu?" M asked, hoping that she would say yes. She would have to honor their desire to be left alone if that was what they wanted.

"Actually, yes. They haven't been able to reach out, to communicate with anyone off planet for over a hundred years. So imagine how relieved they were when the interstellar bot containing our communication portal arrived."

"Have you already made arrangements to for access to their research files? And what about a sample of the disease?"

"We have a full copy of their research files, and I took the liberty of sending a copy to the Suus. They have the largest database we know of so maybe they can help to identify the illness. The interstellar bot has a sample of infected hive tissue. But I have it holding in orbit around Myaad. I don't want to risk spreading the infection by delivering it until requested." explained Lelelu.

"I think it's time to bring Rogsaar up to speed. Brzko, will you please pay a visit? I'd like to contact the Suus and see if they've made any progress. I'd also like to bring Emperor Bartala up to speed since Myaad is basically in his backyard." M said.

"Sure M."

"Lelelu, will you please get a message to the lead on the Suus research team? I want to visit with them and see if they have had any luck identifying the illness."

"Sure M. The lead is Kiik. I'll let you know when I've reached her."

"OK, I'll be on Ploosnar with Emperor Bartala and Empress Nalau." M ended the communication with Lelelu and looked at Brzko.

"Thanks for checking up on Rogsaar?"

"No problem, I'm sure he'll be glad to see me." Brzko said, holding her gaze.

"OK Brzko, I'll catch up with you later. Be careful." M said and embraced her partner.

"Will do M, give Bartala my best."

And with that, they both left Lincoln City, opening apertures directly to their respective destinations.

BACK ON PLOOSNAR

The Muse of Mischief arrived at the bottom of the place stairs on Ploosnar. There was no need for her to call ahead; she and Brzko were always welcome here. Before she got to the top of the stairs, the palace guards had announced her arrival. Emperor Bartala was waiting for her.

"Emperor, it is always a pleasure. I see you still have the new Londo hairstyle. Has it created the excitement you hoped it would?" the Muse of Mischief asked with a big smile

"Yes, it is now the most popular hairstyle on Ploosnar. When I am ready to change I will ask you for another suggestion M; perhaps another style from one of those silly Earth science fiction stories." Bartala said with a chuckle.

"You got it Londo," M quipped "oh I mean Bartala."

This was met with the great joviality she loved so much about her dear friend Emperor Bartala. When he composed himself after having a good laugh at her Londo joke, she continued.

"We figured out what, and who, is sending the random Earth items to Ploosnar."

"It seems the only mystery you and Brzko can't figure out is that of your own origins. Let's go inside and get comfortable, I have a feeling this will take a while." Emperor Bartala turned and walked toward the main entrance of the palace, the long velvet coattails of his bright green jacket rippling behind him.

Emperor Bartala and the Muse of Mischief had settled in one of the many palace sitting rooms. Today they were enjoying the green sitting room. The magnificent room looks as though it is carved out of single piece of marble; there is a green rug under the sitting area. The sofas are a lighter shade of green and the mantle above the fireplace has a collection of green vases. From right to left, they get darker as they get taller. The flames of the fire are even green. But as usual, the thing M finds most impressive is the high vaulted ceiling with windows at the peak, letting in light. Three green tapestries are suspended from the ceiling. The movement of the tapestries and the light coming through the high windows create an effect that M never tires of.

Once they were settled with refreshments, and Bartala's staff had left the room, M began to fill him in on what she and Brzko had learned about the origins of the Earth dump here on Ploosnar.

"What do you know about Myaad?" she asked the Emperor.

"It is a small planet, not far from here. I think it is the size of our moons. It seems like they used to be great explorers but I can't recall hearing anything about them in recent years."

"Yes, they were great explorers. Then, almost two hundred Earth years ago, an illness infected them and their hives. Very few survived and their hives no longer function, which means they cannot reproduce. They lost contact with all of the explorers that were off planet at the time of the outbreak. They shut down their flashports, and haven't allowed anyone to enter or leave the planet in order to make sure they didn't spread the illness." M explained.

"Flashports…" Bartala said slowly, as if he was searching his own mind for details of something that sounded vaguely familiar. "I think I remember these devices. Aren't they transportation devices that run between their ships and planet? The Gaznzulians use something similar. But the Myaads used them to transport commodities back home, and provide supplies to the explorers."

"Yes, and it was wise to shut them down when the illness hit. But between that, and not maintaining their communications equipment, all of their explorers were stranded. They've been shut off from the outside for so long that I presume some of them may have died of old age. But one was a child, trapped on Earth for over one hundred Earth years. Most of that time spent alone."

"Ohhhh that is dreadful, he was alone in a strange place for that long? How did he survive?"

"The Rogsaar's ship still has some functionality. It is able to replicate sustenance and it provides shelter. I think after giving up on fixing the ship Rogsaar started attempting to reach home by sending things through the flashport. The flashports on Myaad were not online to receive, so by tinkering with the flashport anything sent ended up on a nearby planet…"

"Ploosnar!" Bartala said, finishing M's sentence for her

"Yes. I haven't confirmed this yet but it makes sense. Brzko is with Rogsaar now."

Just then Empress Nalau walked in. The Muse of Mischief stood to greet her.

"Empress Nalau, it is a pleasure to see you today." M offered a small curtsey. They may be friends but M still regarded

Nalau as royalty, and she did not enjoy the same level of familiarity with the Empress that she had with her old pal the Emperor. Based on Nalau's appearance alone she deserved this regard. Today she dressed in a long, bright green, flowing gown that trailed behind her. The color matched Bartala's jacket. She wore a short, long sleeved coat of a golden color. She had adopted a hairstyle similar to Bartala's, but hers had golden threads that matched her jacket woven throughout. It wasn't just the royal garments that made her appear so regal, it was also her kind and graceful nature.

Emperor Bartala's greeting was more casual, "My dear, I'm happy you have returned earlier than expected. The Muse of Mischief and Agent Brzko have discovered how and why all of these Earth items are appearing here on Ploosnar. It turns out a being from Myaad has been stuck on Earth for a very long time with no contact to from Myaad, the home world. In fact there was no contact with anyone. Tinkering with a nonfunctional transport device caused the items to start ending up here, instead of Myaad."

With all of the poise and compassion that M had so come to admire about Empress Nalau, she asked only one question, "How are we going to help Bartala?"

THE FIRST ROGSAAR RESCUE

Agent Brzko didn't want to startle Rogsaar so he arrived a short distance from the cloaked opening to Rogsaar's ship. As he approached he could hear Rogsaar humming, sort of. At least he thought it was humming. It sounded more like a cat with a head cold meowing.

He called out to Rogsaar as he approached, "Hello Rogsaar, what are you up to today?"

"Oh, oh Brzko you surprise Rogsaar. I know not when you return."

"We discovered why you haven't been able to return to Myaad, and why your flashport isn't working."

"Tell Rogsaar, tell please."

"Not long after you left Myaad for Earth, there was an outbreak of some sort of infection. It infiltrated the hives and spread quickly. The Bivoors have been working on eradicating it. But it has prevented any breeding for so long that the population of Myaad is down to just a few, compared to what it once was. I'm sorry to have to tell you all of this Rogsaar. It's not going to be as easy as just sending you home. Myaad has imposed a quarantine shutting itself off from the Universe in order to make sure they don't spread the illness." explained Brzko.

"Rogsaar sad, so sad. Just want home, want other Rogsaar."

"I know. Many explorers were cut off from Myaad when the outbreak occurred. If we can't get you home, maybe we can get you someplace where there are other Myaad explorers. How does that sound?"

"Good, very good. Rogsaar not to be alone."

"OK, I'll see what I can do to locate other Myaad explorers. But before I go can you tell me what you're doing with that old tire?"

"Rogsaar find after human leave it under tree. Rogsaar hear loud banging noises, from projectiles launched at this tire."

"Ahh yes, more dumping trash in the forest. Only this time they decided to use if for target practice too. Those projectile launchers are called guns, or firearms. They are very dangerous. But why are you dragging it into your ship?"

"Rogsaar use flashport, try to send to Myaad, not have this material on Myaad."

"About that flashport, when the outbreak occurred, Myaad shut down all of the flashports on the planet. They wanted to make sure they did everything they could to prevent the spread of the illness."

"Where flashport go then?"

"They've been landing on a planet near Myaad, called Ploosnar. Here's a picture of where they end up." Brzko took his tablet out of his pocket, unrolled it and called up an image of the "dump" on Ploosnar. He showed it to Rogsaar. "Have you ever heard of Ploosnar?

Rogsaar shook his head back and forth while shrugging his shoulders "Oh no, no. So Rogsaar's flashport not go to Myaad. But why is this place so blue? It look peaceful."

"Ploosnar is very peaceful; they are some of the happiest beings in the Universe. The blue color is caused by roinad. It's an element that they mine. Myaad is very close to Ploosnar"

"Rogsaar would like to go Ploosnar one day, see the blue planet. Are they angry at Rogsaar for sending items in flashport?"

"Well the Emperor of Ploosnar is a great friend of the Muse of Mischief's so I'm sure we can arrange that, and no, he's not angry at you. Until then why don't you show me more about your ship?" Brzko wasn't really all that interested in Rogsaar's ship, but he could only imagine how lonely Rogsaar must be after so many years alone. Brzko knew that M was working hard to help resolve the disease on Myaad and bring the explorers home, so he could spend a little time with Rogsaar and offer some companionship. Always putting the needs of others before his, Agent Brzko was a true gentleman.

~~~

After discussing ideas for retrieving the abandoned explorers from Myaad with Emperor Bartala and Empress Nalau, the Muse of Mischief retired to her private rooms. Like the owner's table in a fine restaurant, M's rooms at the Ploosnar Palace were always a comfort to her.

The Muse of Mischief had just kicked off her shoes and settled in with her tablet to review the day's correspondence when Lelelu sent her a message.

"Hi M, contact Kiik as soon as you can. She has found some information in the Suus database about the disease that infected Myaad."

M did not waste any time contacting Kiik. She sat down at the interstellar communication portal in her room and sent a communication request to Kiik. The Suus only communicate telepathically, and for that to work with a non-telepath, there had to be a visual link. After just a few moments a video image of a Suus opened.

"Hello, I am Kiik, lead researcher on Suus. You must be the Muse of Mischief. I have heard much about you from our leader, Ciic. It is an honor to be in contact with you." the words appeared in M's head, sent telepathically by Kiik.

"Thank you Kiik, it's a pleasure to meet you." M said.

"We have identified the illness that infected Myaad. It was logged in our database approximately 300 annual cycles in the past, referred to as *Aberidus*. It is caused by spores that live in soil. They can stay dormant for an unknown amount of time. We would like to test the soil on Myaad to see if is naturally occurring. If it is we will attempt to discover what caused the spores to activate. If it is not found in the soil it must have made it through their screening processes. Either way, we are able to provide assistance. Our database contains details of a cure. We've already started synthesizing it." Kiik explained.

"That is great news! The Universe has often benefited from Suus databases. Thank you for working so hard on this." M said.

"We consider it our purpose," Kiik projected "We are experimenting with ways to speed its effectiveness. We have a team ready to travel to Myaad. Once the situation is under control we will also provide them with the knowledge and tools they need to synthesize the cure themselves. That way if there is another outbreak, they can respond immediately. Hopefully there has not been any permanent damage done to the hives."

"Thank you Kiik. I will ask Lelelu to contact Bivoor on Myaad and find out where they would like your team to arrive. We'll be in touch soon."

After exchanging a few more pleasantries with Kiik, M ended her conversation and contacted Brzko and Lelelu. Now that they were both up to speed, and Lelelu was coordinating the Suus team's arrival on Myaad, M went back to catching up on correspondence while she waited for Brzko to catch up with her on Ploosnar.

~~~

"We can welcome them to Lecur. Several of the unused roinad processing buildings still stand at the forest's edge. It is close to the palace and any services they may require. But they will have privacy if that is what they desire. There is plenty of room to hold their ships until they can return to Myaad." Empress Nalau said.

The Muse of Mischief, Emperor Bartala, Empress Nalau, and Agent Brzko were seated in the great green sitting room of the Ploosnar Palace. They were joined by Rogsaar. Brzko had brought him at the request of Bartala and Nalau. They felt was important for a Rogsaar to be involved in developing the rescue plan. The group was discussing the option of a coordinated rescue effort for stranded Myaad explorers.

"I think that is a splendid idea my dear. But it is up to them. Rogsaar, what do you think? Would you and the other Myaad explorers like to come and stay here on Ploosnar while we wait for your home planet to be cleared of aberidus?" asked Emperor Bartala.

Rogsaar was staring intently into the green carpet. Myaads were quite striking with white hair and dark eyes, but even more so with Rogsaar on the brilliant green sofa. The Empress had provided him with a new wardrobe upon his arrival. His black pants and dark grey shirt made him looking even more striking. Looking up and meeting Bartala's gaze Rogsaar said, "No word, Rogsaar have no word to express thank for what you offer. It would please Rogsaar very much to be with other Rogsaars. Rogsaar been alone most of life."

Empress Nalau walked across the room to Rogsaar and extended her hands "It is our pleasure to help you get home Rogsaar. Until other Rogsaars arrive you must stay with us in the palace, stay as our honored guest. Emperor Bartala, the Muse of Mischief, and Agent Brzko will figure out how to find the other Rogsaars and how to get their ships here. While they work on that, let me show you where you will stay. I have the loveliest orange rooms ready for you. Then we can visit with the food staff to make sure we have everything you enjoy." Rogsaar could not have objected if he wanted to, Nalau whisked Rogsaar out of the room.

Brzko turned to Bartala "Will retrieving all of the Rogsaar ships put a strain on your resources? I suspect most of them will be in the same condition as the one you just dealt with on Earth."

"Yes and no mostly no. Some of them will be quick and easy extractions, on advanced planets we do not have to work in secrecy and cloak ourselves. But the extractions will take longer on infantile planets where we have to hide the attractor stream, our ship and the Myaad ship. Can you imagine the chaos that would create on an infantile planet like Earth to see a ship being lifted from the planet by an attractor stream?"

Neither the Muse of Mischief nor Brzko could help themselves, they both let out a good laugh, "Actually yes, we can imagine the chaos it would create on Earth." Brzko said.

"We have contacted Bivoor on Myaad. Once their communications are repaired Myaad will activate the link to each explorer ship. They will transmit a specific message to each one, explaining why they were left to fend for themselves, and how they can contact the rescue team on Ploosnar to find refuge until it is safe to return to Myaad. We know that some of the ships will need repairs but that is no problem. The engineers of Ploosnar can be very innovative when they need to be. We just need to know where the ships are, and if the Rogsaar wants to stay on Ploosnar."

"It sounds like you've got the details all worked out. How many ships did Bivoor say there are?" asked M.

"127."

"Wow! I wonder how many will respond, and take you up on your kind offer." Brzko said as he tried to picture over one hundred identical looking Rogsaars in one place.

~~~

"Rogsaar not remember a Bivoor." Rogsaar was enjoying a live interstellar chat with Bivoor, after over 100 earth years since seeing or speaking to another being from Myaad. Rogsaar was overjoyed. Bivoor looked relieved to see one of the Myaad explorers that had survived being abandoned.

"We are all very relieved to know that you are OK and we working hard to get you home."

"Yas, Muse of Mischief has told Rogsaar about aberidus" Rogsaar said, head shaking. Then corrected the pronunciation "aberidus." For a moment Rogsaar's face glowed with the satisfaction felt from getting the pronunciation correct. Rogsaar was highly intelligent, but a creature of very few words after spending so many years in isolation on Earth.

"That is correct Rogsaar. So are you going to stay on Ploosnar? I hope that you do. Emperor Bartala and Empress Nalau have made a very generous offer to have all Rogsaars stay there until we are ready to have them return to Myaad. There are already teams of technicians from Ploosnar and Suus here working on repairing our communications systems. Once they do, we will be able to send information to all explorers." explained Bivoor.

"This good. Rogsaar wait here on Ploosnar. Empress Nalau give Rogsaar orange room. Rogsaar like Ploosnar very much but still want to be on Myaad."

"You are not the only one that feels that way Rogsaar. All of Myaad thought we would be extinct before we could cure aberidus, we thought our explorers would be lost forever, but the Suus have brought us the cure and we are working at distributing it throughout Myaad. Bivoors had almost given up hope when the

Muse of Mischief's communications bot arrived on Myaad. She and her friends from Ploosnar and Suus are quite amazing, to go to these lengths to help us."

"Yas, yas, Rogsaar very surprised and happy when Muse of Mischief and Brzko find Rogsaar."

Bivoor and Rogsaar chatted for a little longer. Rogsaar had many questions about Myaad, some Bivoor could answer, and some were too complicated for a quick answer. But by the time the conversation was winding down, Rogsaar was starting to accept that going home was a reality.

THE SUUS ARRIVAL

When the team from Suus arrived at Myaad, they placed their ship in a synchronous orbit based on the coordinates provided by the Bivoor. Their cigar shaped ship was stocked with all of the equipment they would need to synthesize the cure for aberidus.

Kiik rarely went out on missions, as the head of research on Suus her responsibilities were quite demanding. But at the request of Ciic she was assigned to a mission that would leave the planet. Kiik didn't know the details, but she'd heard that the Muse of Mischief had saved Ciic from the Viiv when she was a child. Kiik thought there was a good chance that her involvement was approved because the Muse of Mischief was involved. Suus, deeply indebted to the Muse of Mischief, did not hesitate to provide the best of everything to help solve the problems on Myaad. Kiik was delighted to be a part of that. To actually travel to another planet on official business was exciting. And working directly with the Muse of Mischief... that was an honor she never dared dream of.

The cure for aberidus had worked very quickly on Myaad. One treatment was all that was needed to eradicate it from each individual. Unfortunately aberidus had infected all three of the hives on Myaad, and Kiik was sure that the cure had worked on the hives, but there was a very delicate issue that needed to be discussed. While her team was verifying that all three hives were clear of aberidus, she went to find Bivoor.

Kiik found Bivoor in the usual spot, the office. Bivoor's workload was much like Kiik's, Bivoor and the Muse of Mischief were standing near the back wall of Bivoor's office, it was covered with a variety of maps. "I thought I would find you here" Kiik said to both of them telepathically.

"Oh hello Kiik. Yes, there is no rest for a Bivoor." Bivoor said while making an attempt to smile. "How are things progressing with the hives?"

"Very well, tomorrow they will be ready for the new *Caretaker*. But..." now she had Bivoor's full attention "we need to know how, well who, well what you intend to do about..."

Bivoor interrupted, putting an end to Kiik's discomfort "Let me help you out here Kiik. I presume you are about to ask how we will replace each of the hive centers. Or as you say, the *Caretaker*."

"Yes, we are unfamiliar with your protocol. While we understand how parthenogenetic breeding works we do not know how the Caretaker is chosen."

Bivoor paused to think about the answer, "We have never had this problem before, so we do not have a protocol to fall back on. The remaining Bivoors have been discussing options, and we base our decisions on what is best for Myaad. Making decisions for the good of Myaad is our purpose, our function. But we are at the very beginning of a new era. We are going to ask for volunteers."

"A very interesting idea Bivoor." Kiik said. "Assuming there will be more than one volunteer, what criteria will be used to select the Caretaker?"

"We need one Bivoor, one Dumeer, and one Rogsaar, age and health will be used to make the decision."

"How long do eggs incubate?" M asked.

"It takes only a few rotations for the egg to be created. But the incubation takes much longer, 400-500 rotations. A Caretaker must rest after each egg is created; the process keeps the Queen very busy. This is why their food and other necessities are provided for them."

"What are the other functions performed by the Caretaker?" Kiik projected.

"The Caretaker of the hive also monitors the incubation time and quality of development for each egg. They rarely leave the hive, but if absolutely necessary another could step in and perform the monitoring functions for another Caretaker's eggs. In order to speed the repopulation of Myaad we are going to incubate eggs from multiple donors in each hive. The Caretaker may not even provide eggs as the work of caring for so many eggs at once will take a significant amount of energy and time."

"So the long incubation time will give you a chance to prepare for a larger population of young." M said, thinking out loud.

"Yes, Bivoors are working on changes to our rearing methods. Kiik, we understand that the hive skin is no longer showing signs of aberidus, but do you think there is any chance of the new offspring contracting the disease while in the hive? How far into development will the eggs need to be before we can be sure that there is no more aberidus?" Bivoor asked.

"We are confident that the hive is not showing the presence of aberidus. But, the only way to be sure is to complete the incubation process." Kiik projected.

"That's what we thought too. Then ethically we cannot create more than a control group quantity of eggs for each hive until we know for sure. We will not knowingly expose new Myaads to aberidus. Of course with the cure, it may not be such a risk. But Myaad has suffered and we do not want to add to that suffering."

"Is it possible to test just one hive to begin with?" M asked.

"It is possible, yes." answered Bivoor. "But because there is one hive for each type of Myaad, Bivoor, Dumeer, and Rogsaar, we would have to select just one to reproduce. The other two would have to wait up to 500 cycles to begin repopulation. Bivoors have decided it would be better to test all three hives, with a small quantity of eggs in each. This will maintain balance as we begin to repopulate."

The possibility of aberidus still being in the hive infecting the new eggs left a dark cloud over the room. The Muse of Mischief, Kiik, and Bivoor all took a moment to consider this possibility. Bivoors were effective problem solvers and never let possibilities dampen their productivity.

Bivoor suggested it was time for a tour, "This is the perfect time to tour a hive, before we start using them again. I can meet you at the Bivoor hive shortly. If you'd like, you can have Agent Brzko join us. Kiik, would you also like to join us"

"Thank you for the invitation Bivoor. But I must decline, I would like to check in with my team's progress." with that, Kiik turned and left the room.

"Brzko and I we will see you there Bivoor."

~~~

Bivoor, the Muse of Mischief, and Agent Brzko, were gathered outside of the Bivoor hive. The area is beautifully landscaped with a variety of colors and textures. There is a circular patio, lined with benches on two sides, leaving two narrow openings opposite each other. Leading away, from the back of the patio, is a narrow path. The path leads to the main entrance of the hive. The hive is a large dome like structure, except it isn't a round shape, it is more complex. The center, and tallest area is rounded, but branching off of that are several other mini domes. Lines of these domes look like they are attached to each other, spanning out in all directions.

"It smells wonderful in here, like fresh clean air." Brzko said as he turned in the lobby, taking it all in.

The lobby was round with two doors opposite the entrance. Both doors were tall with rounded tops, neither door was marked.

"We will start with the chamber of the Caretaker." Bivoor said as she opened the door on the right. The Muse of Mischief stepped through the door, followed by Brzko, then Bivoor, who came in and closed the door.

"This is a Caretaker's private quarters. There is a communications portal here," Bivoor said gesturing toward the equipment. "There is no need for sustenance preparation facilities, Caretakers are cared for. Through here is the resting chamber." Bivoor walked through the entrance into a small room.

The room seemed to be made of living tissue. Everything was a pale pinkish-orange color, and it looked soft, comforting. "May I touch the surface?" M asked.

"Yes, please do. You may find it pleasing." Bivoor said.

M and Brzko both reached out and ran a hand along the wall near them. The back wall of the room had a bench like protrusion that was made up of the same material. "This is amazing; it's soft and somehow calming."

"Yes. The hive fabric is wonderful for incubating the eggs. Keeping a Caretaker comfortable is important. In the past they would spend their entire adult life reproducing and caring for the offspring. Would you like to see the hive now?" Bivoor asked.

"Yes" M and Brzko said in unison.

They followed Bivoor back out into the lobby and then through the door on the left. They were at the top of a T like intersection; there are long hallways to the left, to the right, and straight ahead. The hallways are rounded and made of the same material they had seen in the Caretaker's sleeping chamber. Bivoor began walking straight ahead. After a short distance she paused, turned to M and Brzko, and lifted both hands, pointing to openings, one on each side of the hall, directly opposite each other. They are small rooms, maybe five feet tall and of course rounded at the top.

"Because the hive is not active it is safe for you to enter an egg chamber." Brzko walked toward the chamber on the left and M to the one on the right, ducking down they each stepped through the entrance. Inside the chamber they were able to stand completely upright. The small rooms look like a miniature version of the Caretaker's resting chamber, bench surface and all.

M stepped back out into the hallway "Is there one egg incubated per chamber?" she asked Bivoor.

"Yes, that's right. The Caretaker will place an egg on the resting surface, and then a thin membrane of the hive fabric will extend over the egg. It is a very pliable material. It will grow with the egg, yet stay translucent, allowing the Caretaker to monitor the development of the egg."

Brzko had re-entered the hallway, "How many eggs can be incubated here at one time?" he asked.

"Close to ten thousand" answered Bivoor. The surprise was obvious on both M and Brzko's face. Bivoor continued, "It sounds like an impossible number of offspring to manage but they are not all incubated on the same schedule."

"How many will be incubated in the first group?" Brzko asked.

"There will be thirty, ten Bivoor, ten Dumeer, and ten Rogsaar. Unlike our normal process of one Caretaker creating all of the eggs, this time each egg will be from a different donor. That way they can all start incubating within a few days of each other. Then, the volunteer Caretaker will have the sole responsibility of tending to them." Bivoor explained.

"Is there anything else we can do to help" M asked.

"You have already given us so much, we can never repay you." Bivoor said with sincerity.

"It's our pleasure Bivoor. Brzko and I don't expect repayment. We do these things because it is the right thing to do, because we can." M explained.

"Myaad will be forever indebted to you and your friends." Bivoor said.

"Speaking of friends," Brzko said, "I'd like to be with Emperor Bartala on Ploosnar when the Rogsaars begin to arrive. Were you able to contact all 127 of them?"

"No, nine of them did not respond, almost every one of them wants to travel to Ploosnar. All of us on Myaad are relieved that they will no longer be alone in distant Worlds."

"We will speak to Emperor Bartala about the nine that did not respond. It's possible that their ships are no longer able to receive communications from Myaad. He may be able to send out search parties." Brzko said.

M continued his thought, "That way, at least we will know if they are still alive. We should also arrange to return their ships to Myaad, or what's left of them. There is still much to do. Bivoor thank you for the tour of the hive. If you don't need us for anything else right now, Brzko and I need to speak with Emperor Bartala on Ploosnar."

"Thank you M. Kiik and her team will be here with us while we populate the hives, and I have a direct line to Lelelu in case I need to reach you and Brzko." Bivoor said.

"OK, then, we'll be in touch soon." M said. And within seconds she and Brzko were gone, instantly arriving at the Ploosnar Palace.

MAKE WAY FOR THE ROGSAARS

"Yas, yas, my friends Rogsaar happy to see you. Please, please come, you must see other Rogsaars in Lecur!" Rogsaar was erupting while running down the palace stairs to meet the Muse of Mischief and Agent Brzko. They were intercepted about halfway up.

"Hello Rogsaar, I'm glad to see you are well, it seems as though you are enjoying your time here on Ploosnar." Brzko said as they embraced in greeting.

"Yas, yas, food good, orange rooms better!"

The Muse of Mischief, Brzko, and Rogsaar stood in a small circle on the landing, laughing about how much Rogsaar loved his orange rooms.

"Muse of Mischief, Agent Brzko, welcome!" Empress Nalau called as she emerged from the palace entrance.

"Empress," M greeted her with the customary curtsy "it is always a pleasure."

Brzko greeted the Empress with his customary bow and kissing of her extended hand "Your Majesty, thank you for receiving us."

Brzko's charm was irresistible to Empress Nalau, she giggled like a young girl. "You look fabulous today Empress, this yellow gown is stunning." She was wearing a bright yellow gown with a tight bodice, high collar and no sleeves. The skirts were full and trailed behind her. The color was stunning against her dark skin.

"Thank you Brzko, now come. We have much to tell you." she said as she whisked them all into the palace.

They were seated in the grey sitting room. This room is a little smaller than the formal green sitting room, but the monochrome effect is similar. Nalau's yellow gown was positively stunning against the drab backdrop of grey. There was no doubt that the sitting room of the day was selected based on the way the color of the room would interact with Nalau's fashion.

"Bartala is out at Lecur this morning, we will join him shortly. There are over 100 Rogsaars here now, more arriving every day." Empress Nalau explained.

"Rogsaar never see more Rogsaars. So many, and we were all on different planets, many stories to share, many stories to share."

"You must enjoy sharing time with them Rogsaar. I'm surprised you aren't in Lecur with them now." M said with just the hint of a question.

Before Rogsaar could explain, Empress Nalau offered an explanation "It seems my new friend here finds the orange rooms too comfortable to leave. Rogsaar has been staying in the palace at night and spending his days in Lecur."

"Yas, yas, I like orange rooms very much." Rogsaar said.

"Rogsaar, was that a pronoun I heard?" Brzko teased.

"Yas, yas, Empress Nalau has been helping Rogsaar... ah, me, speak better. Much in my head, need help to get it out." Rogsaar said looking at Nalau with gratitude.

"It is my pleasure Rogsaar. I cannot imagine how difficult it must have been to be alone for so many years. You did the best you could with the resources you had at your disposal." Empress Nalau said. "Now why don't we take the Muse of Mischief and Brzko on a tour of Lecur?"

Lecur is not far from the palace, close enough to walk. It is located just near the forested area to the east of the palace. The group descended the palace stairs turning toward Lecur. They were of course followed by a small group of palace guards. As they neared their destination, Emperor Bartala came walking down the path toward them.

"My darling, how I have missed you. Thank you for bringing our friends." He said as he greeted his wife with a kiss on the cheek. His arm slipped around her waist with ease. She was still in her bright yellow gown and he was wearing a long red velvet coat. The lapels were stitched with fine yellow accents and the buttons were silver, matching Nalau's jewelry. The lining of Bartala's jacket was the same shade of yellow as Nalau's dress. They were stunning.

Bartala left his wife's embrace and approached M "Hello old friend" he said with enthusiasm as he scooped her up and bear hugged her.

"Ahhhhhhh can't breathe," she said, sort of joking.

"Oh, oh, sorry M, I'm just so genuinely excited today. Being a part of the Rogsaar reunion is fulfilling, each of them has been away from home for a very long time. Now... to be around other Rogsaars... the excitement is electric. Can you feel it? Can you feel the energy? Brzko, tell me you can feel it too." Bartala returned M to the ground and turned to Brzko, grasping his hand and forearm in a passionate greeting.

"Yes, I feel it Emperor Bartala. There is excitement in the air." Brzko answered.

"Come, come, and let us join the group. We have set up a reception area outside of the main meeting hall. The weather is so nice today that all of the Rogsaars have gathered there." Bartala explained as he led the group down the walkway.

Lecur is made up of several large buildings that were once used for processing Roinad. The operation has since moved to more technologically advanced buildings west of the palace, but Lecur has not been left to decay. Quite the opposite was true. Ploosnarians take pride in everything they do. Everything from their personal appearance to the work they perform is done with great care and always a bit of personal flair. You would never find a Ploosnarian outside of their home that is not dressed to the nines, from maintenance workers to interstellar contract negotiators; everyone takes great pride in their appearance and always behaves with grace.

The groundskeepers here in Lecur had absolutely applied some of that personal flair to their work. The gardens are immaculate and amazingly laid out. There is a series of walkways leading toward the central meeting area. The plants lining the walkways are of course blue, as is all indigenous flora on Ploosnar, but the flowers here are remarkable. They begin with very small white flowers on low bushes. They then transition to pale blue flowers; each succeeding planting has a taller plant with larger flowers of a deeper blue. By the time the group reached the main reception hall they were surrounded by shrubs as tall as M that were filled with huge, midnight blue flowers. The reception area is a large round patio filled with round tables and chairs. On the back side of the patio is the reception building, the side of the building along the patio is made of curved glass, angled to match the edge of the patio. There are four evenly spaced walkways converging to the reception patio. Aside from the glass wall of the reception building, the patio is lined entirely with the brilliant midnight blue flowers; these tall shrubs give it the feel of being an outdoor room.

"This is brilliant, what an amazing space." M exclaimed as the group came to a stop. It took her a few seconds to shift her gaze away from the perimeter of the patio to the individuals inhabiting the tables. They were dressed as individuals but it was clear that they were all identical.

Emperor Bartala stepped in front of the group and turned to face them, "You see, you see, is this not amazing? I have never in my life seen this. Almost one hundred genetically identical beings in one place, but each one still an individual. The energy I tell you, well it's… it's like nothing else!" he said as he enthusiastically waved his arms up and down.

The Muse of Mischief tried to suppress the laugh. She averted her eyes, looked to the ground, but it was of no use. The minute she looked back at Bartala she burst out with a hearty laugh. "Have you been watching Babylon 5? Because I swear, you are more like Londo every time I see you."

"Ahhhh I cannot hide anything from you my old friend. Yes, yes, I have been watching this Earth entertainment, just a little."

They all shared a good laugh.

"I can't help it; I have to see what becomes of this Londo. I do not think things will end well for him. Now let us go meet some Rogsaars." Bartala said.

~~~

"So where were you stationed when communications from Myaad ceased?" the Muse of Mischief asked a Rogsaar that was wearing some very interesting garb.

"I was on Xinood 5." Rogsaar said.

"I've never heard of Xinood 5, is there a Xinood 1, 2, 3, and 4?" M asked.

"Yes, but only Xinood 4 is inhabited. Xinood 1, 2, and 3, are too small and distant from the system's suns to sustain life."

Bartala and Brzko were mingling with other Rogsaars on the reception patio. Bartala was right; being in a crowd of Rogsaars was amazing. And not just because they were coming together after over one hundred Earth years of being cut off from their home. Each one had been someplace, away from their kind for all that time; each one had survived on their own on a distant planet. This was the third Rogsaar that M had chatted with. She was sad to see the suns of Ploosnar getting low, soon it would be dark. Empress Nalau was engrossed in the conversation, but thus far, she was fine with just listening and letting M ask all of the questions. M asked what seemed to be the logical next questions, "What are beings of Xinood 5 like and where did you obtained those western clothes?"

"Xinoods are like many other species in the Universe, intelligent beings with an advanced social structure. They are bipedal and as black as a night with no moons. They have bright green eyes, except when they get mad, then their eyes turn red, blazing red. They are not especially tall, about the same size as you or I. Trading is the basis of their economy and so a universal education is highly valued."

"So you were there trading with them when communications with Myaad ceased?"

"Yes, and at first I thought my equipment must have needed repairs. But G'ess and I went over every component and could not find the problem. We realized it must have been a problem on Myaad. So I settled in and took my place in society."

"G'ess? Is that a Xinood?" M asked.

"Yes, G'ess and I used to trade in Technology. He is the sibling of my partner G'ist."

"Partner, like spouse?" asked Nalau. Evidently the idea of interspecies unions had provoked her enough to be more than an observer.

"Yes, Xinoods often partner with other species, it is not uncommon. They are a very accepting of all cultures. When compatible they reproduce with other species. Because Myaads are asexual parthenogenetic breeders we were not easily compatible from the reproductive standpoint. But there is a scientist working on the issue. He thinks we may be able to introduce genetic material from G'ist into one of my eggs."

"Do you have an image of G'ist?" M asked.

"Is G'ist male or female" Nalau asked at the same instant.

They all three chuckled. "We're sorry Rogsaar we don't mean to be rude. We are simply excited to be learning about a new place and species." M said.

"It's fine, really. I understand how strange it must sound for an asexual parthenogenetic being to take a partner. But not all beings enter into partnerships based on romance like your species probably do. For Xinoods the arrangements can be based on logic, or stability. And yes, I do have an image of G'ist. This image is from our last retreat, what some would call a vacation. G'ist is a male." Rogsaar pulled a small pebble looking device on the table. In an instant there was a small hologram generated from the device. G'ist looked pretty much humanoid, the green eyes were brilliant, even in the image.

"You must be very torn, you've integrated into the society on Xinood and taken a partner but you must also miss Myaad, your home. It sounds like you have built a wonderful life, will you return to Xinood?" Nalau asked with clear concern.

"I feel an obligation to help other Rogsaars return to Myaad. Once all of the abandoned Rogsaars are located, I will return to G'ist and my life on Xinood. One day I hope to be able to share Myaad with G'ist. He was never seen a planet with no surface water."

"Oh Rogsaar I had not considered the relationships that may have developed where Rogsaars were stranded. If you need any help to return to Xinood you must tell me. Bartala and I will provide you with transportation or anything else you need." Empress Nalau said with compassion.

"Thank you Empress, thank you."

"But that still doesn't explain why you're wearing Wrangler jeans!" M jabbed.

"I told you... the Xinoods are universal traders." Rogsaar said with just as much jest.

The three new friends shared a good laugh.

The Muse of Mischief excused herself from Nalau and the Rogsaar of Xinood 5; she wandered about looking for Brzko. But she came across a Rogsaar seated alone, their facial expressions could be difficult to read but she thought this Rogsaar looked concerned.

"Hello," she said hoping to engage.

"Hello, you are the Muse of Mischief right?"

M took this as an invitation and took a seat at the table as she answered, "Yes, I'm the Muse of Mischief. And I know you're Rogsaar, but I don't know where you were stranded."

"I was on Jinn," as Rogsaar answered, M noticed a vase or bottle under the table in Rogsaar's hand, "and I want to return to Myaad but I must return to Jinn first. But my ship no longer works; I do not know how I will get back to Jinn."

"I'm not familiar with Jinn, I take it you had a life there? You did not have to stay hidden from the indigenous population?

"No, hiding was not necessary; the Jinns are an ancient, advanced race. Myaad was trading knowledge with them. They are travelers. Jinn star charts are always accurate."

"Why do you need to return to Jinn before going home to Myaad?"

"I brought something, someone, with me that I should have left on Jinn. I did not ask if there was a desire to travel with me. After being on Jinn for so long I was desperate to bring someone familiar along with me."

"You brought someone with you? How? Where is this being?" M asked.

It was then that Rogsaar sat the bottle on the table. The bottle was stunningly beautiful, it was wide and curved at the bottom, with a narrow neck. It was a deep blue color with an intricate pattern of black scrolls etched into it.   "There is a being in there, in that bottle?" M asked.

"Yes, there is a Jinn in the bottle. I took him while he was sleeping, I need to return him to Jinn. He is going to be very angry when he finds out I took him."

"How big is this Jinn?" M asked.

"Do not be fooled by the bottle. A Jinn can be as large as it wants to be, it can take the shape of whatever it wants to be.

Jinn's are highly intelligent; they have traveled the Universe since before recorded time. They mostly stick to themselves, they are laid back and fun loving unless..."

"Unless what?" Bartala asked as he took a seat at the table.

"Emperor!" Rogsaar said surprised that Bartala had joined the conversation.

"Yes, yes, continue, please. What is this Jinn, and what makes them fun loving unless..." he said with a slightly mocking tone. When you've been raised to be the Emperor of an incredible planet like Ploosnar, there is little that you fear.

"Well, unless you cross them. And I have crossed this one by taking him from his home. It's just that, well, they are such magnificent beings that I wanted to keep one."

"Give me the bottle I will have it returned for you." Bartala said as he reached for the bottle.

Rogsaar was quicker, just barely grasping the bottle before Bartala had a firm grip on it "No! You must not open the bottle here, the Jinn may be very angry."

"OK, OK." Bartala said taking the bottle from a reluctant Rogsaar. "But really, how dangerous could a being in a bottle this size be?" he said. Before Rogsaar could even utter a sound Bartala had tilted the stopper at the top just a crack.

Rogsaar uttered a sound as if he'd been sucker punched "No!" he screeched As he pushed back from the table and stood, looking like he was ready to run.

As soon as the bottle was cracked the air around Bartala began to change color, as though it was filling with bright blue smoke. It instantly began to take shape. The Muse of Mischief had never seen anything like this, and it set her on edge. She jumped from her seat in case action was needed.

"Oh Bartala, what did you do?!" M scolded.

Bartala stood up knocking his chair over. This got the palace guards moving, they immediately surrounded the Emperor.

The bright blue cloud had completed its transformation. It was now a very tall, very large being. He was dressed in bright blue, silky pants with a matching shirt. He wore shoes of the same color with long pointy toes that curled up. He towered above Bartala and the guards.

"I am Afrit the Great of Jinn, why have you brought me to this place?" His voice was so loud that the entire courtyard of Rogsaars fell silent.

"It wasn't me, it was him, it was him!" Bartala said pointing to Rogsaar.

Afrit began to turn to face Rogsaar. As he did, M got a good look at him, and knew this being possessed great power. In an effort to diffuse the situation quickly she jumped into his path and attempted to humor him.

"Hey you look like a genie, don't you owe Bartala three wishes? Or is it only the genies of Earth that give wishes?"

Afrit stepped toward her, right up on her really. Uh-oh she thought, that might not have worked. The palace guards, seeing her under threat, began to step toward her. She held a hand up to keep them at bay. Afrit the Jinn continued to stare down at her. "And who is this, with striped legs, speaking to me as though you know me?"

"I'm the Muse of Mischief, nice to meet cha Afrit!" she said jabbing her hand up and forward toward the towering Jinn.

The Jinn's face started to quiver; he was attempting to keep his stern look, but could not. He looked like a human when they try to stifle a sneeze. He released the laughter,

"Haaaaaahahaha. I like you kid!" He said slapping M on the back. Everyone immediately relaxed a little. Afrit seemed to shrink; he was now the same height as Bartala.

M returned to the table and pulled out a chair for Afrit, "Please join us." she said. She touched the Gaznzulian earpiece and activated the earcom link to Brzko. This was code between the two of them, she was in an interesting situation that she knew he would like to part of and wanted him to head this way.

Bartala righted his chair and took a seat, the palace guards stepped back but kept a sharp eye on this new being. M took a chair next to Afrit; the only one in the group that didn't sit was Rogsaar. He was standing with his hands on the back of his chair, clearly concerned that he would be a target of the Jinn's anger.

"Rogsaar, sit. I will not harm you." Afrit said "at least not in front of all these..." Afrit looked left, he looked right, he turned in his seat and surveyed the entire courtyard. "I know I'm late to this party but what the jinn is going on? Are these your clones Rogsaar? I seem to remember you telling me about clones a long time ago on Jinn."

Rogsaar didn't answer; he managed to sit but still couldn't seem to speak. Bartala was up for the task of explaining, "Yes, these are all Rogsaars from Myaad, and yes they are all genetically identical, or clones." Afrit turned toward Bartala, he introduced himself "I am Emperor Bartala, it is a pleasure to meet you, welcome to Ploosnar. I don't think anyone here but this Rogsaar has seen a Jinn before."

"Emperor of what?" Afrit asked dryly.

"Ploosnar, the planet Ploosnar." Bartala answered.

Brzko arrived at the table, he presented himself between Afrit the Great and M, "Greetings and salutations, I am Agent Brzko." He said as he extended his hand toward Afrit.

Afrit slowly turned and looked up at Brzko, "I know you." Afrit said, "I met you on Earth a very long time ago."

"I would remember meeting a Jinn." Brzko said a little perplexed. M had shifted over one seat so that he could sit down. Bartala, M, and Rogsaar all stared at Afrit the Great and Brzko. Could they have met before?

In an instant Afrit the Great was an Earthling, a black man wearing a white t-shirt, jeans and ridiculously bright red athletic shoes. "Remember me now? I used to hang out at Tommie's Barber Shop".

Everyone at the table was dumbfounded. Afrit transformed back into himself, "And by the way Ms. Muse of Mischief, I don't grant wishes. That is a silly fable that the inhabitants of Earth concocted after they met Jinns.

"Yes! I remember you. I used to see you at Tommie's, mostly I remember those shoes. Why would you visit a barber shop on Earth?" Brzko asked.

"There are very few places Jinn's have not been. Given our ability to blend in, travel is generally safe for us. What can I say? I found that barber shop fascinating. It was a meeting place held together by one man, a place of cultural strength. I've seen many oppressed cultures, in many places. But none as strong as the black culture on Earth."

Afrit paused and looked around the table, he realized that everyone was staring at him and only the Muse of Mischief and Agent Brzko had any idea what he was talking about. He transformed back into his natural appearance and continued. "Maybe we could catch up about the barber shop later Agent Brzko."

"Of course, of course." Brzko confirmed. "I'd like to hear more about your travels, I'm sure you've seen interesting things."

"Yes. You might say we Jinn exist to travel. Which is why, Rogsaar, I forgive you for that dirty little deed of yours - capping my bottle and basically kidnapping me. But you brought me to a place I have never been, and it's blue, so vividly blue. I LOVE blue! I'd like to stay here a while and take a look around. Can you arrange that for me Mr. Bartala? I don't take up much space, I can sleep in my bottle."

Bartala, rarely caught off guard, was tripping over his own words, "Um, yes, well... "He cleared his throat and tried again, "It would be my pleasure to host you in the Royal Palace of Ploosnar. I will arrange for you to have a guide that can show you around. But you do not have to sleep in your bottle, unless that is your preference." He motioned to a guard, no doubt to giving instruction to prepare rooms for Afrit the Great.

"Thank you Mr. Bartala. Hey, has anyone ever told you that you look just like Londo Mollari from the Earth show Babylon 5?"

"Yes, I have heard that before," he said looking across the table at M. "It's this fabulous hair isn't it?" he said touching the high peaks of hair at the top of his head.

Everyone at the table, with the exception of Rogsaar, got the joke and laughed. The tension was over. It seemed that Afrit the Great of Jinn might now be an ally.

THE HIVES

After just a few days on Ploosnar, the Muse of Mischief and Agent Brzko were exhausted. The story of each Rogsaar's survival was fantastic. There were many of them that had decided not to permanently return to Myaad. A few had stayed hidden on hostile or infantile planets, like Rogsaar on Earth, but most had managed to integrate into the societies they were in. This was an interesting turn that M wondered if Bivoor had expected. M and Brzko were headed to Myaad after saying goodbye to their hosts.

"Your Majesties, the Muse of Mischief and Agent Brzko have joined us." one of Bartala's many butlers announced, as M and Brzko entered the great green sitting room.

Emperor Bartala looked up, he was seated in an overstuffed, high back chair, with Empress Nalau standing at his side. As usual they were an amazing fashion statement. Today's color was orange - she in a long flowing dress that looked something like the flappers would have worn in the 50"s on Earth, and he in black slacks and a coat with tails. Of course the lining of the coat and the embroidery were of the same color as Nalau's dress.

"I keep telling them to stop announcing you and Brzko, you practically live here." Bartala teased M as she approached his chair.

"Please don't let them stop, it makes me feel so official," she jabbed back, "like a royal visitor to the palace of Genghis Khan back in Earth's thirteenth century."

"I do not know this Genghis Khan you speak of, but by the look on Brzko's face I think you are giving me some tease my old friend." Bartala said playfully with a little suspicion.

"Ahh well, I think we should save the Mongolian history lesson for our next visit." M said with a smile that made it clear she was having fun with Bartala.

"OK, you can educate me about Mongolia and I will teach you how to dress."

"Hey, what's wrong with the way I dress?"

"Oh well technically nothing but, I mean, well, if you want to look like a time and space traveling ambassador that constantly travels around the Universe in striped stockings." he teased.

Empress Nalau, not knowing the Muse of Mischief as well as Bartala was getting a little uncomfortable; she let him know with a skeptical "Bartala..."

"OK, OK, my love I will stop teasing M... for the moment, in this location, but next time we meet we shall drink nekmid and exchange insults until we drop, just as we did when we were young." he said mumbling the last part.

Now all four of the old friends were laughing at the childish challenge Bartala had presented.

"As they say in Oz, it's a date mate." M said, and turned to Nalau, "Empress, as always you are the very definition of grace. Thank you for your hospitality and for all you are doing for the Rogsaars."

M turned to leave the room, as she did Brzko took Nalau's hand, bent and kissed it, "Empress, always a pleasure." he said. She blushed, appreciative of Brzko's charm.

"Be safe my friends!" Bartala called as M and Brzko left the room.

They went directly from Ploosnar to Myaad, Bivoor was expecting them. Over the years the Muse of Mischief and Brzko had learned that it was better to arrive outside of the building where you were expected, and then to walk in. Since other beings could not use apertures, and had to use conventional ships or portals to travel through space and time, they had a difficult time accepting someone just appearing before them, even if they were expected.

The landscaping outside the Myaad administration building was much like it was outside the hive. There were pleasant gardens and benches. Lelelu had contacted Kiik and asked her to meet M and Brzko here.

Kiik was already here when they arrived, seated on a bench reviewing something on a tablet. No doubt work related Kiik took her duties very seriously. While she worked, her long tail seemed to gently sway back and forth like a pendulum behind her. Kiik was holding it upright and they could see the tip of her tail over her right shoulder, and then it slowly swayed and became visible over her left shoulder. M wondered if this was an involuntary, soothing action like when humans rubbed their hands together or tapped a finger.

As they approached, Kiik projected the answer to her question "Yes, it is an involuntary, yet soothing action."

"Pardon, what was that Kiik? What is involuntary yet soothing?" Brzko asked.

"As we approached I was wondering if Kiik's tail movement was involuntary." M explained.

"I took the liberty of keeping my mind open to your thoughts as you approached. I hope you do not feel this was an intrusion." Kiik projected.

"Not at all Kiik. I hope you were not offended by my curiosity." M said taking a seat next to Kiik.

"No, offended by the Muse of Mischief, no never. A curiosity of other beings leads to understanding. It is an honor to be working with you. Your reputation is known throughout Suus. You and Agent Brzko are considered heroes."

"That's flattering Kiik. We were happy to help the Suus." Brzko said.

"One day I would enjoy hearing the story of how you saved Ciic as a child. Today I have some information that I would like to share with you. It has nothing to do with Myaad or the hives, it has to do with your origins. I do not want to offend you so please tell me if this is inappropriate." Kiik projected.

"Not at all" M said quickly. "Brzko and I would be happy to hear anything you have to share."

"Well as you know, Suus has maintained databases of everything we can document, for as long as we have been an advanced race. This goes back centuries, many, many centuries. We record and catalog every detail we know of everything we encounter."

"Right and that helped to quickly identify aberidus here on Myaad." Brzko said.

"Correct. In my free time I have been searching the databases for clues of your origins. I have found a reference to beings that can travel through space and time as you two can. As you know that is a rare talent. We have all heard stories of beings having these abilities, but you two are the only beings that are KNOWN to have the ability, in this time. Of course others can use the time portals on the Planet of Portals, or hire a timeship, but you two are the only beings that can move through time unaided."

"In THIS time, it sounds like that's key." M said.

"Yes. I found a reference to a planet. The data is very old and not as detailed as I would like but the beings were able to travel through space and time and interestingly the males had dark skin and the females had light skin." Here Kiik paused and let that sink in.

She continued "The beings are not named in the reference. I do not know what they were, or are called. It was suspected that they were either immortal or had an extremely long lifespan. The planet was referred to as Clyrea X9." Kiik again paused to let this information sink in.

Brzko broke the silence "Where is Clyrea X9?" he asked.

"There is no reference to this planet's exact location anywhere else in our database. But it is linked to other entries about the Trellan Galaxy. Either this entry has an incorrect name, the planet no longer exists, or it is hidden. I will continue to search for clues as time permits." Kiik projected.

"We can't thank you enough Kiik. I wasn't expecting this today." M said.

"My apologies, I did not want to shock you, or distract you from our work here on Myaad, but I wanted you to know what I have discovered right away."

"Thank you Kiik. You've given us much to think about, but we still have work to do here on Myaad. Your team is monitoring the hives?" Brzko asked.

"Yes, and so far all thirty of the eggs seem to be developing normally." Kiik projected.

"That's great news." M said. "Let's go in and speak with Bivoor."

The three were an odd looking group by Earth standards, but not so odd for those that traveled the Universe. Agent Brzko led the group, with his tall muscular body and dark skin, in his long dark trench coat he looked the part of an "agent." The Muse of Mischief, in step behind him, wearing her black derby, short skirt, and striped stockings, looked playful yet dangerous. In sync with M was Kiik, who was taller than both of them, with glistening green skin, four arms, no mouth, and a long narrow tail. Once inside they joined Bivoor, a petite, pale skinned being, neither male nor female but a clone of all Bivoors, with shocking white hair that stood straight up. M was thinking about the group's diversity when Bivoor greeted them.

"Welcome back to Myaad. Has Kiik told you the eggs seem to be developing normally?" Bivoor asked M and Brzko.

"Yes, we heard the good news. We're relieved. Hopefully development will continue to be normal." M said.

"We have taken every precaution we could think of. As you know the eggs were from thirty different donors, but there is only one Caretaker per hive. This should help to prevent any outside contaminants from entering the hive. Kiik has been kind enough to agree to keep a small team on Myaad to monitor the eggs. They will test each Caretaker weekly to make sure they do not develop aberidus and spread it to the hive. We believe the disease has been eradicated but we want to take every precaution with the eggs and the hives." Bivoor explained.

"It is our pleasure to keep a team here on Myaad while the eggs develop. The team has a direct link to me and even to Ciic, so should anything develop we will know immediately." Kiik projected.

"Bivoors have decided there is no need to wait for the eggs to fully develop before Rogsaars return. Testing has confirmed that aberidus is naturally occurring in our soil, an outside contaminant may have activated it but we will never know for sure. We will continually test the soil for it at numerous locations. If it activates again, we'll catch it early. Now that we have this knowledge, we are ready to welcome the Rogsaars home. I have not shared this news with them yet. We will need help getting them and the ships back to Myaad."

"That is exciting news Bivoor!" M said. Kiik, projected the same excitement to the group.

"The Ploosnarians have been able to repair a few of the ships, and Emperor Bartala is planning to modify one of his roinad transports to deliver the rest. If they travel as a group the journey should be safe enough, but it will take about 25 Ploosnar rotations for the journey, those large transport ships are not known for their speed." Brzko explained.

"We just came from Ploosnar; it was fascinating to be in a group of almost one hundred Rogsaars. Many of them have fascinating tales of their survival." M said. "Have you had contact with any of them Bivoor?"

"Yes, with many of them. We have assigned a Bivoor to gathering and recording their stories. Many Myaads will find these stories interesting. We understand that not all of the Rogsaars want to return to Myaad. Many of them have created lives and relationships on those distant planets, but we still want to capture their stories."

"Do you know how many will return?" Kiik projected.

"Approximately half on a permanent basis and an additional 23 want to return home briefly before returning to their new life." Bivoor answered.

"I would like to meet this group of Rogsaars on Ploosnar, while they are all together. I have a proposal." Kiik projected, "Ciic has authorized me to travel to Ploosnar, my ship can get there in approximately four rotations, if I visit with the Rogsaars for two rotations, I could then bring them all back on my ship, having them here in ten rotations. Emperor Bartala's transport can bring the ships, and any Rogsaars not yet found." Kiik paused to let that sink in.

"That is a very kind offer Kiik. I am sure Bivoors will agree to take you up on it." Bivoor said.

"Great, I look forward to meeting the Rogsaars as a group. Muse of Mischief, will you please contact Emperor Bartala and verify that this plan is acceptable to him?" Kiik projected.

"Sure, right away." M answered. "Brzko, will you be returning to Ploosnar with me or staying here?"

"Actually..." he said turning to face Kiik, "if you have room for an interstellar hitchhiker on your ship Kiik I would enjoy traveling to Ploosnar with you. The technology of various ships fascinates me; I enjoy learning about the ships from the inside."

"Yes, we have plenty of room and it would be an honor to escort an Ambassador of the Universe." Kiik projected.

"While you two prepare Kiik's ship I'll go talk to Bartala, I'll contact you shortly." M said as she headed to the door. Brzko walked outside with her.

"Be careful M, I'll miss you."

"I will Brzko, if Bartala is available I should have an answer right away. Have fun playing spaceship guy with Kiik." she teased as they embraced. Then she was gone.

THE BRUSHER

As always, the Muse of Mischief arrived at the foot of the stairs and was announced by the palace guards. Emperor Bartala was waiting for her. He had a concerned look, almost nervous.

"Quickly M, come inside." he said whisking her through the front entrance of the palace. She followed Bartala down a hallway and palace guards followed them. That was highly unusual, there was virtually no crime on Ploosnar and palace guards did not usually follow the Emperor around his palace. Outside of it yes but not inside.

Rather than one of the usual grand sitting rooms, Bartala led her to his small sitting room deep within the palace, one of his private rooms. Once the Muse of Mischief entered the room he closed the door and the guards took their station outside. Bartala's rooms are very masculine, the lower half of the walls paneled in a dark, exotic looking wood. The upper half of the walls painted a burgundy color. The main furniture consists of two large sofas that face each other over a glass topped coffee table.

"What's wrong Bartala is Nalau ok?" M asked.

"Yes, she is fine, she is unhappy with me, but she is fine. I am worried about you, you and Brzko." he said taking a seat and motioning for her to be seated on the sofa opposite his.

"An unidentified ship entered our orbit yesterday. They did not respond to our communications, when approached by our defensive squadron they left quickly. This has happened before, nefarious individuals end up here, realize where they are, and leave." he said.

"Sure, it happens all over. But what does that have to do with me and Brzko?"

"One of the other security reports of yesterday described an individual who was stopping Ploosnarians on the street and asking them if they knew you or Brzko. Sometimes this individual used your names, sometimes only a description. Knowing that you are dear friends of mine that often stay in the palace, someone alerted the palace guards. They were not able to locate this individual, but they did obtain a description, and an image from security cameras." Bartala said.

"So who was it?" M asked as Bartala took his tablet from his jacket pocket and unrolled it. He turned the screen so the Muse of Mischief could see it. She was looking at a short video clip playing in a loop. The individual in the clip was about the same build as Brzko, he had a long jagged scar running down his right cheek, and also his right forearm. He looked like countless other humanoids, except he was brushing his hair. He had extremely short black hair, and in his right hand he held a small soft bristled brush with no handle. He continually ran the brush over his head, front to back, front to back, front to back.

"The Brusher!" M exclaimed. "I expected his incarceration to last longer, after all the trouble he caused on Cazoova. But I'm not surprised that he came looking for me."

"You apprehended him, and he wants revenge. He's dangerous so I've taken the liberty of contacting Zri. You need protection." Bartala said.

The Muse of Mischief waved her hand and made a dismissive shrug, "I kicked his ass once, and I'll do it again. I might be female, but I'm not feeble."

It took just a second for Bartala to realize what she had said. He let out an enormous laugh, and stomped his feet. So loud in fact, that a palace guard opened the door and stuck his head in. "Emperor? Is everything OK?"

"Yes, yes, yes. The Muse of Mischief just cracks me up! Please alert us when Zri arrives from Gaznzul."

"As you wish Emperor." the guard said and closed the door.

"You've never told me what happened with the Brusher. I just know that you apprehended him alone on Cazoova and turned him over to the Gaznzulians."

"Pour me a shot of nekmid and I'll tell you the story." M said playfully. "But first I need to ask you a question.

Bartala raised his eyebrow at that, "Kiik has offered to transport all of the Rogsaars to Myaad. She has a ship large enough to take them all. Then your *barge* could take all of the ships back to Myaad sometime..."

"*Barge*? What is a barge?" Bartala interrupted.

When the Muse of Mischief smiled at him, he knew he was about to receive a playful insult. M removed her tablet from the pocket in her jacket, unrolled it, and called up an image of an Earth garbage barge. She turned it so Bartala could see it.

"Oh very nice M, very nice. Are you saying my state of the art transport ships are meant for hauling trash?" Bartala said, pretending to be insulted.

"So what do you think are you OK with the Kiik visiting Ploosnar for a few days and transporting the Rogsaars to Myaad?" M asked.

"Yes, yes, of course. I approve of this plan M. I have never met a Suus. Will Kiik be able to stay in the palace for a few days? Nalau will be very upset with me if she does not get to entertain a Suus,"

"Kiik is planning to stay on Ploosnar for two rotations, and then it will take her four to get here." M explained.

"Excellent, Nalau will have time to prepare. What will Kiik need to be comfortable? How big is a Suus? I heard they have four arms and that their skin is like needles, is that true?" Bartala asked, clearly excited by the idea of meeting a new species.

"Jeez, relax would ya?" M jabbed "I don't think you need to do anything special for Kiik. The Suus are entirely telepathic, they do not have mouths. Kiik will provide her own sustenance, vapor, while she is here. And yes, Suus have four arms, and their skin is covered with fine *needles*. But as long as you don't go around hugging them, you'll be fine."

"Oh no, will she be able to read all of my thoughts? How will I converse with her, I am not telepathic" Bartala asked.

"Yes, she has that ability but she will not *read* your thoughts unless you are conversing. Suus are very disciplined. Unless you two are alone, you will converse by speaking for the benefit of the non-telepaths in the vicinity. Suus "hear" non-telepaths just fine, they have ears." M explained.

"Please tell her I look forward to her arrival. I will notify the Rogsaars that they should prepare for departure in approximately six rotations. And I suppose that story I want to hear will have to wait, I must go speak to Nalau." Bartala said as he stood. "You are staying here I assume?"

"Ummm yeah! You still owe me a nekmid. And... I should wait for Zri." M said.

"Excellent, please inform Kiik that we are eager to have her here on Ploosnar. I will break the news of guests to my beloved Nalau and be back here to hear your story. DO NOT get into that nekmid before I return!" Bartala said while wagging his finger at M. He was clearly cracking himself up as he turned to leave the room.

Rather than go through the trouble of activating her earcom link to contact Brzko, M just went to Myaad. She had a hunch that Brzko and Kiik would be at the Myaad administration building making plans for their departure. Brzko was not surprised to see her.

"Hello M, how's Bartala?" he asked.

"He's fine, good. He is delighted by the idea of meeting you Kiik, and very grateful for your offer of help." she answered.

A general feeling of feeling honor emanated from Kiik.

"Are you going to stay and help us prepare for the trip?" Brzko asked.

"No, I have to get right back, before Bartala returns. He stepped out for just a minute to speak to Nalau. Also I need to be there when Zri arrives."

"Zri? What's wrong? Why are you waiting for Zri?" Brzko asked with serious concern.

"The Brusher is free and has been asking about us on Ploosnar. Bartala took the liberty of contacting Zri to meet me on

Ploosnar while they look for him." M explained, trying to put his mind at ease.

"So he's free and he's looking for you. No doubt he's pissed he got his ass kicked by a girl, even though that girl is the planet jumping, time traveling, Muse of Mischief, it would still piss most males off. I don't like it M, please go straight back to the palace and wait for Zri. If anything happens contact me." Brzko said kissing her cheek.

"I will, you two have a safe trip, and have fun playing spaceship Brzko." M said giving him a big hug. Then she was gone

~~~

"Why can't you use a communicator like everyone else?!" Bartala asked. "You've missed the first round of nekmid.

The Muse of Mischief had arrived back on the sofa where she had been seated when Bartala left the room, but she wasn't fast enough. Bartala had returned before her. He sat across from her, attempting to look perturbed. "Why use a communicator when I can just go talk to someone?" she fired back.

"I see your point; I guess if I had that ability I would do the same thing. But now Brzko and Kiik will be on the ship for four rotations, and Nalau will be preparing for their arrival, so you and I have plenty of time for those stories you owe me!" Bartala exclaimed.

"Pour me a nekmid and I'll tell you about the Brusher." M said.

Bartala eagerly complied, pouring nekmid for them. He knew they would want more before M was done with her story, be brought the bottle back to where they were sitting. The old friends settled in, Bartala kicked off his shoes and put his feet up on the coffee table, M kicked off her heels and drew her legs up on the plush sofa, towards her.

"Brzko and I received a request from the Ruling Council on Cazoova," she began, "they had been receiving consistent reports of young Cazoovians being removed from their parents, stolen. We went to Cazoova and started looking for patterns in the disappearances."

"How old is a Cazoovian before it can be raced?" Bartala asked.

"Even though they can communicate within their first year, Cazoovians don't begin to express free will until they are four or five years. They cannot race until they are seven, this ensures that they choose to race, and have plenty of time for training." M explained. "The Ruling Council is advised by Cazoovians and is tasked with making sure they are not exploited."

"I don't see how there could not be exploitation involved in non-indigenous beings using them for racing, and for the sole purpose of betting. It's preposterous!"

"This from the man that bets weary travelers he can return faster than they if they depart together through a portal on the Planet of Portals?" M asked.

"OK, well, I see your point. Maybe exploitation is too strong of a word." Bartala said, making a dismissive gesture with his free hand.

"It didn't take long for us to see that The Brusher had been lurking near the family of each Cazoovian that had lost offspring. With the help of the Gaznzulian surveillance, Brzko and I were able to catch The Brusher in the act." M said, as if it were no big deal.

"But there was an altercation between the Brusher and you, was there not? Rumor has it that you are responsible for that scar on his arm." asked Bartala.

"Yes. Brzko and I separated in order to trap him. I was alone when I confronted him and demanded that he release the infant Cazoovian he had just stolen. He complied and released the Cazoovian, but came after me. He made the mistake of assuming that I was weak. I shooed the Cazoovian away from the area so it would not be injured and the Brusher attempted to restrain me from behind. His elbow and his nose were broken in the struggle. By the time Brzko and Zri arrived he was in restraints. I suppose it devastated him that he got his ass kicked by a human girl."

"But you're not human."

"He doesn't know that." M said grinning.

"You will never cease to amaze me M, as tough as the best on my security team yet, always a lady with compassion and sometimes even grace. Maybe someday you will finally tell me the story of how you and Brzko met." Bartala teased.

"That would take some time Bartala, it was long ago, and it is a long story…" there was a knock at the door.

"Yes, what is it?" Bartala called.

The door opened and Zri entered, "Muse of Mischief, I am relieved to see you are safe. Emperor Bartala." he said, nodding in the Emperor's direction. "We are sweeping Ploosnar for the Brusher now. It should not take us long to locate him. As per the terms of his parole he has an embedded tracker. Coming after you is a violation of his parole agreement. He will be reincarcerated on Gaznzul." Zri said, taking a sentry post near the door.

"Thank you Zri." M said.

"So have you been to the races on Cazoova?" Bartala asked M.

"I've never attended the races as entertainment - sporting exploitation doesn't really appeal to me. But I've seen a few of them while working with the Ruling Council."

"I enjoyed them a few times many years ago, but they have lost their appeal. At first they seemed to be good fun. After awhile it seemed that they were just exploitation. I know they participate based on their free will, and that they are paid well, but I suspect that they do not understand the lifelong repercussions that this type of extreme physical activity will have on them later in life."

"It's interstellar NFL." M said, leaning forward to reach for the bottle of nekmid.

"Oh yes, I've heard of this Earth NFL. They call it football, no?"

"Yes, football. And it's similar, the exploitation of young athletes for the entertainment of others. Only the athletes often end up with bodies that seem to age much too quickly. Humans, like Cazoovians, are rather fragile."

"I wish I had seen you kick the Brusher's ass my friend! The shock you must have given him when he thought he could subdue you as easily as a human female."

"Well I look human." M replied with sarcasm.

"More like a freak of nature eh?" Bartala teased, "Especially with those striped stockings."

"You do realize that you are the only being that could say that to me and not be swallowing his teeth right?" M asked, sort of kidding.

"Oh yes, oh yes, I know that M. But we go way back, back to when you were but a child. A child with abilities you didn't understand. I suspect the only being you have known longer than me is Brzko. I have always done everything I could to protect you. Not that you need much protection from the likes of the Brusher!"

"I think Zri would argue that point, wouldn't you Zri?" M said turning towards Zri standing at the door.

"Muse of Mischief it is true that you need very little protection; however, you do sometimes, well, tend to... "Zri was looking slightly uncomfortable "rush in and then deal with the consequences."

At this Bartala couldn't help himself, he let out a very hearty laugh "Ha! I see that Zri knows you very well indeed."

"Yes, Zri has been looking out for me for quite some time and..."

Zri turned from the door and stepped toward where the Muse of Mischief and Bartala were sitting "M, my team has located and apprehended the Brusher. He was hiding on one of the moon outposts. He has been placed in the secure holding cell on my ship, he will be returned to his incarceration cell on Gaznzul within the hour."

"Great news Zri! Let's go talk to him." M said.

Bartala had known M for so long that he should not have been surprised that she wanted to face her stalker, but he was. He watched the conversation between Zri and M quietly.

"It will infuriate him to see you, but since he is back in our custody I suppose you will be safe enough."

"Great! Bartala, as always thank you for the hospitality. I should return within the hour, and then I will tell you story of how Brzko and I met if you still want to hear it, and you can tell me why your lovely wife is unhappy with you."

"I will be right here waiting M, drinking my nekmid." Bartala said with a smile.

M turned to Zri "Is your ship in a standard orbit above us?"

"Yes." Zri answered.

"Perfect, I'll see you there..." and with that M was gone from the room.

Zri disappeared a second later.

Gaznzulians were not able to create and use apertures, but they do have a few tricks up their sleeves. They have perfected transporters that are similar to the ones the Rogsaar ships used to return findings to Myaad. They can easily and instantly move between the surface of a planet and one of their orbiting ships. Which means, that even though they have some of the fastest ships in the Universe, there is no chance of them being able to keep up with the Muse of Mischief, even if she stays in the present.

~~~

"You! I should have killed you when I had the chance!" the Brusher was clearly very agitated by the Muse of Mischief's presence outside of his holding cell.

She had arrived on Zri's ship just a second or two before him. But it wasn't shocking to his crew. They all knew the Muse of Mischief well.

"Ahhh I missed you too Brusher." she teased "I just stopped in to say hi and ask how that arm healed. I see the break left you with a nasty scar."

He just glared at her through the invisible force field that sealed his cell. The Gaznzulians had taken his brush so he resorted to running his hand over his head. It was like watching a nervous dog lick its paws. The Brusher just kept running his hand over his head, front to back, front to back, staring at the wall in front of him.

"I wonder how long your incarceration will be this time, now that you've broken the terms of your release and come after me." That did it, M got a response.

The Brusher turned toward her, then tilted his head back and let out blood curdling roar.

M walked away, over to where Zri was standing, watching the exchange. "Zri, is that a smile I see?" M asked.

"Smile? No, of course not. I take your security very seriously, there is no room for humor." he said, busting out in a full on smile.

"And I appreciate the hell out of my friend." she said extending forward and kissing his cheek. "Do you need anything from me?"

"No, not at this time. I'm sure the Universal Security Council will contact you for a statement before they decide on the Brushers fate. Take care of yourself and call me if you need anything. I'll be close."

"Lucky for me, you always are my friend." and she was gone.

A LONG OVERDUE STORY

"Trella is where it began." The Muse of Mischief said.

"Hey wait a minute, you changed your clothes! Do you keep a wardrobe on Zri's ship?"

This made M laugh, "Uhhh no. I went home and changed before returning. I'm no longer in the mood for striped stockings."

"Mmmmm I do like this garment better. You actually look like a lady."

M had changed into a simple floor length skirt, and blouse. What Bartala couldn't see though was the left side of the skirt had an intermittent tear away seam. Beneath the skirt she wore solid black leggings. Time traveling, planet hopping superheroes just never know when they will be called upon to take action. "So anyway," she continued, "Trella is where it began."

"Trella? How did you ever find such a remote planet as a child? I remember it seemed like absolute paradise but it is in such a remote area, I've not been there since I became the Emperor of Ploosnar." Bartala said.

M chuckled at her friend's arrogance, as if an Emperor should maintain the freedom he had as a child. She continued.

"I never wondered how Trella came to be, or how I found it. It was always an escape for me. Sometimes I've wondered if it was hardwired. Some kind of safety feature, so that when I started traveling I would be sure to end up someplace safe. Can you imagine if I had ended up on the Black Sea Planet or Chyke 2C95 when I was a child? I may not have survived."

"Oh I can imagine that! I remember a tough but frightened adolescent that appeared in my father's palace after stumbling upon Ploosnar." Bartala recalled.

M smiled at her old friend and continued, "I never spoke of Trella to the humans around me. I didn't understand what I was doing when I opened an aperture and traveled, but I knew that they wouldn't understand it either and would surely not believe me. They probably would have locked me up and attempted to treat me for mental illness, which means prescribe mind altering drugs.

Anyway, once when I was very young the pretend family took a trip to the ocean, a place called Lincoln City, Oregon. We all piled in a gigantic green station wagon; that's a hideously ugly gas combustion automobile. I hated these family trips. They didn't provide me the hiding space I was used to. I loved my time at the ocean, the hugeness of it made me think of the possibility of other planets. I had been to Trella several times, but I had never had contact with a sentient being. For all I knew at the time, Trella could have been solely in my imagination. After the trip, life went back to *normal*, boring public school, bland food, and being surrounded by mindless zombies that were perpetually watching sitcoms."

"Sitcoms?" Bartala asked.

"Yes, a super Earth invention." M said sarcastically, "it stands for situation comedy. They are unimaginative drivel that's broadcast endlessly on the idiot box or television as it's actually called. It's basically a communication system gone bad. Originally it was able to provide worthy information and reasonable entertainment. But over the years, the greed of the Earth corporations turned it into an addictive propaganda machine. Humans spend their entire lives being programmed by the corporations, their standards are lowered, they're told what to eat, what to wear, even what to think."

Bartala recoiled in disgust, "No wonder you have such a dim view of the planet. It's disgusting that those responsible for the oversight of Earth didn't control the greed. You see, there is something to be said for a monarchy! Why do you and Brzko stay on that planet?"

"I cannot disagree with that, assuming it's the *right* monarch, and we stay because we were hidden there as infants. What if whoever hid us comes looking for us? Anyway, back in this *normal* day to day routine I start to daydream about the time I spent alone walking on the beach, I longed to be back there with the sand under my feet and the sound of the waves crashing. Imagine my surprise when I was there, I thought it, and then I was there."

"That must have been quite shocking. Were you frightened or excited?"

"Both. I panicked and thought of the room I had just been in, and then I was there. It was then that I realized I could go to specific places. I started traveling as much as I could. Mostly I just went back to the beach at Lincoln City. There is a very short river there. The D River, they call it the World's shortest river.

It's only a few hundred feet or something like that. Anyway the area is absolutely stunning, with the ocean and huge trees, big hills.

But there were a few times that traveling was a little, well concerning. Humans don't react well when you just appear in front of them. They have no concept of the Universe, most of them think they were created by the divine intervention of a god. So... if you just appear you too must be of a god status, they worship both good and evil gods. You see how that could work for or against you. But either way it tends to draw unwanted attention."

"Absolutely barbaric. Did you know that you weren't human at that time?"

"No but I was beginning to suspect. I started thinking about Lincoln City in the past; I knew the population was virtually nonexistent 100 years prior. Of course there was no way for me to verify the date the first time I went back in time but it was obviously the same place - the trees grew right down to the sand though, the highway wasn't there and neither were the buildings. I went as often as I could sneak away. It was fantastic, until I realized I was seeing someone else's footprints next to the river. After that, I started jumping to the forest and walking a short distance to the beach. I assumed it was just someone of that time, living in the area - maybe one of the local Native Americans from the nearby Yaquina tribe."

"Was it Brzko?" Bartala asked as he leaned forward. The story of how his dearest friend met her mate was clearly exciting him.

The Muse of Mischief smiled, not allowing herself to be deviated from the way she wanted to tell the story, she continued "Brzko had been hidden on the East Coast of North America. He was desperate to escape from an unhappy home. He had been experimenting with travel as well. We had never seen each other on Trella, but evidently we were both exploring the planet. After learning about the Oregon Trail in history class he started exploring Oregon."

"Oregon Trail?"

"I'm going to have to bring you a book about Earth history, although it would probably disgust you. Early settlers of the continent where we were raised spread from east to west, as they slaughtered the indigenous population. Their travels mostly followed the path that was called the Oregon Trail, as the farthest western point that was inhabitable, it was the destination. Anyway, Brzko had seen pictures of a place called Depot Bay, that is just south of where I was hanging out. He was intrigued by the rocky outcroppings and native people, but he branched out and started exploring. He was also raised by pretend parents that didn't really seem to care what he did, that left him plenty of time to explore.

The first time we saw each other I was sitting on a boulder next to the D River. I had arrived at the forest, and after making sure the coast was clear, as the Earth saying goes, I went down to the river. I was just enjoying the sound of the water and the fresh air. I saw movement not far from me, I looked up, and there he was, no further than you are now. I panicked and opened an aperture back to my bedroom."

Bartala poured them both another nekmid as he whistled through his teeth.

"When I saw him, it was like every cell in my body was electrified. I'd never experienced anything like it. I was obsessed, I had to meet this person but I wanted to be prepared this time. It turns out he had the same reaction. He felt the connection the minute he saw me, he was devastated when I disappeared. We both went back to that place as often as we could, I knew he was trying to find me, I could feel him. The problem was the time, how could we get there at the same time. I decided to leave a note for him. Even back then I wore a derby. I wrote a note telling him to meet me on May 27, 1912 at 10:00 AM at the D River. I wasn't sure he'd find the note, and I wasn't sure that I'd be able to travel precisely to that time but I had to try."

"And it worked didn't it?"

"Yes, I discovered that if I thought of the specific time, as well as the specific place, I could travel there. But you know how mischievous I am. I wanted to arrive first, so I arrived a few hours early at my usual spot in the forest. As I walked down to the beach I saw him. He was sitting on my favorite boulder, wearing a derby and holding mine, he had also arrived hours early. I knew I had met my match."

"Stop, stop, you will make me cry. No, don't stop, don't stop!!"

M smiled and giggled at Bartala's reaction. "So he stands up when he sees me and he is the most attractive being I've ever seen - tall, dark, confident, and wearing a long black trench coat with his derby. I boldly walked up to him and before I could speak he said "*I've been looking for you, my Muse*" I asked him how he knew my name and he said he hadn't stopped thinking about me since he saw me. He knew we were not from this planet, that we had been hidden here, and that we were connected, we were partners.

And that's it, we went back to our *normal* lives until we were of the age Earth considers a human to be independent. Then we left our pretend parents and we've been together since."

"How could you stand to be apart after meeting?"

"Brzko and I spent every minute we could together. Every time one of us could break free from the pretend parents we would meet in the past in Lincoln City or travel to Trella together. We spent as much time together as we could. Eventually we built our fortress, the Island, in Lincoln City. When he couldn't get away to meet me I'd come find you and stir up some trouble. Remember that time you hid all of your father's bisporks, wow, he was PISSED!"

"Hahaha yes, he was very pissed. But he saw the humor in it later after he calmed down. Did you meet Brzko before or after we met?" Bartala asked.

"Brzko and I met a few years before I stumbled my way to Ploosnar."

"I remember that day very well. My father was informed of a being that had appeared at the palace entrance, I went out to see what the commotion was, and there you were, surrounded by armed guards and still defiant. Ha! You were a sight, striped stockings, high heels, and a derby - a petite little lady struggling with the guards. How old were you?"

"I was eleven. You know I really hate being restrained. I was on Trella skipping rocks, just killing time, when I suddenly found myself here. Brzko and I have wondered if the ones that hid us on Earth may have placed something from Ploosnar on Trella to facilitate our meeting."

"An interesting idea. Perhaps there are clues of your origins on Trella. We should take a trip there together and see if we can find anything."

"Where are you planning to go now Bartala darling?" Empress Nalau had entered the room.

The Muse of Mischief stood and faced her "Empress Nalau, it's a pleasure to see you."

"Hello M, dinner is being served, will you join us?"

"It would be my pleasure." M said as she and Bartala joined Nalau. Today's story hour was over.

THE EMPEROR MEETS A SUUS

While waiting for Kiik and Agent Brzko to arrive, the Muse of Mischief and Emperor Bartala had spent their time between the Rogsaars and planning a trip to Trella. The time, of course, passed very quickly. Empress Nalau was busy running the palace, preparing for Kiik's arrival, and maintaining her benevolent presence among her loyal subjects.

The Suus have transporters capable of transporting beings between the surface and their ships but the logistics of loading almost one hundred Rogsaars and their provisions, made landing Kiik's ship a more logical choice. Bartala had cleared them for using his private landing pad directly beside the palace. The proximity to the palace made this space off limits to all but the highest ranking dignitaries. The Muse of Mischief, Emperor Bartala, Empress Nalau, and a handful of palace staff and guards, had gathered to meet the ship. It landed without incident but before the portal opened someone grabbed M from behind and swept her off her feet.

It was Brzko, he couldn't wait for the portals to open to be near his beloved Muse of Mischief. "I missed you M." he said lifting her up and kissing her.

He put her down and she regained her balance, "Hi Brzko, you know I missed you too. Did you have fun playing Suus spaceship with Kiik?"

"Actually yeah, it was really interesting. The Suus are brilliant, and they actually have a great sense of humor. They take their work so seriously that it rarely shows. But mostly I'm relieved to be with you again my love."

Bartala couldn't resist a chance to tease M "OK stop, stop, or go to your room! You two love birds..."

"Hush Bartala," Empress Nalau interrupted "you know you enjoy a good love story." she teased.

The laughing friends turned toward the Suus ship when they heard the sound of the ramp descending opening. Suus ships of this class are oblong, grayish in color and large, very large. The portal being used today was on the narrow end closest to the receiving group. The ramp descended from the open portal, a small group of Suss exited, slowly walking down the ramp in a tight formation. In front were two of Kiik's team, then Kiik, then two more of her team. The front two Suus were carrying large red banners. Once they cleared the overhang of their ship, the banners automatically extended. They were fantastic, seeming to be ever changing shades of red as they billowed in the breeze.

The sight of five four-armed, green beings with long tails was shockingly beautiful. So beautiful in fact that the receiving group stood and watched in captivated silence. Emperor Bartala escorted Empress Nalau to the edge of the landing pad to receive their guests, the Muse of Mischief and agent Brzko stood just a step behind, M behind Bartala and Brzko behind Nalau.

As the they neared the group the front two Suus stepped aside and Kiik stepped forward, bowed, and projected her greeting "Your Majesties, on behalf of the Suus I thank you for receiving us and allowing us this opportunity to experience Ploosnar. We appreciate your hospitality."

Emperor Bartala stepped forward and extended his right hand, as was the traditional Ploosnarian custom. Kiik stood, and followed his lead, extending her lower right arm and hand. Bartala grasped her hand and raised it high above their heads. "May you be honored with good fortune and long life my new friend, welcome to Ploosnar." He then brought her hand down and to the center of his chest, holding it just for a moment, above his uppermost heart. With the official greeting over, he released Kiik's hand, stepped back and let Empress Nalau, M and Brzko approach.

Empress Nalau, being the ever compassionate hostess approached Kiik boldly, grasped both of her lower hands and welcomed her "Welcome to Ploosnar Kiik, I am Empress Nalau. I hope your journey was without incident."

"It was Empress, thank you." Kiik projected.

"Please follow me to the palace, we have the most wonderful guest rooms prepared for you." Empress Nalau said.

"Thank you but we really could not impose on you," Kiik projected "we will be fine on our ship."

"You are honored guests, the first Suus to visit Ploosnar. Please, allow us to honor you as the dignitaries you are."

Kiik knew she was outranked by the Empress. There was no use in trying to resist Empress Nalau. "We are honored to be your guests Majesty and we thank you for your hospitality." Kiik projected.

M detected a feeling of excited intrigue. She suspected it was emanating from Kiik's crew. The Suus took their work so seriously that they probably rarely, if ever, had the opportunity to enjoy the kind of lavish hospitality that was about to be bestowed upon them. She caught Brzko's eye, he was detecting the same feeling.

"Wonderful, if you will follow me, I will show you to your rooms. After you have had a chance to refresh we can gather in the great golden sitting room for refreshments."

"Of course Empress." Kiik projected. She then turned toward her crew and seemed to pause. No doubt she was giving direction, the Suus carrying the banners turned and headed back to the ship, "Two of my crew will secure the ship and join us later." she projected.

Empress Nalau headed up the walk toward the palace, Kiik fell in sync with her and two of her crew followed directly, and two palace guards followed the group. That left Emperor Bartala, the Muse of Mischief, and Agent Brzko.

"Are you hungry Brzko, or did the Suus have something other than vapor to feed you?" Bartala teased.

Brzko laughed and said "No, no, I'm not hungry Emperor, we stocked the ship with acceptable supplies before leaving Myaad. But I would like a drink. Suus do not consume alcohol of any sort."

"Ech, I would not have enjoyed that trip!"

"I enjoyed the Suus, they are some of the most fascinating beings I've encountered. The amount of data they've amassed about the Universe is stunning." Brzko said.

"Come, let's go to my private sitting rooms for drinks while Nalau plays hostess. We should have plenty of time to make up for the last four days you spent sober. And we can plan our trip to Trella." Bartala said as he began walking toward the palace.

Brzko and M followed. "We're going to Trella?" Brzko asked.

"Yes! While Zri and his team were rounding up the Brusher, I actually got M to sit still long enough to tell me the story of how you two met. That caused us to reflect upon our first meeting and how M stumbled upon Ploosnar. Perhaps there was a reason, some link from Trella to Ploosnar." Bartala explained as they approached the palace.

"First, let's make sure everything is ready for the Rogsaars to return to Myaad." M said.

"Bah! M! You are a party pooper. I want to talk about a fun trip, not logistics. But of course you are correct. As long as we can plan with a nekmid in hand."

The trio entered the palace through the private side door, it led directly to the royal chambers, was heavily guarded and the biometric scanners ensured it could only be used when one was with a royal. The two palace guards that had followed the group back to the palace stayed at the door, there was no need to follow Bartala around his own home. They entered a long white hallway. It was lined with statues of previous Emperors on the left and Empresses on the right. The statues were in color, they seemed to be alive, although made from something that felt like marble.

"OK Bartala," M said stopping in front of the third or fourth statue, "I've been here a few times before and it's amazing but also kind of creepy. The previous royals seem so lifelike. It's as if they are looking at us."

"You get used to it, but when I was a child, my great-grandmother…" Bartala turned and stepped back a few steps to stand in front of an Empress that was presented in an amazing gown of silver. He nodded toward the statue of his great-grandmother, "…she told me these statues would honor me when I became Emperor. As I walked down this hallway every morning I would gain strength from the presence of each one. I did not believe her when I was a child, but now, I see that she was right. I am honored by the presence of my ancestors. Nalau and I will teach the same understanding of this honor to our child. But a child is a conversation best left for another day."

Other than Brzko, Bartala was by far the best friend M had; they knew each other extremely well. She could tell something was amiss when he mentioned having a child, there was a momentary look of deep sadness. When the timing was more appropriate she'd ask him about it.

The group continued on down the hall to Bartala's private sitting room.

"I love this room Emperor Bartala, it just feels comfortable." Brzko said as he entered.

"Thank you Brzko, please make yourself at home." Bartala said as he closed the door.

The table had been set with fresh fruits, lusimis, and of course nekmid. M settled into her usual spot, Brzko sat beside her and Bartala settled into his usual spot across from them. He poured them each a nekmid. Raising his glass to his friends he began a toast, "To my dearest friends, and our successful endeavors on Myaad."

"To us!"

"Here here!"

Bartala refilled the glasses the moment there were set upon the table. He leaned back and yawned. "Tell me about the Suus Brzko, what was it like to be on a ship with them for four days?"

"By the end of the trip I was feeling a little confined, I'm not used to traveling by ship." he answered.

"Oh poor you! Having to travel like a normal non-time traveling being." Bartala said sarcastically. They all laughed.

"Exactly! They were kind enough to grant me access to the Suus database. I spent some time searching for references to Clyrea X9. There is only one specific reference, the one Kiik told us about," he said looking toward M "but there were other incomplete references to planets that no longer exists I started attempting to cross reference that data to see if I could get anywhere."

"Clyrea X9?" Bartala asked.

"On Myaad, just before Brzko and Kiik left, she told us that she had found a reference to a planet called Clyrea X9 in their database. The beings of this planet had the ability to travel through space and time. The seemed to live a very long time or to be immortal, the males had dark skin and the females had light skin." M explained.

Bartala was very excited, he leaned forward "Great stars! We've got to find this place, it must be where you are from. What else do they know about Clyrea X9?"

Brzko offered what little information there was, "Unfortunately that's about all we know. There are references to an unnamed planet on the far side of the Trellan Galaxy that could have been Clyrea X9, or it could hold some clues. I'd like to have Zri send a crew out that way to start scanning and see what they can uncover."

"That settles it. "We're going to Trella after the Rogsaars are settled back on Myaad." Bartala said, "This will be splendid, it has been far too long since I've been on a mission with the two of you. Oh, the fun we will have!"

"Easy Bartala, you wouldn't want to mess up that pretty Londo hair of yours. Is Afrit still here on Ploosnar?" M asked. There was a knock at the door.

"Come." Bartala beckoned.

The door opened, a member of the royal staff presented himself, "Emperor Bartala, Empress Nalau has asked me to inform you that your presence is requested in the great golden sitting room." With the message having been delivered, he turned and left the room.

Bartala stood, "Yes, Afrit the Great is still here. I rarely see him, I think he has been out exploring every corner of Ploosnar. We will plan our Trella excursion another time. Now it is time to play royal host to our guests from Suus." He straightened his jacket and smoothed his ridiculously tall hair on the way to the door.

~~~

The great golden sitting room is the grandest room in the Ploosnar palace. As the name suggests, it is decorated with gold. The golden sofas seem to sparkle, if it wasn't for the black accent pillows they would have be too much. The ceiling peaks in a tower, there are golden tapestries suspended from the top.

Empress Nalau, Kiik, all four of Kiik's crew, and two of Bartala's staff were already present. Emperor Bartala turned on his official charm upon entering the room, giving Kiik and her crew a warm welcome to his palace. There was no need to serve refreshments to beings that sustained themselves off of vapors. Once everyone was seated Bartala's staff served nekmid to all but the Suus.

The group exchanged pleasantries about their recent trip but everyone seemed very uncomfortable. It was as if there was an elephant in the room, as they say on Earth. The Muse of Mischief decided to try something she'd never done before.

She attempted to project a thought to Kiik, "You seem uncomfortable, is everything alright?" She didn't really think it would work, so when she "heard" Kiik's answer it literally made her jump.

"Yes, we do not frequently socialize with other species, especially those of royalty. We are cautious to ensure we do not offend." Kiik projected back to M. It would be terribly rude to continue communicating this way while in a group. M decided to take control of the situation and attempt to put everyone at ease.

She asked aloud, "Kiik is there anything you or your crew would like to do while on Ploosnar? There are amazing blue forests filled with intoxicatingly beautiful flowers that may interest you."

Empress Nalau's look expressed her gratitude and relief toward M for initiating a comfortable conversation.

Kiik projected her response to the entire room, "Yes, thank you for asking. We are of course anxious to spend time with the Rogsaars but we will have plenty of time for that on the journey to Myaad. I am very interested in the flowers of Ploosnar, as you know the cultivation of scents is very important to us. For me personally, it is a hobby. Because Ploosnar adheres to acceptable scanning and safety standards, I have been authorized to obtain specimens if they are available."

Empress Nalau did not allow this opportunity to escape her, "Absolutely Kiik! We will arrange for you to tour the palace gardens with our lead botanist first thing tomorrow. She will provide you with any specimens you would like." She nodded to one of her staff. He promptly left the room, no doubt to arrange the botany tour.

"You are most gracious Empress, thank you. My first has an interest in bisporks. Ruur would like to meet one, and possibly ride one, would that be possible?" Kiik projected.

"Absolutely. We will arrange for a tour of the bispork stables tomorrow. Do you have transportation animals on Suus?" Bartala asked.

"No" both Kiik and Ruur projected at the same time. "This is why they intrigue me so, Emperor." Ruur answered, "My field of study is mammalogy. I am familiar with the mammals of many planets but I have not yet seen an animal that is used for transportation and able to communicate with language. I find this concept very intriguing." Ruur projected.

"Oh yes, you will find them intriguing. I don't care for them as transportation but the Muse of Mischief and Agent Brzko sometimes ride them when they are here."

With the entertainment plans set for tomorrow the conversation stalled. Smalltalk was not the forte of the Suus.

There was a brief knock, the main door to the great golden sitting room opened. A palace butler stepped in to announce a visitor, "Your majesties, Afrit the Great of Jinn." Afrit entered the room. Both the Emperor and Empress stood, as did the Muse of Mischief and Agent Brzko, this was a formal meeting of dignitaries. All five of the Suus stood as well, at first M thought they were following the example and behaving with formality, but then she saw that they were actually recoiling from Afrit. Every needle like hair on their green skin was sticking straight out. Kiik's thoughts were projected throughout the room.

"Danger! There is a shapeshifter among us. Maintain your defenses."

"Oh relax sister! That stuff on Suus happened a very long time ago, before either of us was born... or hatched?" Jinn shrugged and as he casually plopped down in a large armchair.

Kiik was a little confused by his familiarity, his comfort at taking a seat amongst them, "You know this shape shifting being?" she projected.

Bartala, as the lead dignitary answered "Yes Kiik, he is our guest. We have no reason not to trust him. But it seems that something happened to cause the Suus to distrust Jinns. Please sit I assure you nothing will happen here."

The Suus had been huddled in a small group, their posture reminded M of hissing cats. They relaxed just slightly and took their seats again. Before everyone was seated Afrit the Great offered an explanation.

"OK so check it out, a long, long, long time ago some of my ancestors thought it would be fun to explore Suus. They of course presented themselves as Suus in order to move freely about the planet. The only problem is that Jinns are not telepathic. Things got a little frantic when real Suus tried to communicate with them. There was a lot of name calling, and banishing, and things like that. No big deal really. I mean we pissed them off and they banished up from Suus forever." he shrugged as if it had been no more than a childish game.

"That is not quite accurate shapeshifter." Kiik projected.

"My name is Afrit, but you can call me Afrit the Great."

"Afrit the Great, the Suus version of history includes the Suus that were hurt during the apprehension of the Jinns. To our knowledge, Suus has never been infiltrated by an unknown at any other time."

"Well at this point it's vapor in the clouds kid. We have to get past it, it wasn't me and it wasn't you. I think we could learn a lot from each other. Jinns have a huge database of navigational charts and I hear the Suus have a huge database of everything. As a gesture of goodwill, I offer you full access to the navigational databases of Jinn. I'll even have a copy of it sent to you."

After a moment Kiik stood and walked toward Afrit the Great, "Afrit the Great you are correct in your assessment that we should put the past behind us. It was not you that caused the chaos on Suus. You are also correct that we have much to offer each other. I request that you forgive my inappropriate judgment of you, and I offer you my friendship." Kiik bowed her head and waited for his reply.

"No issues here sister, the past is the past." Afrit said.

Kiik returned to her seat and this time Brzko jumped in to move things along. "How many Rogsaars are here Emperor Bartala?"

"I think the last count was 118. Some of them will be returning to the planets they were on when we found them, and a few have requested to become residents of Ploosnar. I will of course grant them residency. For those that want to return to other planets, they will need to know if Myaad will allow them to take their ships. If they will, I can have their ships refurbished, if not I will provide them with transportation."

"Emperor Bartala, your generosity is remarkable. You and Empress Nalau are very giving." Kiik projected.

"My beloved Nalau has brought about much change. She has helped me settle down and taught me the value of giving."

Empress Nalau, seated in the chair beside her husband's turned to face him. As she did, the Muse of Mischief caught her gaze - their eyes lock for just a second, but that was all it took. They both burst out laughing.

"Oh darling Bartala you never cease to entertain me." Nalau said reaching for his hand. He looked a little bewildered. "You, settled down?" M asked. "How long ago was it when we found you betting with weary travelers on the Planet of Portals?"

"Oh well, that was different. I was, well it was.... Um that is to say... OK I concede, let's just go with the giving part then." He said dismissing the subject entirely.

The visitors were no doubt a little lost with the conversation. Once again Brzko jumped in and saved the day, "While you are showing Kiik and Ruur around Ploosnar tomorrow, M and I will visit the Rogsaars and make sure they are ready to depart. We can also check with Myaad about the old Rogsaar ships."

"Your majesties, we feel the need to retire. We must rest in preparation for tomorrow's activities." Kiik projected as she and her team stood. "Thank you for an enjoyable evening, the hospitality is appreciated."

Both the Emperor and Empress stood, Bartala addressed the Suus. "It is our pleasure to have you visit the Palace of Ploosnar. If there is anything we can do to make your stay more comfortable, please do not hesitate to let us know."

The Suus projected their gratitude.

Empress Nalau stepped toward the door, "If you'll follow me, I will show you back to your rooms. The palace can be a little confusing."

The group left the room. As soon as the door was closed Bartala addressed Brzko, M, and Afrit "I'm starving! Let's go to the kitchen and eat. Do you mind a casual meal without all of the ceremony?"

"Nope, that sounds great to me. Are you hungry M?"

"Hell yeah, always."

They headed for the door. Kitchen meals were nothing new to them. It was often how they had dined after excursions. Raiding the refrigerators of a foreign planet was always an experience.

~~~

"Ewwww! What is that? It looks slimy, like squid." Agent Brzko said with disgust, as he watch the Muse of Mischief eating long strips of something out of a bowl that Emperor Bartala had handed her.

They were having a great time raiding the royal the refrigerators. They had thus far killed off the lusimis, a bowl of salad, and a couple of fruit trays.

"You've got to try this! It's pragma, kind of a cross between grass and fruit. It only ripens once per year and it doesn't keep well. You have to eat it while you can." the Muse of Mischief explained.

"It is quite a delicacy hear on Ploosnar." Bartala added.

"Hmmmmm" Brzko was still skeptical, but given the way Bartala and M both loved food, he knew they could not make a bad suggestion. He also knew that it was not squid, all Ploosnarians were vegetarians. They considered the eating of animals, or products derived from animals, to be barbaric. "OK, hook me up M." He tilted his head back and opened his mouth. M took a piece of the pragma from the bowl and dangled it above Brzko's mouth after it unraveled it was easily a half meter long. She slowly lowered it into his mouth.

Bartala and Afrit were both laughing at this exchange.

He began to chew, and all three fixated on him, waiting to see what he thought, "SHIT, that's good!" He took the bowl and fished out another piece, and then he handed it to Afrit, "You've got to try this!"

The friends laughed. "Yes it is delicious. We grow fields of it to the north of the palace, after it's harvested, we let it ferment slightly. Some say it has a flavor that starts sweet and then becomes savory, others say it is just savory. It is a very healthful food, full of vitamins and minerals. But most important, the taste is divine." Bartala explained.

One of Nalau's personal staff entered the room and approached Bartala, "Emperor."

"Yes, what is it?"

"Empress Nalau has asked me to inform you that she has retired for the evening. She will not be joining you for dinner."

"Thank you. Please tell her I will retire soon."

"Certainly Emperor." he said leaving the room.

"That sounds like a good idea. I think I'll retire too. M are you ready?" Brzko asked.

"Not yet, I'll help Bartala straighten up and then join you." M said.

Brzko knew that meant she needed to have a private conversation with Bartala. He kissed her cheek and headed to their rooms. "G'night Bartala, Afrit."

Afrit the Great also took his leave "Later kids."

"Rest well my friends."

Alone with Bartala, M decided to approach the subject of a child. They had known each other for long enough that there was no reason not to just ask him, "So what's the story behind your comment about having a child when we were walking through the hall of ancestors earlier?"

Bartala was placing the empty dishes near the sink for his kitchen staff to deal with. He paused and looked at the Muse of Mischief "Empress Nalau has invoked her right to use a surrogate to have our children." He was clearly disappointed.

"Isn't that an old custom, a really old custom?"

"Yes very old, it has not been done for generations. I think that my great-great-great grandmother was the last one."

"So what does it actually mean? Is it just the way it sounds, you're and Nalau's child is carried to term by another? M asked.

"Precisely. And we now know that the bond between mother and child is not as strong when a surrogate is used. That is why the practice was abandoned long ago."

"Why does she want to use a surrogate?"

"She does not want to be a mother."

"Ouch."

"Yes, ouch. She sees women like you, free of parental responsibilities and she wants the same thing."

"But she understands that as Empress of Ploosnar she is obliged to at least attempt to produce a child, an heir."

"Yes, but she does not have to actually "mother" the child. It is a great disappointment."

"I can understand both sides of this Bartala. Not all women are meant to be mothers. But without an heir your family line will end with you. This seems like an honorable solution. Why can't you be the main parental figure? There is no requirement that it be a mother. In fact we both know that there are many species where the male cares for the offspring. Besides it is better that she knows what she wants before she has the child. Otherwise the results could be disastrous. A poorly raised child is of benefit to no one. This way you still have an heir and she maintains her happiness - and some of her freedom."

"How do you do that?"

"Do what?" M asked.

"Take away my self-pity and show me the logical side of my wife's decision."

"C'mon Bartala, I'm the Muse of Mischief!" M said ribbing him with her elbow "And I've known you since we were young. I also have a little bit of insight into the female mind." she said rolling her eyes. "I'm female…"

"Not feeble!" Bartala finished one of her favorite sayings for her. "Thank you my friend." he said embracing her in a bear hug. He let her go and they began walking toward the door. "I hope Nalau is not asleep yet. I must tell her that I have come to terms with her decision and I will embrace it with my usual gusto."

"Gusto? Really? You have been watching way to much Earth television my friend!"

BISPORKS, GARDEN TOURS, AND AIRCOACH RACES

The Muse of Mischief and Agent Brzko were downstairs for an early breakfast with Emperor Bartala and Empress Nalau the next morning. It was going to be a busy day. The Empress would make sure that her Suus guests had a delightful time. Emperor Bartala, the Muse of Mischief and Agent Brzko would visit with the Rogsaars and make sure they were ready for the journey back to Myaad. Afrit the Great had departed the palace early. Today he was off exploring the moons of Ploosnar.

The Emperor and Empress were, as usual, a stunning fashion statement. She wore an ankle length teal dress with flared sleeves; she wore a brooch with her family crest on the left side of the high collar. There were ribbons of the same color woven through her hair. He wore black slacks with a long black velvet jacket. The jacket was lined and accented with the same teal color as the Empress's dress. The Emperor had donned his family's crest for today's activities. He displayed it proudly on a chain, just under his teal necktie.

As today was going to be busy, breakfast was served buffet style. There was no time for elaborate, formal service that was customary at most palace meals. Nalau, M, and Brzko sipped their morning tea as Bartala made his way through the delights that were presented on the buffet table. As he neared the end, Nalau began working her way down the buffet spread, she called to M.

"Muse of Mischief I hope you will try the pragma fruit this morning. It is perfectly ripe right now. I find it delightful with gashi grain."

"Gashi?"

M stepped forward to see what the Empress was talking about. When she came up alongside Nalau, the Empress leaned toward her and whispered, "I don't know what you said to him last night but I must extend my sincerest gratitude. We have been struggling with the conditions of having a child. It has been frustrating and painful for both of us. But somehow you were able to help my beloved husband see the issue from a different perspective." Empress Nalau slipped her free arm around M's waist and leaned toward her, giving a sideways hug. "Thank you M."

M noted that Nalau had casually called her by the nickname M. "You're welcome Empress, I've known Bartala since we were children and when he's acting like a child I'm able to call him out." The ladies started giggling, they couldn't stop, it escalated into full blown laughter as they each pictured the many childish ways of Bartala.

"What is so funny about breakfast you two?" Bartala asked from his seat at the head of the table.

"Nothing to share here…"

"Just girl talk."

"Uh-oh Bartala, I think they may be plotting against us today. M, what are you up to? Brzko asked playfully.

"Nothing, just getting some breakfast. You should really try the pragma with gashi grains."

Knowing their efforts to be let in on the joke were futile the men exchanged looks. They both knew continuing to push wouldn't work, so why bother?

With everyone seated at the table they conversed about their plans for the day. "The final count of Rogsaars returning to Myaad with the Suus is 86." Bartala announced. "The kitchen staff has packed three times as much food as they will need. It is better to be prepared. Once we finish eating I would like tour the Suus ship and see if they need anything else to accommodate the Rogsaars."

"I'll go with you. Do you need help with anything Empress Nalau?" M asked.

"Thank you for asking M. I do not think I need any help this morning. I am going to tour the gardens with Kiik and our botanist. It is a luxury for me to spend time touring the gardens. I cannot resist an opportunity to see it through the eyes of a Suus. It should be thrilling to tour our extensive flower gardens with a species that appreciates of scent of individual flowers."

"This pleases me Nalau. Thank you for giving yourself permission to enjoy today. You work so tirelessly to please others." Bartala said.

"I was thinking about accompanying Ruur on his mission to become familiar with bisporks. I'm curious to see how they react to a Suus." Brzko announced.

"So you're wondering if they bisporks will talk back to a Suus, they way they always seem to talk back to you?" M asked.

"Yep, uh-huh, that's it. And I think it's about time to depart for the stables, so if you'll excuse me your majesties, M." Brzko said as he stood and prepared to make his exit.

"Enjoy your day Brzko." Bartala said.

"Thank you for offering your companionship to Ruur, Brzko. You and M are like family to us, and we sincerely appreciate your efforts." Empress Nalau said.

"It's my pleasure Empress. We certainly appreciate all that you do for us. Bye M," he said as he bent down and kissed her cheek.

"Bye, have fun. Bartala I'm sure it's time for us to go too." M said.

As Brzko departed a palace butler stepped into the room, "Your majesties, Kiik and her companions are waiting for you at the entrance to the palace."

"OK thank you." Bartala said.

When the trio arrived at the entrance Brzko and Ruur were already gone. Empress Nalau, Kiik, and another of her team, headed down the stairs with the botanist, their tour would start with the gardens at the bottom of the stairs. Nalau had arranged for several members of the gardening staff to join them with various carts and storage containers. It looked like they were going to be quite busy.

The other two Suus were waiting for the Muse of Mischief and Emperor Bartala at the top of the stairs. "I am Taat and this is Lyyl, we will be assisting you with preparing our ship to transport the Rogsaars to Myaad." the Suus on the left projected. Luckily he had gestured toward Lyyl during the introduction. Otherwise they would have not been able to determine which was which as the communication was telepathic.

"Great, let's go to the ship. The supplies should have been delivered early this morning." Bartala said as he headed down the stairs. It was a short walk to the private landing zone where the

Suus ship was. "Have you enjoyed your stay on Ploosnar thus far?" he asked them.

"Yes," Lyyl projected. "We do not often have time to freely explore the gardens of other planets. We both work in transport. Our time is spent moving cargo to and from Suus. This has been a very enjoyable diversion from our normal duties. There are many flowers, and many scents here that we have not previously encountered."

"It will not take long to load the cargo today. And if your ship needs no modifications we will have a lot of free time. We also have all day tomorrow. Is there anything either of you would like to do or see while you are here?" Bartala asked.

The response to the question was odd. There was no direct telepathic communication. Instead a general feeling of conflict seemed to emanate from one of the Suus. It was like an answer was on the tip of the tongue as they say, but it was being suppressed.

"What is it, you can speak without fear of reprisal and our conversation will stay confidential." Bartala assured them.

It was Taat that answered. "We understand that there are races with the aircoaches, we would both like to see these races and if possible operate an aircoach in a competitive manor. We do not have this type of activity on Suus."

"So you want to be race coach drivers? You're going to love it." M said.

"We will need to obtain permission from Kiik." Lyyl projected.

"Really? Where is the fun in that? Hmmmm, let me take care of getting permission from Kiik. I have an idea she will not be able to refuse."

"As you wish Emperor."

They had arrived at the Suus ship. "Good. Now let us get this freight loaded so we can continue on with our day."

Once the Suus had the ship open it didn't take Bartala's crew long to load the stockpile of food, basic medical supplies, and other consumables.

The Muse of Mischief was curious about the actual space the Rogsaars would be in for four days. "May we tour the space where the Rogsaars will be staying during the trip?"

"Yes, the dormitory is this way." Lyyl walked toward an opening in the wall of stock room, it looked like a closet space but it was rounded. Once M, Bartala, and Lyyl were inside a force field covered the doorway they had just walked through. M had just the slightest sensation of dropping. She noticed the area outside of the doorway had changed. It was some type of elevator system and it was smooth. They stepped out into a long hallway. It was lined on both sides with small rooms. Each room had a bed, a sink, and a sitting area with a desk and communication portal.

As the group made their way down the hall Lyyl projected the answer to the question that both M and Bartala were pondering, "We have modified the cargo space to hold 110 individual rooms. Down here at the end of the hallway is a community area and kitchen facility."

"Wow, this is quite impressive, all for a four day journey. The Rogsaars will be traveling in style." Bartala said as he looked over the community area.

"You said the space was modified, so these rooms were installed just for transporting the Rogsaars?" M asked.

"Yes" Lyyl projected. "We transport a variety of freight around the Universe. The Suus are often called upon to provide aid services to refugees, sometimes we transport groups that do not have access to their own ships, and sometimes we provide evacuation transportation. The rooms that you see are modular; we are able to set them up in this space to accommodate a variety of needs."

"I'm beginning to like you Suus more and more all the time!" Bartala exclaimed. "Is there anything else that needs to be prepared prior to your departure?"

"I do not think so. Taat, is all of the cargo loaded?" Lyyl projected. Taat had entered the room behind them."

"Yes, all cargo is loaded and secured. The only remaining cargo to load is the personal items that the Rogsaars bring with them. We will begin loading them and their personal items midday tomorrow. Tomorrow night we will all sleep on the ship, with an early departure planned for the following morning." Taat projected to all of them.

"Excellent, then you two are free until midday tomorrow. I need your help with something." Bartala said. M knew from his tone of voice that he was up to something. "I've already sent a message to Kiik and asked for her permission to have you two help me this afternoon. She of course gave her approval."

"It is our pleasure Emperor Bartala, how may we assist you?" Lyyl projected, thinking that the Emperor really needed his help.

"I'm short by two drivers at this afternoon's aircoach races. I need you two to fill in as drivers." Bartala said with a chuckle.

"Oh way to go Bartala, I knew you would find a way to help Lyyl and Taat get to race." M said. Bartala was absolutely beaming. "While you boys are playing *go speed racer* I'm going to go visit with the Rogsaars and let them know when they will be moving to the Suus ship. Have a great time and be careful."

"Are you two ready?" Bartala asked as he headed toward the exit.

Both Lyyl and Taat projected affirmation and excitement as they followed Bartala to the door.

The Muse of Mischief activated her com link to Brzko once she was outside. "Hey Brzko where are you? Back at the stable yet?"

"Yes, we returned a few minutes ago. Ruur and I are feeding the bisporks. Is everything OK?"

"Yep, the cargo is loaded. I'm heading to the stables now." The Muse of Mischief said as she arrived at the front entrance to the bispork stables.

~~~

"So how was the ride Ruur, did you enjoy yourself?" The Muse of Mischief asked.

Ruur was clearly beside himself with joy as he brushed the bispork he had been riding. "I enjoyed the ride very much. I had no idea what it would be like to ride such a large being that has free will. It was... exciting."

"Were you able to communicate with the bisporks?" M asked.

The bispork answered for him "Green been, good ride, like him but heavy."

The Muse of Mischief, Agent Brzko, and the bisporks all laughed out loud, while laughter emanated telepathically from Ruur.

"How far did you ride?" M asked Brzko.

"We went all the way out to the dump."

"Oh that's a pretty long ride, but the trail through the forests is beautiful."

Ruur agreed, "Yes, we took some extra time and I was able to investigate the forest. There are some magnificent flowers there. The scents are quite intoxicating."

"How did thing go with loading the ship? Is everything ready for departure the day after tomorrow?" Brzko asked.

"Yep," M said as she climbed up on the stable fence and sat cowboy style. "The only thing left to load is the Rogsaars and their personal items. That will commence at midday tomorrow. I'm headed over to fill them in after this."

This caught Ruur's attention, "If you would not mind, I would like to accompany you. I should first check in with Kiik, but after that."

"Sounds good, do you need me to have someone locate her and the Empress?"

"Thank you, no. I can reach her telepathically." Ruur projected.

"Just how far can you be from each other and still communicate?" Brzko asked.

"It is dependent on many factors, possible interferences, but certainly we would be able to communicate anywhere on this planet without having visual contact." Ruur projected, "Once you involve atmosphere the variables can have more impact. But we are also able to communicate across long distances if we have a visual link, like with a communications portal."

"Impressive!" Brzko said.

"Well if you two are ready then, let's go to Lecur. Hmmmm Ruur, we can contact the palace to send us an aircoach, or if you're up for an adventure you can go with me." M said.

"You can transport beings with you?" Ruur projected, his excitement could be felt.

"Yes, we have to be in physical contact and you have to be willing."

"I don't know what to say, that would be excitement I had not anticipated. Yes, I am certainly willing." Ruur projected, "what do I need to do?"

"Keep me from getting poked by those little needles on your skin." M said sort of jokingly. "Actually just relax, I'll take your arm and you won't even notice we're moving...." M stepped forward, alongside Ruur; she put her left hand on the forearm of his upper arm, and placed her right hand in his lower hand. "... until we're there."

And they were. Moving others in mid sentence was a mischievous little thing she liked to do. It kept the hitchhiker from having a chance to get nervous, or doubtful. That happened with Bartala when they were young, he'd get nervous, she'd go and arrive without him. She kept having to go back and get him; so, she learned not to build up to the departure.

She kept a firm grip on Ruur's arm and hand, just in case he was unstable upon arrival. To be in a different location in the time that it takes to blink can be a little unnerving for some. Brzko was right there with them, on the edge of the courtyard where they had met with the Rogsaars a few days ago. Ruur was stable, she stepped back and looked at him, "Welcome to Lecur, how do you feel?"

"Like I want to do that again!" Ruur projected. "Suus believe that we have an advantage over some beings because we are telepathic. But the ability to move yourself to any location by far exceeds telepathy."

Brzko patted Ruur on the shoulder, "That's what almost everyone says. Are you ready to meet some Rogsaars?"

"Yes, I look forward to it." Ruur projected.

The trio began walking toward the central courtyard; there were a few dozen Rogsaars in the area. The only way to tell them apart seemed to be their age and the style of their garb. Several of them turned and looked towards the trio. Then they began staring. At first the Muse of Mischief was confused, what could be wrong? Then she realized that most of these Rogsaars had not previously seen a Suus. Four armed, green beings tend to attract attention around fair skinned two armed bipeds.

"Muse of Mischief, Muse of Mischief, do you remember I, ahhh remember me? I am Rogsaar of Earth!" A Rogsaar had run up to the group as they approached the courtyard.

"Rogsaar, hello! Yes of course we remember you. Are you ready to return to Myaad?" M asked.

"Yas, yas, I enjoyed Ploosnar and the orange rooms in the palace but I have not been to Myaad since I was a small Rogsaar. Will we leave soon?"

Brzko fielded this one, "Yes, tomorrow at midday all Rogsaars that are returning to Myaad will board the Suus ship. You will depart early the following morning."

"Oh very good, very good, we are excited to go home." Rogsaar said. "I will tell the others to prepare, when we are leaving. Thank you for finding me Brzko." He just about jumped into Brzko's arms to hug him. He was clearly very grateful that M and Brzko had found him after spending so many years alone on Earth. Before Brzko could even introduce Ruur, Rogsaar ran off to tell the others of the pending departure.

The trio continued on, "Let's take a seat at one of the tables. I suspect there are a few Rogsaars that would enjoy meeting a Suus." M said as the group took seats at one of the first open tables. She was right.

A Rogsaar dressed in a black jumpsuit, with red stripes running down the side, approach the table. "May I join you?"

"Of course." Brzko answered as he stood, Ruur followed his lead and also stood.

"I am of course Rogsaar I was on an outpost on Smd which is a moon of Drolla O0. There is a small trading colony there, they gather precious elements and trade for other supplies. After being stuck there I began helping a local sarfet with his trading shop. I am pleased to be returning to Myaad, and I suspect it is you that I have to thank for that? Are you the Muse of Mischief and Agent Brzko? The ones that found the Rogsaar of Earth?"

"Yes, that's us. I'm glad you're excited to be returning to Myaad. With the help of the Suus aberidus has been eradicated and now there is an opportunity to rebuild your society." M said.

"Suus, I have not met a Suus, but I think you might be a Suus?" Rogsaar said as he turned toward Ruur.

"Yes, I am a Suus. My name is Ruur I am the first to the captain of our ship, Kiik. Much pleasure will be received from helping Rogsaars return to Myaad." Ruur projected.

Rogsaar looked a little perplexed, "That was in my head. I was told that Suus are telepathic but I did not understand what communication would be like. This is very fascinating. Can you read my thoughts?"

A small group of six or seven Rogsaars were now surrounding the table. They were all very curious about the species that would be taking them home to Myaad. "Suus are trained to only read the thoughts of others when they are conversing with telepaths. With non-telepaths we use our ears to hear words, or thoughts."

"What do you eat? One of the Rogsaars standing near Ruur asked.

"Vapor, Suus obtain their sustenance from vapor." Ruur answered.

"What will we eat on the way back to Myaad?" another asked.

M fielded this one, "Emperor Bartala has been kind enough to stock the ship with more than enough provisions for your journey home. There is a common area with a large kitchen where you can prepare your meals."

"Can we see the ship? We are curious about it."

"That is up to Ruur." M answered.

"Yes, you can see where you will stay on the ship. I will confirm with Kiik. It is not too far from here, we could walk. How many of you would like to go?"

There were only about twenty Rogsaars that wanted to see the ship. M suspected that the remaining Rogsaars wanted to maximize their time in the fresh air.

While Brzko and the Muse of Mischief were not official representatives of Ploosnar, they did have a standing here and would always do what they could to represent the palace. It did not seem right to let Ruur and a group of Rogsaars wander over to the Suus ship unescorted. Brzko stepped up.

"I'll go over to the ship with you Ruur, in case you need anything from the palace along the way". He said.

"Thank you Agent Brzko, I do appreciate your attendance." Ruur projected.

Brzko bent down and kissed M's cheek, "I'll see you in a while M."

"Bye Brzko."

The small group departed, M was left sitting at a table with a few Rogsaars. "Have any of you decided to stay on Ploosnar?" she asked the group.

"Yes, I will be staying and I know of several others." answered a Rogsaar that was dressed in Ploosnar fashion. M couldn't help but wonder what his white hair would look like if he took on the Londo style that Bartala was so fond of.

"Where were you before?" M asked.

"I was on Wrexna. Have you heard of it?"

"Yes, I've been there a few times. They invent some great gadgets but the food was not much to my liking."

"I agree the food is very bad. That alone is enough of a reason not to return!" Rogsaar said.

"And you don't want to return to Myaad?"

"Maybe someday. But after struggling to survive on Wrexna for so many years I do not have an interest in being on Myaad while society is rebuilt. There is a lot of work to do in order to rebuild. I am not young, I want to contribute in a way that I enjoy but I do not want to struggle again. The Emperor Bartala has been kind enough to offer us places in his society. I have already been given private quarters, and an assignment that is much to my liking. I will be a member of the palace kitchen staff. After so many years with the food on Wrexna I am looking forward to the assignment."

The Muse of Mischief chatted with the Rogsaars for a while. They were all much more relaxed than during her previous visits. It didn't take long for Brzko to return the small group of Rogsaars that been on a tour of the Suus ship.

"Where's Ruur?" she asked Brzko as he returned.

"He was summoned to meet up with Kiik and his crew at their ship. They have some final preparations to attend to before the Rogsaars board tomorrow. I'm sure they want to load the flora specimens carefully. It sounds like they will be taking a large collection home with them."

The Rogsaar that had been on Wrexna spoke up, "If you will excuse me, I must also prepare for tomorrow. I am not departing on the ship but I am moving to my private quarters here on Ploosnar. I'm sure the returning Rogsaars need time to prepare as well."

"Of course! Thank you for chatting with while the others toured the ship." M said. "I'm sure we'll see you again, we are often on Ploosnar. We will be here to see the others off tomorrow."

The remaining Rogsaars made their way back to their temporary quarters to prepare for departure, leaving Brzko and the Muse of Mischief alone in the courtyard. The silence and blue flowers were peaceful, but it didn't last long.

"Ah ha! I thought you two might be here." Bartala called as he approached.

"Hey Bartala, did you manage to turn the Suus into aircoach racers?" M asked.

Bartala let out a very hearty laugh as he took a seat at the table. "Ohhhh yes and I think it will be a new passion for them. I may have ruined them. It was as exciting for them as it was for me. Luckily no one was hurt."

"Good. I bet they had a fantastic time. I don't think Suus do a lot of racing on their home planet, or any type of recreation for that matter." M said.

"Speaking of home....." Brzko said, "We're probably not needed here until tomorrow M, let's go home for a while."

"Great idea, I can hear the ocean waves calling!"

HOME ON THE BEACH

The fortress that the Muse of Mischief and Agent Brzko call home is amazing. The house is large and sits high atop the rocky cliffs overlooking the Pacific Ocean. On a clear day the view continues for miles. And the sunsets... they have found none better in the Universe.

From the outside, the home looks like any other large home along the coast. It sits far off from the entrance gate, so the house cannot be seen from the road. There is a large stone fence surrounding it. Inside that fence is another that cannot be seen, it's basically a force field, Gaznzulian technology to keep them safe from intruders.

The front of the house overlooks the Pacific Ocean. The front all is two stories tall and all glass, providing an endless view. The decor is interstellar eclectic. Most of the art looks like it's from Earth but it is in fact a collection of things from throughout the Universe. There is a collection lining the windowsill in the dining area, to the casual observer they look like shells with a few glass pieces mixed in. But the items that look like glass are actually the discarded shells of the sw'dell of the Black Sea Planet. But the seas of the Black Sea Planet are very different from the seas of Earth.

A selection of the art has been created by Brzko. He is an amazing artist, and enjoys painting whenever he has the time, which of course, is not often. The main hallway is lined with a series he painted, representing the Birdohnirc of Drolla O0. These are amazing little freshwater hive beings. They look a lot like the exotic goldfish of Earth but they connect to make one being, and then separate to gather food and explore. They never stray far from their group. Each group combines to make one amazing being, each one is unique. They look like colorful underwater flowers with their long fins flowing in the current; each has a unique pattern of color.

The Muse of Mischief was sitting on the window bench in the living room, looking out over the ocean, when Brzko brought her a champagne flute a sat next to her.

"Champagne? What are we celebrating?" she asked.

"Clyrea X9 M. It's the first real clue to discovering our origins, to discovering *what* we are." He clinked his glass against hers and they both sipped.

"It's exciting isn't it Brzko? But sometimes I think I need to just accept what my life is and not worry about trying to figure out *where* I'm from, or *what* I actually I am."

"Are you saying you don't want to research Clyrea X9, or the area where it may have been?"

"Hell NO! I can't wait to start. I guess I'm just preparing myself for the possibility that we'll never know what we are or where we came from. And that has to be OK because look at our lives. We can go anywhere, and anytime, we want to. We have an amazing group of friends and colleagues throughout the Universe. And we get to spend our time doing things like apprehending criminals like the Brusher, helping Rogsaars get back to Myaad, and saving the future leader of the planet Suus from villains. I can't imagine a better life."

"I see your point M, and completely agree. To us, to our awesome life…!" Brzko said raising his glass and clinking it against M's again. "Once the Rogsaars leave Ploosnar we should have some time to ourselves, we should start on Trella if…"

He was interrupted by an audible alert from the interstellar communications portal "Attention please: Incoming message marked urgent."

They were far too comfortable kicking back on the window bench overlooking the Pacific Ocean to get up and go to the office and receive the message. M picked up her tablet, "Display the message on Muse of Mischief Tablet, authorization M5B7pigsinflight."

Brzko laughed at the comical password she used.

It was a video message from Bartala "Hello, I know you two must be enjoying a little rest before the Rogsaars depart tomorrow but I must tell you something as soon as possible. Please call me!"

"OK, either he discovered coffee and drank way too much of it, or he's got some really good news." Brzko said, chuckling at the excitement that was oozing from Bartala in his message.

They both laughed.

"OK, don't frighten me with the idea of Bartala on high doses of caffeine!" M said. "Can you imagine what would happen if he discovered something like Red Bull? I'll call him back."

"While you do that I'll make dinner. How does stir fry sound?"

"Fantastic."

Brzko made his way to the kitchen, and M donned her communication link and activated it. She could tell that Brzko was on earlink com while cooking, he'd be able to listen in. M sat down in front of the interstellar communication portal in the office and initiated a link with Ploosnar. Bartala must have been waiting by his portal, he answered immediately.

"M, M, M, she's done it, she's done it!" he was just about yelling, and standing, in front of the communication portal that was meant to be used while seated. She could only see his belly.

"Hi Bartala, who has done what, and sit down would you? I don't want to stare at your belly." M said.

The Emperor sat down; his Londo style hair was an absolute disaster. It looked like he was wearing pajamas. "Empress Nalau, she initiated the surrogate rituals. I will be a father in 300 cycles. Can you believe it M, I'm going to be a father. We are going to have a son."

"Congratulations Bartala, I know you've waited a long time for this. How is Nalau?" M asked as she heard Brzko's words in her ear, *tell him I said congratulations.*

"My beloved Nalau is fine. She did not tell me until they were sure that the process was successful. Now we just wait for the child to develop with the surrogate. I want to celebrate, when will you return?"

"Brzko says to tell you congratulations. We were planning to return tomorrow just before midday. But we can return in the morning if you like. I guess we should take that trip to Trella right away. You're going to be very busy once your son arrives." M said.

"Yes, yes, let's go to Trella. I want to explore again, before I am a father." Bartala said.

"You look like you could use some sleep too. Are you going to be able to sleep?" M asked her old friend.

"No, yes, I don't know. So many things are circling in my head. We must decide on a name, we must hire a nanny, we must prepare a nursery. I have to go M, I have much to do."

"OK Bartala, give our best to Nalau and try to get some sleep. We have a big day tomorrow." M said. Just as she ended the communication link she heard Brzko through her earcom link.

"Dinner's ready."

As she walked into the kitchen the smell hit her and she realized just how hungry she was, "It smells fantastic. It smells like fresh niptdyn but we didn't have any. Did you aperture out to the market on Drolla O0 while I was talking to Bartala?" M asked.

"Yep, guilty as charged."

"What do you want to do after we eat?" M asked as they took seats at their dining table.

"Paint, you?"

"Beach walk then sleep."

THE TRELLA PLAN BEGINS

"How many of your ships are going to make the trip?" The Muse of Mischief asked, as she paced around Bartala's private sitting room.

"Protocol mandates three ships, mine and two guards. But I don't want to dominate the group. Maybe I could take only two?" Bartala asked with a leading tone.

Brzko took the bait, "what are you suggesting, aperture travel? We won't be able to take enough gear, not to mention food."

"No, no. I wish it were still that simple. But as Emperor I have to be escorted by palace guards. Trelod ships are almost as fast as Gaznzulian ships, and you just happen to work with a Trelod that has her own ship...."

"That's a great idea Bartala!" M said. "We could invite Lelelu, it's been a long time since she went exploring with us."

"Yes, that is a great idea, she'll be here soon. We can talk to her about when she gets here." Brzko said.

"Ahh you see, sometimes I do have good ideas, even though I'm JUST an Emperor and not a... a... whatever you two are."

They all appreciated Bartala's humor, when the laughing subsided M continued with the planning, "We can't make it to Trella and back before the Rogsaars are to return to Myaad, but we can leave right after that."

"I completely agree. Bartala you will not be taking any trips prior to the Rogsaars returning to Myaad."

They all turned toward the new voice in the conversation. M was the first to stand and approach.

With her usual curtsy she greeted Empress Nalau, "Your highness, always a pleasure. And congratulations. I think you may have found a way to tame that adolescent wild streak in your husband."

Nalau stepped forward and embraced M, "Thank you M, I appreciate the support that you and Brzko always have for us. But, please, there is no need for formalities, I consider you one of my closest friends. Please address me by my name."

"All right Nalau." M said as she returned the hug. She stepped back and Brzko approached the Empress.

"You however, may keep up the formal greetings and kiss my hand my anytime you like!" Nalau said giggling.

Brzko bowed and kissed her extended hand, "Your highness."

As he stood Nalau said, "I shall never tire of your charm Brzko."

"Hey wait a minute, are you flirting with my wife" Bartala said as he approached the trio. "If it makes her happy then don't ever stop my friend." He said patting Brzko on the back.

They all took seats on the sofas, Brzko and the Muse of Mischief on one sofa, Bartala and Nalau on the other facing them.

"I understand you are anxious to explore Trella. Bartala has told me that you will be looking for clues to your origins. That is exciting." Nalau said.

"Yes, we've been to Trella many times but we've never really *explored* Trella. I can't wait to go as an adult and really look around. But I think we need to get ready for the festivities on Myaad. What do you have planned so far and how can we help?" M asked.

"The plan is just for a reception to welcome them home. They have not been home in a very long time, and Myaad does not currently have the resources available for much of a reception. So we are taking care of the details. The Gaznzulian security team we sent was kind enough to transport all of the food and decorations; they will arrive on Myaad the day after tomorrow so there is plenty of time to set up. Lelelu has been a huge help in coordinating everything with Bivoor."

"Do they have housing for all for the returning Rogsaars?" Brzko asked.

"Yes, the Dumeer have been very busy making sure there is enough housing, food, clothing and other consumables for almost one hundred additional Rogsaars. Of course the Suus will be there for the reception, and I just learned a few minutes ago that Ciic will be attending. She is already enroute to Myaad."

"Really?" M said, clearly excited. "We haven't seen Ciic since her wedding!"

"What? You were at her wedding? I thought Suus ceremonies were generally private, or species specific. Please tell me you did not wear those striped stockings." Bartala said.

This made Brzko laugh, "What is it with you and M's stockings Bartala?"

"Truly? I'm jealous. She dresses playfully and I cannot."

"I'm sure I could find them in your size Bartala, would you like a pair of striped stockings for your next day of celebration?" M asked sarcastically.

"No, no, no. I'll just continue to dress with the regal poise of an emperor." he said with a fake *poor me* tone.

"The notion that Suus weddings and other ceremonies are species specific is a false rumor. They are actually quite open to including others, as long as they are worthy. And when you save their lives, you're deemed worthy. What can I say? That's just how Brzko and I roll."

They all laughed. "One day you must tell me the story of how you saved Ciic, I still have not heard what happened; perhaps on the way to Trella."

"Maybe then Bartala, although I'd like to catch up on my sleep." M said.

There was a knock at the door. "Come!" Bartala called.

One of the palace butlers stepped in, "Excuse me for interrupting. It is time for embarkation; your presence is requested for the event. Also, I am to inform you that Lelelu has arrived and is in orbit awaiting..." M disappeared before his eyes.

The butler was visibly shaken by M's mischievous activity. "Don't worry, you get used to it with these two. She likes shock us non-aperture travelling, gravity based beings. You were saying..."

The butler cleared his throat and picked up where he left off, "In orbit and awaiting landing instructions."

The Muse of Mischief returned as he was speaking, she had Lelelu in tow. Even though the flora on Ploosnar was blue, and Ploosnarians had bright blue eyes, commoners were not accustomed to seeing blue Trelods. Shock at Lelelu's appearance showed on the butler's face.

"No instructions needed, this is Lelelu and she'll just leave here ship in orbit until the Suus depart." M said.

The butler opened his mouth to speak, closed it, opened it, closed it, and then finally managed "It is a pleasure to meet you Ms. Lelelu, welcome to Ploosnar." With that, he quickly ducked out of the room and closed the door.

"Oh M you are mischievous today aren't you?" Nalau said cracking up.

"Hey, just living up to my name! I know it's been a while but I'm sure the two of you remember Lelelu."

"Of course, of course. Welcome to Ploosnar Lelelu."

"Welcome to the Palace Lelelu, I hope you will be able to stay with us while you are here."

Lelelu looked spectacular whenever she traveled, a bald, bright blue individual wearing a form fitting black jumpsuit. "Thank you Emperor, Empress. It is a pleasure to see you again. And it will be my honor to stay with you in the Palace while I am here." She said offering a slight bow to each in turn.

"You've arrived just in time for the Rogsaars to embark, will you join us?" Bartala said.

"It would be my pleasure." The group stood and made their way to the door with Bartala in the lead. He took a right as he left the room, leading the group through the royal chambers of the palace it was a much faster route to the landing pad. This meant they would be walking through the hallway with statues of the previous Emperors and Empresses.

Bartala and Brzko were in the lead, having a masculine chat about something that no doubt would not have interested the ladies, who walked in a small group behind. After they passed the third or fourth statue Nalau turned to the Muse of Mischief and Lelelu, "Does this hallway creep you out, or is it just me?"

"Oh this is really creepy, the statues are a little too lifelike for my taste!" M answered. "I'm always expecting one of them to come to life and start scolding me."

"Definitely creepy, I'm glad you said that Empress. I was worried I might be the only one with prujelst bumps." Lelelu said.

This caught the Empress off guard she stopped, "Prujelt bumps?"

"Right, prujelst bumps - you know little tiny bumps that cover your body when you are cold or creeped out. Named after prujelst birds" Lelelu explained. "On Earth they get goose bumps - a water dwelling bird."

"Right." M said "What are there here on Ploosnar Nalau?"

"Creepy bumps! Just creepy bumps, we don't have them named after an animal. Because *that* would be creepy."

The three ladies busted out in serious laughter. They were laughing so hard they didn't realize that Bartala and Brzko had turned and walked back to them.

"And just what is it that is so funny that it will make us late?" he asked.

"Oh nothing dear, we were just admiring the statues of your ancestors." Nalau said clearly lying as she regained her composure.

Bartala looked from Nalau to M to Lelelu, considering if he'd be able to get an answer out any of them. "Brzko, I think your wife is starting to rub off on my wife."

"Ha! I couldn't agree with you more Bartala. And for that you are lucky!" he said slipping his arm around M's waist.

"Damn straight!" M said, sending off a new round of laughter amongst the ladies.

"C'mon ladies, shake a leg or we'll be late." he said pretending to be annoyed.

"Shake a leg? What is that supposed to mean?" Lelelu spoke for both her and Nalau, who found the saying quite odd.

"I'll explain on the way." M said, picking up the pace.

ROGSAAR EMBARKATION

The group approached the Suus ship from the palace side, opposite the side where the Rogsaars were gathered. All of the Rogsaars were there, even those staying on Ploosnar or returning to where ever they had made new lives. The Suus stood in formation next to the ramp; today they were using the doorway on the long side of their ship. The ramp was decorated with the tall banners they had been carrying when they arrived on Ploosnar a few days ago. Kiik was standing at the base of the ramp, as the group approached she stepped forward and address Bartala.

"Emperor Bartala on behalf of the Suus I would like to thank you and Empress Nalau for your hospitality and generosity. The Suus are better for having made this alliance with Ploosnar. Should you need our assistance in the future please do not hesitate to call upon us." she projected as she bowed toward the royal couple.

Bartala stepped forward and clasped both of Kiik's lower hands in his own, "It has been our sincere pleasure to host you and your team Kiik. We will see you on Myaad in a few days."

With pleasantries exchanged the group prepared what looked like a receiving line. Kiik's team boarded the ship, no doubt to direct the Rogsaars once they were onboard. Kiik stood at the base of the ramp, Emperor Bartala next to her, then Empress Nalau, then the Muse of Mischief, then Agent Brzko, then Lelelu.

Nalau leaned toward M and whispered in her ear, "M switch places with me. You have had more to do with the Rogsaars returning home than I have." She stepped behind M, intent on taking her place.

M shifted over next to Bartala just as the Rogsaars approached in single file. First in line was the Rogsaar from Earth. Agent Brzko extended his hand. "Rogsaar, I'm so glad we were able to help you return to…"

Before he could finish speaking Rogsaar lurched forward and embraced him. "Rogsaar so happy, so grateful. Brzko you saved me from a sad, lonely life." He continued on down the line without further comment, as did the remaining Rogsaars that were returning to Myaad.

"Well I guess that's all of them Kiik. I understand you want to have everyone settled in before you leave for Myaad in the morning. Should you need anything…" Bartala was interrupted by someone yelling.

"Hey, hey Kiik, don't leave yet sister! Kiik wait a minute." It was Afrit the Great of Jinn running toward them waving his hands in the air. In a flash, the palace guards were in front of him blocking his path as he neared the landing pad.

"It's OK let him pass." Bartala called to the guards.

Afrit the Great was smoothing his clothes as he walked toward them, as though the guards had soiled him, "I don't understand why your guards are so tense."

"I am the Emperor and you cannot just run up to an emperor." Bartala said.

"Emperor, right." Afrit said dismissively, waving his hand as if being Emperor were no more important than a pesky insect. He approached Kiik, "I just wanted to say goodbye and thank you Kiik. I'm glad to have met a Suus that I like."

Kiik projected, "Goodbye Afrit the Great, thank you for the navigational charts you have shared with us. We are grateful. You are not going to attend the reception on Myaad?"

"No, nope, I'm just not feeling" it sister. I'm hitching a ride back to Jinn with that Rogsaar over there," he pointed to one of the Rogsaars that was staying behind. "I appreciate Bartala's hospitality but eh… I've seen enough of Ploosnar. Besides I need some good food. The food here!" He said rolling his eyes.

Bartala took a step forward, ready to confront Afrit the Greta's comment about the food. Nalau stopped him by pinching his arm. It would only draw things out. Brzko turned his head in order to stifle a laugh, the scene was quite comical.

"Thank you all, we will see you soon on Myaad." Kiik projected as she turned and walked up the ramp, entering her ship. The ramp lifted, closing the entrance.

"Well that's that then. Hey if you guys are ever near Jinn feel free to stop in and look me up." Afrit the Great said as he walked away.

They stared after him, all a little dumbfounded at Afrit's casual departure.

"Who wants nekmid?" Bartala called loudly as he began walking toward the palace.

SCHATORREN DESIGNS

Kiik's ship left Ploosnar before anyone awoke. Zri was on his way but he would not arrive until late this evening or early tomorrow. That meant the group had a free day. They had gathered for breakfast in the great dining hall.

"Lelelu, I know you've been to Ploosnar before, is there anything you'd like to do today?" Empress Nalau asked her.

"Yes Empress. You may not remember this but many years ago when I was here we visited your personal tailors. They made me the most amazing jackets. If it is possible, I would like to visit the tailors again." she answered.

"Absolutely. That sounds wonderful. I am always up for a visit to the tailors. M will you be joining us?"

"New clothes? Hell yeah, count me in. What about shoes?"

"Uh-oh, next they are going to be deciding what color to paint their toenails for the reception." Brzko said to Bartala.

Lelelu spoke before Bartala could respond, she cleared her throat, "For your information I don't have toenails."

They all laughed.

"Touché!" Brzko said.

"We cannot win with three of them Brzko."

"Let's go to Smd and get some fresh niptdyn for dinner." he said.

"That sounds much better than a visit to the tailors."

Bartala and Brzko stood to leave the room. Bartala kissed Nalau's cheek, "Have a wonderful day my love. I will see you for refreshments this afternoon."

Brzko reached for M's hand and pulled her up to standing. He literally swept her off her feet as he leaned her back giving her his best Hollywood movie star kiss. As he righted her he said, "Until later my darling Muse of Mischief."

She was a bit dazed as he turned and left the room with Bartala. Nalau and Lelelu were laughing as M plopped back down in her chair. "OK are you two ready then?"

"Yes, I'd like to walk. It's not very far and the weather is perfect right now." Nalau said.

As the trio walked through the foyer to exit the palace, M caught a glimpse of them in the mirrors that line the wall. "Wait, look." she said.

The other two turned toward the mirrors, confused.

"We look good!" she said.

And they did. Empress Nalau was dressed in her usual fashion, a royal blue ankle length dress. The skirt had a slit up the left side and both it and the short jacket were lined with black. The jacket had tabs and black buttons on the back. Lelelu was wearing a short grey skirt with a short, cropped shirt of the same fabric. She also had short boots and a fantastic hat that M had never seen before. The Muse of Mischief was wearing a short red and black dress, the bodice was tight, resembling a corset, the skirt was short and ruffled. She also had a matching jacket. It was

Trella

black lined with red and black heels. The stockings she wore today were not striped.

It was indeed short walk. The ladies arrived at Nalau's favorite tailor, Schatorren after a quick walk through the streets near the palace. Everyone they encountered recognized the Empress and gave right of way to the group. It was difficult to blend in when you were followed by palace guards. The shop is a huge unattached structure. The entrance is grand with two large arched doors, a butler stood in attendance to greet shoppers. As the trio approached, the doors swung wide and the butler welcomed them.

"Your Majesty! We are honored to have you visit Schatorren Designs today. Please enter." He bowed deeply as he gestured for the group to enter the doorway.

They had barely stepped over the threshold when they were greeted by Schatorren himself. "Empress Nalau. To what do I owe the pleasure of your visit today? It must be clothing for your friends, as you already look so divine today that I cannot suggest a single improvement." At this the Ploosnarian sporting a Londo hairstyle bowed deeply and kissed Nalau's hand. M was impressed to see that Bartala's new hairstyle was catching on.

"Schatorren, surely you are not suggesting that my wardrobe is too large? It would upset me deeply if I were not able to add to it," she teased.

Her sarcasm caught him off guard, for a moment he thought he was in trouble, "I apologize Empress. I did not mean…"

She interrupted him, "Relax Schatorren, I was being humorous. A day out with the ladies makes me a bit playful. May I present the Muse of Mischief and Lelelu." she said gesturing toward her friends.

Schatorren approached M first, he bowed, "Ahhhh the Muse of Mischief! You are famous throughout the Universe. You honor me with your visit today. And you are the most fascinating creature I have ever seen." He said turning to Lelelu, reaching for her hand. "What are you? Other than absolutely divine?"

"I am a Trelod." Lelelu said, enjoying the attention.

"Are all Trelods as blue as you are? You look like you were meant to be on Ploosnar where everything is blue. Where are you from?" Schatorren asked.

"Trelods are indigenous to the Planet of Portals, but most of us live in many places throughout our lives." Lelelu explained.

Schatorren, seeming a little out of sorts due to his infatuation with Lelelu, stepped back to address them as a group, "What can I do for you ladies today? Are you looking for something specific?"

"I am in the mood for new shoes." Nalau said.

"I would like something purple." M said.

"I would like new jumpsuits for traveling. With matching hats in a style no one else has ever seen." Lelelu said, clearly having fun with Schatorren.

He clapped his hands and instantly he was surrounded by a small crowd; two designers and three design assistants. "For you, the very best shoe designer we have." he said motioning toward one design team. "For you, my superhero team." he said to M. "And you, I will design for you myself" he said to Lelelu as he grasped her arm and escorted her off to a design center with an assistant following close behind.

M and Nalau followed their designers to the appropriate design center.

Each designer has a small sitting area in an absolutely grand room. The ceiling so high you can hardly see it. The room is large and open, but each designer's area is clearly defined by their style. A variety of chairs, sofas, and stools placed around each design table. The design tables were tall, with a slanted top.

The process at Schatorren Designs starts with an interview. The designer enjoys refreshments with the client, getting to know them and "breaking the ice." As the client describes what they want, the designer begin to sketch ideas. With the client able to see the designs develop, and offer input prior to completion, they are assured of getting something they love that is uniquely tailored to their desires.

"My name is Kilome. It is an honor to have been selected to design for the Muse of Mischief." Kilome said as he gestured toward a small sofa in his design area.

"It's a pleasure to meet you Kilome. How long have you been with Schartorren?" M asked taking a seat.

"I have been at Schartorren Designs for many cycles, close to twenty, ever since this new location was opened. Before that, I was designing on Drolla O0. I find Ploosnar more to my liking."

"Drolla O0, are you Sarfet?" M asked.

"Yes, partially." he answered. "My mother is from Ploosnar and my father from Drolla O0. As far as I know I am the only being that is Ploosnarian and Sarfet."

"I guess that would explain why your eyes are not blue. At first I thought you might be wearing contact lenses."

Kilome is an intriguing being, tall and thin with dark hair. He wears his hair all one length but slicked back, away from his face. As M took a closer look, she could see that his nose is at a slight angle and the nostrils are slightly flared - both traits of the Sarfet.

"Well then I guess I will have designs like no one else has even imagined!" M said.

"Oh yes! Of that I can assure you Muse of Mischief. Are you looking for a certain type of garment? Where will it be worn? What type of activities will be performed in the garment?"

"I was thinking of something new for the reception on Myaad when the Rogsaars arrive home. You are aware of the Rogsaars I presume?" she asked.

"Yes, several of the Rogsaars had new garments designed during their stay on Ploosnar. A few of them are even employed here. So you are thinking of something formal?"

"Hmmmmm I do like formal clothing, very much. But… sometimes I am called upon to deal with situations at a moment's notice. I don't have time to change out of restrictive clothing."

"I have an idea…" Kilome took a seat on the high stool at his design table and began sketching. It only took a few moments before he had enough of a design to show M. "What do you think?" he asked as he tilted the sketch toward her.

"Wow! I think you nailed it!" She said as she stood to take a closer look.

"Nailed? Is that a positive reaction?" he asked with slight apprehension.

M laughed, "Yes, it's slang from the planet Earth. To nail something is to get right, exactly right."

He looked relieved.

The design sketch was of M, she even had her hands on her hips with one foot extended making her look like the sassy time traveling, aperture jumping being she was. The skirt was a little longer than she usually wore, it was hard to run in long restrictive skirts, but the bottom half of this one was designed to be fringe, so it moved.

"What do you think?" Kilome asked.

"I'm impressed Kilome. It looks like I will have complete mobility even though this is a little longer. And this…" she traced her finger over what looked like a train.

"Is a short train to more formalize the garment. But it will be removable in case you need more mobility."

The top part of the garment looked like a corset with bows made of ribbon running in a line down the back. The same ribbon would be run in three straight lengths down the front of the corset.

"You will of course need a matching jacket or wrap, shoes and stockings." Kilome quickly sketched those things. The shoes were amazing - pointed toe high heels with several shades of purple.

"Kilome, this is magnificent! How did you manage to create designs that are so perfect for me after only speaking for a few moments?" M asked.

"Ahh, you haven't spent much time with Sarfets have you?"

"No, not really. Just a little trading on Smd, I love niptdyn."

"Some of us are empaths. In fact all Sarfets used to be empaths but the skill has been waning with the last few generations. For a race that functions primarily as traders, it is a valuable skill - and for me as a designer as well."

"You can design for me anytime Kilome!"

"It is my honor Muse of Mischief. If you will excuse me, I will begin the creation process. The garments will be delivered to the palace later today." Kilome said as he stood.

"Of course Kilome, thank you." M said as she stood, planning to go look for her friends. But as Kilome walked away, Lelelu approached.

"Hi Lelelu, how did your designs turnout?" M asked.

"I think they will be the best garments I've ever worn. I went all out, seven new sets!" Lelelu said, sounding exhausted. "But it will be money well spent."

"Money well spent?" inquired Empress Nalau from behind them, "Oh no Lelelu, today's outing is at the courtesy of the Palace. It is truly a pleasure for Bartala and me to be able to provide you two with these gifts. You do so much for the Universe, and you never ask for a thing in return."

"But Empress...." M attempted to object.

Empress Nalau dismissed her objection with a wave of her hand, "I'm pulling rank here M. As Empress of this planet I insist. Now let's go down the street a few doors and have some tea before we return to the palace." She began heading toward the entrance of Schatorren Designs.

"Wait tea?" Lelelu asked a little confused. "Isn't that an Earth beverage?"

"Originally yes, but Ploosnarians know a good thing when they find it. Some of our early explorers brought back samples from our first Earth missions. We've been cultivating it ever since." Nalau answered as the trio stepped out on the sidewalk.

"Well, not just cultivating," M interjected. "I'd say they've been improving it. They've enhanced the flavors."

Once out on the sidewalk a pair of palace guards fell in step behind them. The trio returned to the palace after enjoying their tea, they returned in plenty of time to enjoy the niptdyn with Brzko and Bartala.

THE ROGSAAR RECEPTION

"OK, who's riding with me and who's riding with Zri?" Lelelu asked the group.

"Well who has the faster ship?" Emperor Bartala asked.

"They are both as fast as lightning compared to your *barges*." The Muse of Mischief teased.

"Lightning, what has lightning got to do with this?" Bartala asked, clearly confused.

Everyone but Bartala laughed, "My dear Bartala, sometimes you miss the point." Empress Nalau said.

"I think the two of you should travel with me." Zri said. "The ships are of equal speed, but my ship is larger. Your cargo is already loaded and I can accommodate your staff. My ship also has more advanced defenses"

"There are only two Rogsaars that want to travel to Myaad for the reception, Rogsaar of Xinood 5, and a Rogsaar that was somewhere in the Glion Galaxy. Lelelu, are you OK with transporting them?" Brzko asked.

"Yes, of course. It will take less than a day to get there."

"Were you able to locate G'ist?"

"Yes, he's on board now. Rogsaar is going to be very surprised."

"If you want to arrive before Kiik does you'd better leave now." M said.

"Agreed." Zri said. "Emperor, Empress, are you comfortable with a transport or would you like me to have a shuttle land to take you up to my ship?"

With the animation of a child, Bartala answered for both of them, "Ooooh transport, transport! Yes, that will be fine."

"Excellent, if you're ready then." Zri took a step closer to Bartala and Nalau, working the controls built into the sleeve of his flight suit. The trio disappeared.

"I'll take Lelelu back to her ship if you want to round up the Rogsaars." M said to Brzko.

"Deal."

The Muse of Mischief took Lelelu's arm and they also disappeared from the palace, arriving instantly aboard Lelelu's ship.

"Thanks M." Lelelu said once on the ship, "Have you met G'ist?" She gestured toward him.

"No, I haven't had the pleasure yet." She stepped toward him with her hand out "I'm the Muse of Mischief; I'm so pleased you could come. I know Rogsaar will be excited to see you, the separation has been difficult."

G'ist was taller than M, He reached out and took her hand. When he spoke she was surprised at how gentle his voice was, not feminine, but gentle. "It is my pleasure to make your acquaintance Ms. Muse of Mischief. What can I possibly do to thank you for this opportunity? Rogsaar and I did not think we would have the funding or the available free time for me to visit Myaad in the near future. But when you called upon my employer and asked for my assistance on a mission? Well… how could they deny a request from the Muse of Mischief?"

"That was Lelelu's idea. Brilliant, isn't she?" M and G'ist turned toward Lelelu; she looked up and smiled but continued to prepare for departure. "I know it's been difficult for Rogsaar to be away from you, to be away from home."

Brzko arrived with the Rogsaar they were speaking of, the partner of G'ist.

"Ahhh, oh. We're here. Oh, that's…." Rogsaar trailed off.

"It startles everyone the first time Rogsaar." Brzko reassured him. "I'll be back in a minute." He left to escort the final Rogsaar that would be traveling with Lelelu.

Rogsaar was facing M, he hadn't seen G'ist yet. He jumped when a familiar voice spoke from behind him.

"Rogs, I have missed you." G'ist said.

Rogsaar turned and couldn't believe eyes. Lelelu stopped pre departure to watch the reunion. "G'ist!" Rogsaar rushed toward him, "how did you get here? It is comforting to see you!" he said as they embraced. They stood holding each other, as a couple they were striking - Rogsaar with pale skin and white hair, and G'ist completely black with bright green eyes.

"Lelelu contacted me and offered to provide me with transportation to attend this reception with you. I asked Lelelu not to tell you, I wanted to surprise you, to be with you for this momentous event. How I have missed you…." he stepped back and took a long look at his partner, Rogs, as he called him.

Rogsaar turned to M and Lelelu, "Thank you, thank you so much. This is unbelievable, I…. I…"

"You're welcome Rogsaar." M said

Brzko returned from Ploosnar with Rogsaar from the Glion Galaxy.

"We are ready to depart. Do you require anything prior to us leaving?" Lelelu asked.

"No, thank you" they responded in unison.

"You may sit here on the flight bridge." she gestured to an out of the way seating area. "Or, you may ascend those stairs and enjoy the scenery from the observation deck above." She pointed to spiral staircase in the wall.

The trio exchanged looks and headed for the stairs. The offer of an observation deck was just too tempting to pass up.

"OK, Lelelu, we'll see you there." M said. "And you were absolutely right about those new flight suits!"

This made Lelelu grin. Blue, bald, grinning, and donning a fantastic greenish brown flight suit, she was absolutely stunning. "Thanks M, see you in a few hours."

The Muse of Mischief and Agent Brzko arrived outside of the administration building on Myaad. Instantly they were approached by Bivoor.

"Oh Muse of Mischief and Agent Brzko I am thankful that you are here. The Rogsaars are to arrive tomorrow and we are not ready." Bivoor said sounding almost frantic.

"Hi Bivoor, don't worry. We're here to help! And more help and supplies will be arriving in a few hours." M said.

As usual, it was Brzko that had the biggest calming effect, "Hey Bivoor, I'm sure you've got a plan, a timeline of sorts? Let's go sit down and take a look at it and see where we can fit in to help."

That did it, Bivoor was instantly calmed! The trio went inside and sat down at the meeting table in Bivoor's office. Bivoor handed Brzko something that looked like a clipboard.

"Hey before we get started Bivoor, how are the eggs developing? Is development going as planned?" M asked.

"Oh yes, thank you for asking. There are no signs of aberidus and the Caretaker's seem to be doing fine." Bivoor answered.

"OK, let's run down the list." Brzko said.

"Housing for the returning Rogsaars, is it ready?"

"Yes, the Dumeers have been very busy. We have a separate dwelling for each Rogsaar, as well as a few extras."

"Food supplies?"

"Yes, but I am not sure what we will need to provide for the reception."

M jumped in, "Don't worry about that. Ploosnar is providing more than enough food and beverage for the reception."

"What have the Bivoors planned for the reception? Will there be a speech or any type of ceremony?" Brzko asked.

"A speech to welcome them home, then we would just like to enjoy their company, hear the tales of their survival, and allow them to renew their appreciation of home, of Myaad."

"OK then it sounds like you are as ready as you can be. Don't worry about the setup. The Empress is an amazing planner and hostess. She is bringing a small army that will take care of all the details so that you and the other Bivoors can enjoy the reception." Brzko said.

"The generosity of you and your friends is…" there was a knock at the door.

Another Bivoor opened the door just enough to lean in, "Apologies for the intrusion Bivoor. We have just been notified that a Suus ship has arrived in orbit. It carries someone named Ciic. They have been cleared to land their transport shuttle; it will be here in moments."

M instantly felt butterflies in her stomach. She was excited to see Ciic again, it had been several years. Brzko and M last saw her at her wedding on Suus, after rescuing her from Mahb in ancient Ireland.

The trio stood and headed toward the door. But instead of turning right to head out the front door, they turned left out of Bivoor's office. There is a clearing behind the Myaad administration building. The shuttle was touching down just as they stepped out of the building.

~~~

The Muse of Mischief and Agent Brzko stood in the front of the group, there were five or six Bivoors and at least that many Dumeers standing behind them. None of the Myaads had ever received dignitaries from another planet before. Today they would meet several. You didn't have to be telepathic to feel the excitement of the group.

The Suus shuttle was the same shape as their standard transport ship, just smaller. The oblong ship had landed; the large door on the long side opened and the ramp extended. First to exit were two Suus carrying tall red banners that billowed in the breeze. After descending the ramp they stepped to the side and Ciic walked down the ramp with Muum just a step behind her. M and Brzko began to walk forward, they paused, about to offer a curtsy to the leader of the Suus when they received a telepathic message from Ciic, "Please do not bow to me, we are equals, we are friends."

Neither of them gave any outward indication of the communication. Instead, they stood in place and let Ciic approach, she eagerly embraced M.

"Hello friend," M projected to Ciic, knowing that she would be open to *hearing* her thoughts, "it has been too long and I am pleased to see you are well."

Ciic continued the embrace, "The honor is mine Muse of Mischief, the honor is mine. Without you and Agent Brzko, I would not have lived long enough to ascend to the throne of Suus. I will always be grateful and indebted to you."

Finally released from the awesome embrace of this tall four armed being M responded verbally as was the custom when in mixed telepathic company, "There is no debt between friends! Welcome to Myaad."

Ciic stepped to the side of M and embraced Brzko, M greeted Muum. Once the old friends had enjoyed their private reunion a small army of Suus began to disembark the shuttle, each was carrying a tall vessels overflowing with Leel vines, heavily laden with flowers. The smell immediately permeated the entire area.

Brzko and the Muse of Mischief escorted Ciic to the waiting group. M made the introduction, "I present Ciic from the house of Naan, Ruler of planet Suus. Ciic welcome to Myaad, this group has gathered to receive you with honor." The entire white haired group bowed in unison, the choreography was perfect.

The Bivoor selected to speak for the group stepped forward, bowed again, "Welcome to Myaad Your Majesty, I am Bivoor. It is a great honor to have you here. Should you need anything while you are here please let me know."

"Thank you Bivoor, we are honored to be included in this grand event. It is a privilege for us to attend. We have brought Leel flowers for your reception. The center of each flower contains a unique nebula, and the smell is pleasing to most species. It is our hope that this gift from Suus pleases you." Ciic projected to the entire group.

"It does, it does very much Ciic. Thank you. But you have already done so much for us. Without Kiik and your research team we would not have recovered from aberidus. We do not know how to repay your kindness and generosity." Bivoor said.

"There is no need to repay the Suus." Ciic projected, "It is our pleasure to help when and where we are needed. In the future Myaad may be called upon by the Muse of Mischief and Agent Brzko to offer assistant, it is in that way that you can repay the Universe. If you would like to show my crew to the area of the reception, they can begin to place the Leel flowers."

"Of course, yes. I will take them to the Theatre myself." Bivoor and the other Myaads joined the Suus that carried the Leel flowers, forming a large group - half of them with stark white hair and black eyes and the other half tall green four armed beings carrying vessels filled with Leel flowers. They set out down the walkway on the north side of the administration building with Bivoor in the lead. This left the Muse of Mischief, Agent Brzko, Ciic and Muum alone.

"Lelelu and Zri should both arrive within a few hours. As you know Kiik will arrive tomorrow. Is there anything the two of you would like to do prior to their arrivals?" M asked looking up at Ciic.

"Yes" Ciic projected. "I have a personal favor to ask of you."

"Please, ask Ciic." M said.

"When you helped me escape from Mahb you took me to your home, your island, I think you called it. I will never forget the beauty of the ocean. There is no place on Suus such as this. I have attempted to describe it to Muum but…."

Brzko jumped in, trying to make this easy for Ciic, "But describing it just doesn't do it justice. You'd like us to take you there so Muum can see the ocean?"

A feeling of relief came from Ciic, "Yes" she projected. "But I understand that this is your personal space and I do not want to intrude on your privacy. But when I was previously there I had a cloaked appearance, cloaked to look like a human child. We cannot hide that we are Suus."

"I don't think that will be a problem." M said. "We should be able to get in and out without having any contact with Earthlings, you won't be able to walk on the beach but you will be able to see the views from the windows. We just need to tell Bivoor that we will be gone for a while, we wouldn't want to cause any concern."

"We can have our crew share the information. They have been told that we will be away from Myaad for a short time." Ciic projected.

Brzko stepped forward toward Muum, "Right telepathy. That must come in handy! Well Muum have you ever traveled through an aperture?"

"No, what do I need to do?" Muum projected.

"Nothing really, I'll take your arm," Brzko said as he took hold of Muum's lower arm, "and…"

They were gone. M knew that Ciic already knew what to expect from aperture travel, there was no need to explain. She placed a firm grip on Ciic's lower arm, and went home.

~~~

"... then just relax." Brzko finished the sentence he had started on Myaad. But before he could explain to Muum why they had left mid-sentence he had to attend to their security system.

"ENTER AUTHORIZATION CODE NOW 30... 29... 28..." Brzko was already at the panel near the front door that was rarely used. He entered the code to disarm the system.

"ADDITIONAL LIFE FORM DETECTED, ENTER SECONDARY CODE 30... 29... 28..." Brzko entered the second code.

The Muse of Mischief and Ciic had arrived while he was disarming the system. Brzko turned and address Muum. "I hope that sudden departure didn't startle you too badly Muum. We've found that most beings are quite apprehensive the first time and because we can only travel with willing participants, it's better if we don't let the tension build."

There was no response from Muum. Brzko figured it was just an issue with telepathy, maybe Muum had forgotten to project for the non-telepaths.

"Muum" Ciic projected to them all, "what is wrong are you ok?"

Muum pulled his gaze from the front windows of the house, "It is better than you described Ciic. I have never seen a place like this, the water.... the water is mesmerizing." He turned back to the windows.

They could all feel Ciic's satisfaction, gratitude and deep love as she stood beside Muum and they embraced with their lower arms around the back of the other and their upper arms embracing in front of them.

M and Brzko just let them stand and take in the view. It was early evening in Lincoln City so the setting sun was reflecting off of the Pacific Ocean, creating an intense golden glow. After a few minutes they stirred and M took the opportunity to further their experience.

She walked over to one of the sliding glass doors and opened it. Knowing that Suus have a superior sense of smell, she figured they would enjoy the smell of the ocean breeze. M stepped back and let them soak it up.

The telepathic feelings that emanated from Ciic and Muum were amazing. M and Brzko could feel what they were feeling. It occurred to M that this was similar to Brzko's ability to calm others. She wondered if he had some sort of telepathic ability, at least where conveying calm was concerned. The four friends just stood and looked out at the ocean for quite some time.

After a while Ciic broke her gaze and turned toward M and Brzko, "We cannot thank you enough for sharing this with us. You are lucky to have a home like this."

"Yes we are." Brzko said. "We could live anywhere in the Universe but this is home. We know we are not human but we don't know where we're from, but there has to be a reason we were both hidden here on Earth as children. Until we discover our origins it seems logical to keep this as our home base."

"You two are amazing beings, no matter what you are." Muum projected. "Thank you for sharing this with me, Ciic has described it many times but I now I understand why it had such an impact on her as a child."

Ciic was taking notice of the artwork on their walls while Muum was projecting. When he finished she commented, "Your decor has changed since I was here, it is beautiful, it fits you. Is this a Burdohnirc? I have read about them but not seen them in person. I find the water intimidating."

"Yes, that is one of Brzko's paintings." M said.

Muum walked over and took a close look at the painting that had caught Ciic's eye.

"This is remarkable, such fine detail. Brzko you are quite talented." Ciic projected, Muum concurred.

Brzko walked over to where they were standing, "Thank you, I appreciate you compliments. These creatures fascinate me and I enjoy creating artistic representations of them." He continued on down the hall with Ciic and Muum, showing a few more of his Burdohnirc paintings.

M went into the kitchen and made two cups of jasmine tea. There was no need to offer tea to their guests, or so she though. She sat the brewed tea on the counter and even though Ciic and Muum were around the corner and out of earshot, very clear communication echoed in her brain.

"What is that intoxicating smell?" It was Muum.

She answered out loud, "This is green tea with jasmine flowers." Muum and Ciic were already standing next to her, Brzko followed looking slightly bewildered.

Ciic stepped right up to the counter and projected "May I?"

"Of course" M answered.

Muum took that to be permission for him as well. Each picked up a cup, bent over it, and inhaled deeply through their nostrils. They both radiated glee. M and Brzko watched in silence, they were watching Suus consume for the very first time. Once the tea had cooled the steam (or vapor) ceased to rise from the cups.

They sat the cups down. Ciic addressed M, "This is something you would consume as a beverage?"

"Yes."

"The flower in this is quite delicious, and there is slight stimulation from the vapor."

"We call that caffeine. It comes from green tea, the dried leaves of the camellia sinensis plant."

"And the flower?"

"Jasmine, or jasminum flowers."

"Is it possible for us to procure this product? We would like to take some back to Suus."

"Of course, you can take what we have here back to Myaad and after the reception we can track down live specimens of the plants so you can cultivate them on Suus."

"Thank you Muse of Mischief. How much time do we have before we need to return to Myaad?" Ciic projected. Muum had already returned to the window gazing at the sun setting over the Pacific Ocean.

"We have about 30 minutes before we need to return." M answered.

Ciic projected her acknowledgement of this information and returned Muum's side, gazing out the window.

M and Brzko took the opportunity to freshen up. M donned the new purple outfit she had recently obtained on Ploosnar.

Brzko hadn't previously seen the outfit. "Damn girl! You look good! Is that what you had made at Schatorren?"

"Yes, do you like it?"

"Oh hell yes. I think I'll change the hat band on my derby to match your purple, and then I'll be ready to go."

"All right, I'll go see if the big green lovebirds are ready."

~~~

The Muse of Mischief and Agent Brzko returned Ciic and Muum to Myaad after an enjoyable excursion to their home on Earth. A few minutes after their arrival their earcom links came to life.

"I've established orbit around Myaad and have been cleared to land the shuttle. I will be there shortly with two Rogsaars and G'ist." Lelelu broadcast over the earcom link.

Before either M or Brzko could answer, Zri announced his arrival, "We have also established orbit. We've been cleared to land but without a sentry ship in orbit Gaznzulian protocol prevents us from landing. We will begin transporting our guests, and the supplies, to the landing zone as soon as you have landed your shuttle Lelelu."

"OK, we are on the way." Lelelu answered.

"So how did your guests behave Zri?" M teased, knowing that Bartala could at times be a chatterbox.

"There were no problems Muse of Mischief, I had many duties to attend to in the control room." Zri answered. That meant he hid from Bartala and left his crew do deal with the chatter.

M, Brzko, Bivoor, Ciic, and Muum gathered at the landing site near the administration building just as Lelelu's shuttle landed. The doors opened and she stepped out. She had changed on the way, wearing one of the new outfits she obtained on Ploosnar, she was absolutely stunning. She was wearing a long green skirt with a slit up one side and a cropped top of the same color. She was also donning a fantastic hat with interesting angles.

The two Rogsaars that traveled with her stepped out; one was arm in arm with G'ist. He was as black as night but his bright green eyes could be seen from far away.

Ciic commented and since no one else reacted, M had the feeling that the communication was projected only to her. "A Xinood! I have not had the pleasure of meeting a Xinood in person. Are they partners?"

M answered with her mind, knowing that Ciic would be listening for her thoughts. "Yes, Rogsaar of Xinood 5 created a life on the planet, finding work and entering a partnership. They are even trying to find a way to combine their DNA for the purpose of procreation."

That surprised Ciic so much that she turned and looked at M. "Fantastic, I wish them the best of luck." She projected to M.

The small group was upon them. Lelelu at the head of the group bowed deeply toward Ciic and Muum, demonstrating the proper protocol for greeting such dignitaries. Both Rogsaars and G'ist followed her lead. "Your majesties, it is my honor to see you again." She straightened up, "May I present Rogsaar and G'ist of Xinood 5 and Rogsaar of Glion Galaxy." She stepped to the side and allowed the others to approach.

The Rogsaars and G'ist looked a little uncomfortable with Ciic. No doubt they were intimidated by her station as ruler of Suus. Muum came to their rescue by projecting a calming welcome. "We are honored to meet you all, we do not often get to travel and meet well traveled individuals such as yourselves."

That seemed to relax them. Bivoor could hardly wait for the pleasantries to be exchanged before approaching the Rogsaars. After a quick introduction of G'ist, they were off to mingle with other Myaads.

Zri and five of his team arrived on the landing pad near Lelelu's ship. After a quick survey of the area, four of his team stationed themselves at even intervals around the landing pad. The fifth stayed near the arrival point, ready to begin receiving passengers and supplies.

Zri approached Ciic and bowed, "Ciic, Muum, it is a pleasure to see you again. I am thankful it is for an event such as this."

They had hardly finished exchanging pleasantries when there was a commotion on the landing pad. M knew before she looked that direction, it had to be Bartala.

"Ahhhhhhhh I just LOVE instant transports, they don"t even mess up my hair." Bartala said smoothing his hand over his tall Londo style hair. "I have to get one! My darling, what do you think? Do you like moving this way?" He asked Nalau.

"This way please Emperor." The Gaznzulian stationed at the arrival point attempted to push Bartala along, there were several others and many supplies, waiting to come down to Myaad.

M watched her dearest friend approach. As the Emperor of a planet himself, she knew that Bartala could always be counted on the follow the customs of any official introductions. By the time they arrived at the group Bartala had completely recovered from his excitement. They were looking especially fine today. Nalau wore a maroon gown trimmed in black. It had many layers that fluttered in the breeze. Her jewels were modest today, a simple pendant of blue crystal hung on a piece of black silk around her neck. Bartala was of course wearing a long formal coat, also maroon, heavily embroidered with black trim. His broach was of the same crystal as Nalau's pendant. He and Nalau came to a stop and as they were about to bow before the leader of the Suus, Ciic projected a message to them, "Please do not bow to me. We are equals, and it is my hope that we will become friends."

The telepathic message was only intended for Bartala and Nalau, but M and Brzko could tell by the looks on their faces that it had been received. M stepped up to make the introduction.

"Ciic, Muum, it is with great pleasure that I present to you Emperor Bartala and Empress Nalau of Ploosnar." she said as she stepped back.

Ciic stepped forward and grasped Bartala's hand, and held it close to her chest in the traditional Ploosnarian greeting. She had been studying their customs. This simple action, by the leader of a planet, showed great respect to Bartala and Nalau. He would not forget such an action. She had won his respect.

While the group chatted about the trip from Ploosnar to Myaad, palace staff continued to arrive. There were around twenty of them standing near the arrival point. The supplies were arriving in large black cargo containers. It looked like Nalau had thought of everything.

Empress Nalau broke from the small group and caught M's eye, they stepped off the side. Lelelu instinctively followed. "I think it's time to get started on the set up. How soon are we expecting Kiik to arrive with the Rogsaars?"

Lelelu took the tablet from the pocket in her skirt, consulted the tracking application and answered, "Maybe about an hour, Empress."

"Oh we have no time to waste then!"

"The reception is going to be in what they call the Theatre, it's a large outdoor stadium. It's not far from here, just a short walk over that hill." M said. "Lelelu, will you please show Empress Nalau and her staff the way to the theatre?"

"Of course M, my pleasure." The two of them walked away, toward the waiting palace staff and supplies. The cargo containers were stacked in threes; each stack was loaded on a hover lift, ready for transport.

M returned to the small group, while Lelelu, Nalau and her staff left for the Theatre with the cargo.

"It is time for final preparations, is there something we can do to help?" Ciic projected to the group.

"Oh don't worry, when my beloved gets going, if you are anywhere near her she will put you to work!" Bartala said. "I am going to the Theatre now; will the rest of you be joining me?"

Everyone offered affirmation and followed Bartala toward the hill behind Lelelu's shuttle.

Nalau was only a few minutes ahead of them but when the group rounded the corner, and looked down on the theatre, it already looked ready to receive the returning Rogsaars. The theatre has a half circle of stadium style seating on one side, the other side is wide open with a low platform. There is a large, open field behind the platform. The plan was to have Kiik land in the field, have the Rogsaars enter the Theatre via the platform and then disperse and mingle on the seating side of the theatre.

Each of the vessels used to transport the Leel vines had a telescoping rod that was extended from the center. They were all extended and the vines loosely wound around the rods. There was a long red ribbon attached to the top of each rod, they billowed in the breeze. The vessels lined the platform and went half way down each side of the seating area. The smell was intoxicating! There were tables set up at the back of the open area; they were modular setups that literally folded out of those black cargo containers. Nalau's staff only had to extend them and then lift the food and beverage from under the table and place it on top. They were genius inventions. They even had linens that draped the tables to hide the containers. It was a little too soon to place the food and beverage on the tables. There was a Ploosnarians stationed next to each table, ready to attend to the guests.

Nalau saw the group approach and eagerly came to them, "OK, we are ready, doesn't this look fabulous?"

"My darling, once again you have outdone yourself. Thank you!" Bartala said.

"Well it wasn't only me, Ciic, these Leel vines are amazing! I have never seen flowers with nebula centers. They are stunning! A wonderful finishing touch." Nalau said.

"It is our pleasure to provide them for this momentous event." Ciic projected.

Lelelu approached with three Bivoors, "OK, it looks like we're all set. Which is good because we just got word that they arrived early! Kiik is in orbit, waiting to land."

"Oh stars! We need a few more minutes." Nalau said with just a hint of panic.

Brzko easily took care of that. Placing his hand on her forearm he said, "Just tell us what you need Empress."

Her demeanor instantly changed, she was once again calm. "I need you all in a receiving line. Here is the order in which you should stand, first Muse of Mischief, second Agent Brzko."

M almost spoke.

"No, I know what you are going to say. I've already discussed this with Bivoors and we all agree. Without the two of you the Rogsaars would never have been found and returned." There was clearly no point in arguing with Nalau, she was in charge. "The order will be Muse of Mischief, Agent Brzko, Rogsaar of Earth, Emperor Bartala, Ciic, three of the Bivoor,

Lelelu, me, and Muum. The remaining Bivoors, the Rogsaars that came with Lelelu, the Dumeer, and the remaining Suus, will mingle in the open area. Zri will of course be lurking wherever he is needed."

The entire group turned and looked at Zri, he smiled and shrugged. Lurking was what he did. It was how he kept everyone safe. They all chuckled.

"OK, places!" Nalau said and clapped for emphasis, she nodded to her food staff and within a minute the food and beverage displays were on the tables, complete with little enclosed waterfall centerpieces. That was a brilliant choice for a planet that had no surface water!

Everyone hurried to where they were supposed to be. Nalau walked up and down the receiving line, making sure everyone met with her approval. She fussed over the broach on Bartala's coat. Making sure it was perfectly straight. She took her place in line just as the ship set down.

The large center door opened, four Suus stepped out, two carrying the tall red banners that were customary. They flanked the walkway. Kiik exited the ship and began walking toward the platform. A long, single file line of Rogsaars followed behind her.

She stopped in front of M, "Kiik, welcome back to Myaad, thank you for all you've done."

"My pleasure Muse of Mischief, I would love to stay and chat but….." They shared a moment of humor before Kiik moved on. To stall the returning Rogsaars at this point would throw several of the attendees into a tailspin.

Because the Rogsaars were most interested in seeing the Bivoors and the Dumeers, the line moved quickly. Besides, they had all been on Ploosnar together a few days ago. After the last of the Rogsaars passed through the line, Kiik's crew came and joined the reception.

M and Brzko stood back and watched the group. With the returning Rogsaars and the others that had survived on Myaad, there were now hundreds of identical beings in one place. The only Myaads that could not attend were those filling the positions of hive Caretakers. With all they had been through, it was just too risky to have them leave the hives, even for something as joyous as the reception.

Bartala approached M and Brzko, "Ahhhh again the misfits gather and watch. Why do the three of us dislike crowds?"

"Four of us." Lelelu said as she joined them.

"Five of us." Zri said as he joined them.

The *misfits* as Bartala called them, stood in a group watching the festivities. Empress Nalau and all of the Suus seemed to be having a grand time mingling with Bivoors, Rogsaars, and Dumeers.

"It's not that I dislike crowds..." M said searching for the right words, "it's just that I'd prefer to be doing something specific.

"Like planning a trip to Trella?" Zri asked. "It will be the five of us that go right?"

"Oh yes, oh yes, let's go very soon!" Bartala said. "Once my son is born I will have less freedom. And maybe we will find clues to your origins." he said nodding toward M and Brzko.

"I don't think Brzko and I have anything pressing after this reception. Do we Lelelu?" M asked.

"No, not really. The dignitaries of Drolla O0 have asked for you or Brzko to attend a ceremony of sorts, but I've given the proper excuses to get you out of it. I know how much you two love attending ceremonies." Lelelu jabbed.

"How long do you need to prepare Zri?" Bartala asked.

"I can be ready within two days." he answered.

"OK then we..." Bartala was interrupted.

The group was so engrossed in planning for their next expedition that they didn't notice the Theatre platform had been cleared and turned into a stage of sorts. There were three Bivoor, one standing front and center had a wireless earpiece microphone unit, ready to address the crowd.

"May I have your attention please, attention please." The Theatre went silent, all eyes were on Bivoor.

"Not long ago we thought Myaad would die. After aberidus took so many of us and prevented us from repopulating, we truly thought we were lost. But thanks to tenacity of one Rogsaar we are here today, with eggs developing in the hives and our long lost travelers returned home. We still have so much work to do, but before we begin I want to thank Rogsaar of Earth. Rogsaar please come forward."

The crowd scanned, looking for Rogsaar; once spotted the crowd gladly parted for Rogsaar to pass. This was a different Rogsaar than M and Brzko had first encountered in Scorchbrooke, there was no more loneliness and despair.

"We owe it all to this Rogsaar constantly tinkering with a flashport. For those of you unaware of how this all came to be, let me explain. Rogsaar continued trying to contact home by sending various items through the flashport, but they did not arrive on Myaad, they were sent to Ploosnar. This attracted the attention of Emperor Bartala, through the hard work of the Muse of Mischief and Agent Brzko, the mystery was solved. The Suus then came to our rescue by sending Kiik to help eradicate aberidus and restore the hives. Muse of Mischief, Agent Brzko, Emperor Bartala, and

Kiik, please join us on stage." The entire crowd turned their eyes toward the group that preferred to stay out of the spotlight.

"Oh yea! This is the part we all love." M mumbled sarcastically to the small group.

"Ha! How do you think I feel? I have to take the stage next to you in those purple shoes and that ridiculous derby!" Bartala jabbed.

"Yeah but at least my hair doesn't stick straight up!" she jabbed back.

His hands instantly went to his hair, smoothing it.

The trio slowly walked toward the stage, meeting up with Kiik at the steps. They stood in a line next to Rogsaar of Earth.

"Please join me in thanking the group responsible for returning Rogsaars to Myaad and curing aberidus." Bivoor said. The crowd went wild, they began stomping in unison. You could feel the vibration; luckily it didn't last too long. And even better, Bivoor didn't ask anyone from the group to speak.

Once the crowd quieted down Bivoor addressed them again. "As many of you know, not all Rogsaars chose to return to Myaad, we hope that one day, they will at least come to visit their home. But we understand that they have established new lives around the Universe and we wish them happiness. Emperor Bartala has offered to provide repairs to the Rogsaar ships that his team was able to salvage. Thank you Emperor, thank you. Many Rogsaars were forced to call these neglected ships home while they were stranded. It is my pleasure to announce that Bivoors have decided to make these ships the property of the Rogsaars. Once the ships are repaired they will be free to travel where and when they desire. It is our hope that this gift will inspire more Rogsaars to visit their homeland, and even better, to inspire Rogsaars to begin exploring again!"

This announcement was met with great enthusiasm from the crowd. Once the stomping subsided, Bivoor made the final statement, "Welcome home to all of the Rogsaars!"

They all left the stage, glad to be out of the spotlight, and accepted that mingling with the crowd was necessary.

G'ist and Rogs were standing near a table, snacking on the fresh fruits Empress Nalau had provided when the speech began. Afterward G'ist turned to his partner Rogs, "Did you hear that Rogs? We've just been provided an opportunity."

"What are you talking about?"

"Your ship. Your ship now belongs to you. Once it is repaired we can travel. You can introduce me to some of the places you seen."

"I cannot think of a better way to spend my life G'ist."

M and Brzko were standing near a table snacking on lusimis when Ciic and Kiik approached. "Friends" Ciic projected, "we have come to say our goodbyes. We must return to Suus."

"I guess things here are winding down. We will be leaving soon too." M stepped forward and took Ciic's lower hands in hers, "Ciic thank you for the help you have provided Myaad. We could not have saved them without help from the Suus."

"Muse of Mischief it is always my pleasure to assist you and Agent Brzko, please call upon me anytime. If you ever slow down, I hope you will come to Suus just to visit." Ciic projected.

M released Ciic's hands and turned to Kiik, "Kiik, it has been a pleasure getting to know you. I look forward to our next adventure! The help you have provided the Myaads is invaluable. Ciic is lucky to have as the lead researcher. I hope you will lead the team that returns to Myaad when the eggs are fully incubated."

M's compliments rendered her silent for a second or too, gratitude emanated from her. "Thank you Muse of Mischief. I do not often get to work in the field, and working with you has been an honor."

It was Brzko's turn, he grasped one of Ciic's lower hands, bent and kissed it, the same way he did with Empress Nalau, "Your Majesty, it is always a pleasure to see you. Safe travels my friend. Please give Muum our best."

Ciic was taken aback, she did not know how to respond to an exchange such as this, he didn't wait for a response. Instead he moved on to Kiik, "Kiik, it has been a pleasure. I wish you the best my friend."

He had flustered them, joy and excitement emanated from them. They turned and began walking up the hill to return to the landing pad, all of the other Suus joined them at the bottom of the hill. The power of their minds joined together, projecting the same message as they looked down on the crowd from the hilltop, "Goodbye friends, we are better for knowing you."

The entire crowd turned toward them, waving, and wishing them well. With the Suus gone, the crowd began to disperse. The reception was over. The Rogsaars had finally made it home.

TRELLA ON THE HORIZON

With most of the Rogsaars back on Myaad, life at the Ploosnar Palace had returned to normal. Empress Nalau had done a spectacular job of hosting the Rogsaar reception. She was back to her usual philanthropic duties. Emperor Bartala on the other hand, was back to his usual unsettled behavior, always wanting to be on the go.

The group of travelers had gathered at the palace to plan for the expedition to Trella. They were in Bartala's favorite sitting room, his personal room. The Muse of Mischief and Agent Brzko were sitting on one side, across the table Lelelu was seated next to Emperor Bartala. Zri of course, had stationed himself between the group and the entrance. He was one of them, but he never stopped guarding them either.

"Why can't we leave today?" Bartala said with the tone of a pouty teenager.

"Because, we need time to pack some gear." Lelelu said. "I'm going home to pick up some supplies."

"And while she's doing that, I need to travel back to Gaznzul to reload some supplies and make some changes to my crew." Zri said.

"Are you going to bring us the latest in Gaznzulian technology Zri?" Bartala asked with no shame.

"Of course Emperor. I have some new things that you may enjoy."

"Good I want to ride with you Zri! Who is riding with whom and can we be ready to leave tomorrow?" Bartala said impatiently.

"OK Emperor, I'm happy to have you on my ship. How many palace guards will be on board with you and how many of their ships will follow?"

"Two guards will be on board with me and two ships traveling with us." Bartala answered.

Zri nodded in acknowledgement, "I assume you're ready since the only thing you will pack is nekmid?" he teased.

"Ahhhhh, you will thank me for that nekmid while we are bored out of our minds on the way to Trella!" Bartala said.

"Or we could introduce you to espidrun, although you may sleep the whole way." M interjected.

"Espidrun? What is that and why have you not shared this before?" Bartala said, sounding truly offended.

"We only just discovered it on Smd; it's made from fermented niptdyn. It's very potent." Lelelu said.

"And quite palatable!" Brzko added.

"That sounds like the perfect thing for a long journey. Maybe it will slow you down enough to finally tell me the story of how you and Brzko saved the ruler of Suus when she was a child." he said to M.

"Maybe, if you're lucky." M said teasing him.

"I need to depart, but I didn't bring the shuttle down. M?"

"Oh right, sorry Lelelu. I'll take you back." M said standing and walking over to Lelelu.

They disappeared, and then M reappeared and took her seat again.

"I will be departing now too. Contact me if you need anything before I return." Zri said.

"OK Zri, safe travels." Brzko answered for all of them.

After a slight manipulation of his armband Zri transported himself back to his ship. It was back to just the three of them, M, Brzko, and Bartala.

"Break out that espidrun. I want to try this stuff!" Bartala said.

"What makes you think I have any here at the palace?" M asked.

Bartala waved his hand at her, dismissing her question, "Who do you think you're talking to? I know you have some here M, break it out."

"OK, OK." She disappeared from the sofa, and was back a few seconds later with a bottle in her hands. "You don't have glasses ready yet?"

"You are such a show off!" Bartala said.

Brzko was laughing at the two of them. M loved to tease her old friend and he had no problem throwing it right back at her. They truly deserved each other. Brzko retrieved the glasses from Bartala's side table.

"Here you two, here are the glasses. Now stop bickering long enough to try this." Brzko said taking the bottle from M. The bottle appeared to be made of heated titanium, it was blue and pink, it was short and wide, there was a lever on top that opened a spout.

"Oh that is pretty slick!" Bartala said.

"Slick?" M asked. "Are you watching Earth television again?"

Bartala just looked at her and rolled his eyes, that meant he was busted, he had been watching trashy Earth television again.

Brzko tilted the bottle and poured the hot pink liquid into the waiting glasses. Upon contact with air it immediately began to release blue steam. He pressed the protruding spout back in to the bottle and sat it down, then handed a glass to Bartala and one to M. Lifting his own he toasted his friends, "To long life, good health, and a safe journey."

They all sipped.

Bartala lost his mind! "Ooooohhhhhhhhhhhhhhh this is good! It's sweet but not too sweet, it's savory but not too savory and the texture is like, well it feels like electricity in my mouth! But in a good way."

M and Brzko both chuckled. Their friend's reaction was priceless.

"Just don't drink it too fast." Brzko said. "It's really potent. A glass this size is the equivalent of drinking six or seven nekmids."

"Do you have enough to take to Trella?" Bartala asked.

"Yes, we have plenty." Brzko answered.

The friends sat in silence for a few minutes. They were comfortable enough with each other that they did not need to fill the time with pointless chatter. After a while the Emperor spoke.

"The surrogate will enter phase two of gestation before we return. My son is developing as expected."

"I'm glad to hear that Bartala, but what is phase two?"

"As the child develops the host becomes somewhat incapacitated. Once the second phase begins she will remain inside, with limited movement."

"I've never seen a pregnant Ploosnarian, the child develops in a sac on the back of the mother or surrogate is that correct? Brzko asked.

"Yes, which is why my beloved Nalau did not want to carry the child herself. The second phase of the pregnancy will last for almost two hundred days."

"Interesting, so *sac* is the correct term, and is it opaque?" M asked.

"No, we do not call it a sac. The child develops within a membrane." Bartala explained. "Yes, it is opaque; you cannot see the actual child until birth. When it is time, the membrane will begin to peel away and the connecting cells will retreat back into the mother or surrogate, leaving the child ready to survive on its own. The process usually takes two days."

"Are there ever complications? Does the infant ever need to be extracted?" M asked.

"That is extremely rare. I believe it happens less than one time in over ten thousand births." Bartala said. "It is not a risky process, but it is a great inconvenience to the mother and the other members of her family. So we do not procreate without a plan. That reminds me. Have you heard anything from Rogsaar of Xinood 5? I am very curious to see if Rogsaar and G'ist will be able to reproduce."

"No, I haven't heard from them since they stopped by here to pick up Rogs refurbished ship. They are both ecstatic about having their own ship now, thanks to you." M answered.

None of them heard the door open, so they were startled when Nalau spoke, "They won't return home for a few more days. But I've been in touch with the doctors on Xinood 5 and asked him to let me know if there is anything we can do to help."

Bartala eagerly stood to greet his wife, "My darling, you look ravishing this evening!" And of course she did. With no official duties pressing, she was a little more relaxed than usual with her hair was gently pulled back in a loose ponytail. She was wearing a simple, ankle length black skirt and matching short sleeved blouse. The only color was in her casual attire was the bright orange and white broach she wore.

Always the gentlemen, Brzko stood to greet the lady of the house, well palace. "Empress, you are looking lovely as always this evening." He bent and kissed her extended hand.

"Oh Brzko, I shall never tire of the way you treat a lady. You could take a lesson dear Bartala. Now which one of you is going to pour me a taste of this new drink?" She said as she sat down on next to Bartala.

Her unusually casual demeanor had completely caught Brzko and Bartala off guard. Nalau looked at M and winked; she knew what she was doing and found it very entertaining.

Bartala caught the wink, while Brzko retrieved a fourth glass and poured an espidrun for her, "I think you have been spending too much time with my wife M. Your mischievous side is beginning to rub off on her."

Before M could defend herself the Empress spoke, "Perhaps it's not her that's *rubbing off on me* Bartala." She said as she lovingly grasped his leg. She took a sip of the espidrun. "Wow!" She covered her mouth and coughed lightly. "This is amazing. It's very strong but I like it very much!"

Bartala beamed with pleasure. "Have we found a drink you like well enough to transform you into a *drinking" buddy?*" He said the last two words in this insanely funny fake John Wayne Earth like accent.

They all looked at him and laughed. They were still laughing when a butler entered, "Excuse me Your Majesties," they quieted and turned toward the butler, "the kitchen has asked me to inform you that dinner is ready." He turned and left.

Nalau stood, "I hope you will be staying for dinner." she said to M and Brzko.

"I'm sorry Empress, we must return home to prepare for our trip to Trella." Brzko said. "We hope to leave tomorrow afternoon.

"About that trip," Nalau said, and the room paused, was she going to put a damper on Bartala's fun? "What if I were to tag along? I've never been on one of your excursions. M, tell me the truth - do you think I would enjoy the trip?"

Knowing how much having Nalau join them on the trip to Trella would mean to her best friend, M did not hesitate to answer, "I think you would have the time of your life, Empress." Bartala continued to beam. Brzko looked back and forth between M and Nalau to see if there was more to be said.

Nalau turned to Bartala with her drink in one hand, she pointed at the espidrun bottle with the other, "Bring the bottle and come love, we will discuss the trip over dinner. Goodbye M, goodbye Brzko, we'll see you soon." She turned and walked toward the door.

Bartala scooped up the bottle and trotted behind her, at the door he turned to M and Brzko, giving them an exaggerated wink, and then he was gone. M and Brzko returned home to prepare for the tip.

~~~

The Muse of Mischief and Agent Brzko returned to Ploosnar before Lelelu, she was stopping by Smd to pick up a supply of espidrun. The last thing they wanted to do was run out on an expedition like this. M and Brzko secured their home and returned to Ploosnar, arriving at the bottom of the palace stairs as was their custom.

As they reached the top of the stairs, they were announced by the palace guard, "The Muse of Mischief and Agent Brzko Your Majesties."

Emperor Bartala came running out of the palace, "Where's Lelelu? Are you ready to go?"

Empress Nalau was right on his heels, "Relax darling. We are on schedule to leave later today."

"Emperor, Empress, good afternoon." M said. "Jeez Bartala, at least let us put our bags down."

Brzko kissed the Empress's hand, "Hello Empress Nalau, a pleasure to see you again. I'm excited to hear that you will be traveling with us."

The two of them were more casual than M had ever seen them. Bartala was wearing simple brown slacks and a brown shirt with pale green paisley, no jacket or tie. Nalau was wearing a knee length skirt made of the same fabric as Bartala's shirt. Her shirt was a solid green, the same color as the paisley pattern. Even though the attire was more casual than usual, their garments were still crisp and there was not a single hair out place. M and Brzko must have been staring at them.

Empress Nalau stepped forward and twirled, "What do you think? I just don't think formal gowns and palace jewels are the correct fashion for an expedition. I had Schatorren make us new, casual wardrobes for the trip."

"I think you both look fantastic." M said. "Well except for that hair of his." She said as she thrust her thumb in Bartala's direction.

"I concur!" Brzko added.

"Let's go inside, lunch is ready and Zri is already in orbit." Empress Nalau said.

"Oh, Zri is here." Brzko said. "Please start lunch without me; I'd like to visit with him for a few minutes." He didn't wait for a response from the group. He was gone almost instantly, leaving both of his travel bags where he had been standing. M knew what he was up to. Brzko wanted to converse with Zri about the ship's defenses before the group was on board, there was no need to cause them any concern.

He arrived on the flight bridge. Zri was there with two of his crew. "Hey Brzko, I figured you'd pop in before the others." Zri said.

"You know me well Zri. How go the preparations?" Brzko asked.

"We're just about ready, preflight tests are complete. We are stocked with supplies, and all of the gear is loaded and stowed. It will only take a few minutes to transfer your personal gear aboard and of course whatever the Emperor is bringing."

"How big is your crew?"

"There are five officers with me - you've met ShyUst before right?" Zri said motioning to his second in command.

ShyUst walked over to them, "Yes." Brzko said extending his hand "It's a pleasure ShyUst, I think the last time I saw you was when we apprehended the Brusher."

"Yes, it was. Hopefully this will be a much quieter trip!" ShyUst said shaking Brzko's hand before returning to his position at the main console.

"Zri is there anything else you need before we go?" Brzko asked.

"No, thank you Brzko. I'll come down after I run a check on the transporters."

"Sounds good, I'll see you soon then." and with that Brzko was gone immediately back in the palace foyer.

It is a short walk from the foyer to the formal dining room, Brzko was surprised when he entered and found the room empty. He continued on to the kitchen, as he went down the hallway he heard Bartala's voice from up ahead, he was laughing. Brzko continued on, following his voice.

"There you are," Brzko said stepping outside to join the group on the back patio.

"Hi Brzko, how's Zri, all ready to go?" M asked as she stood and went over to properly greet her partner.

He grabbed her and tilted her back in his arms, one of his best Hollywood style kisses planted on her lips. He stood her upright, she was visibly shaken. She hadn't expected such an exciting greeting.

"Wait, what were we talking about?" This caused a burst of laughter from Bartala and Nalau. "Oh Zri, that's right."

Brzko smiled at his love, "He's pretty much ready. Once Lelelu arrives, he just needs to load Bartala and Nalau's supplies, and we're off. But first... what's for lunch. I'm starving. Emperor, are your guard's ships ready?

"Yes, they are loaded and ready, holding in orbit."

Brzko helped himself to the royal buffet that had been laid out on a side table. He took his seat next to M at the table, "I hope you are all ready to fend for yourselves, Zri will do his best to keep us safe, but his food is not this good!"

"As long as we have plenty of espidrun, who cares!" Bartala said.

"Speaking of espidrun....." Lelelu surprised them by stepping out onto the patio.

"Hey Lelelu, how did everything go?" M asked. Which was code for *did you get all of the espidrun we ordered?*

"Everything went as planned, everything..." she was interrupted by Zri.

"... Lelelu brought is loaded." Zri said as he walked out of the palace.

Bartala jumped to his feet, "Let's go. C'mon we're ready it's going to take a few days to get all the way to Trella."

Nalau tried to calm him, "Darling please, perhaps Lelelu or Zri would like some lunch."

They both declined.

Zri walked over to the table with something in his hand, "I'd like you both to wear these at all times." He handed Bartala and Nalau Gaznzulian arm consoles. "I've already distributed them to your guards."

"OK!" Bartala said excitedly. He loved gadgets.

"Notice these two buttons at the top." Zri said demonstrating with his own console. "If you press the one on the right, you will be transported to my ship. But if you press the one on the left, at the same time, everyone in the group is alerted that you have an emergency. If you are away from the ship you will automatically be transported back to the ship. On the screen you can navigate to the communications menu to page or send a message to anyone, or everyone."

Bartala managed to pull his eyes away from his new toy, "Hey why don't they have to wear them?" he said, nodding toward M and Brzko.

"The Muse of Mischief and Agent Brzko can transport themselves to anytime or place they desire. They also have earcom links that keep them in constant contact with me, my crew and Lelelu." Zri explained. "If you would like to give up the ability to transport, and several other functions, I can switch your console for an earcom link Emperor." He said teasing Bartala.

Knowing that he had been bested, Bartala let it go, "No, no, this is fine Zri. Thank you."

"OK then, gather any personal items, and press the top button on the right when you are ready to board. Questions?" Zri said.

"No, thank you Zri." Nalau answered. "We will join you momentarily."

The Muse of Mischief, Agent Brzko, Lelelu and Zri all left the patio at once, leaving Bartala and Nalau alone.

Bartala stood and pulled her chair out for her, "Are you ready for the adventure of a lifetime my love?"

"Yes Bartala. I am a little nervous, but I am also excited."

She wrapped her hands around his upper arm, and they walked toward the palace. Several of their staff were standing just inside the door. They had not both been gone from the palace in a very long time, but they trusted their staff. Everything on Ploosnar would be fine while they were gone. Once they reached the front steps, they faced each other and pressed their buttons simultaneously, two guards followed them directly. It was the first step of what was going to an exciting journey.

~~~

Zri's ship was built for safety and speed, but no creature comforts had been overlooked for this trip. The ship is long and narrow, but wider at the front. There is an upper deck at the front of the ship, this serves as the command bridge. There are lifts on both sides of the bridge, basically elevators that run automatically if the sensors detect anyone in the lift. With only two levels, there is no command to give in the lift. If you are on the main level and step into a lift, you are taken to the bridge. If you are on the bridge and step into the lift, you are taken to the main level.

The command bridge is like most, the outer edges are lined with consoles and workstations. There are three seats facing the front of the room, and the main display. The display can show the view from the cameras that line the exterior of the ship, or it can show information from any of the ship's systems.

The Gaznzulians work in rotating shifts on the bridge, there are always two on duty. Each is fully trained for all duties. The only exception is the second in command, ShyUst. He has been trained to assume command if needed.

There is a large community room at the front of the ship on the lower level. There are windows lining the front of the room, and many comfortable places to sit. The view from the room is spectacular when the ship is in motion. On the left side of the ship there is a large dining table and chairs with a kitchen area. This is the room where the group will spend most of their time. Both of the lifts are just outside this room, in a long hallway with individual rooms on either side. The rooms become progressively smaller toward the back of the ship, the smallest are the crew quarters. The very end of the hallway provides access to the cargo bay; which is basically a huge warehouse, with a large ramp that can be used for loading and unloading both passengers and cargo.

The explorers had gathered in the community room for a departure toast. Zri directed their attention to the view, "Emperor, Empress, I've instructed the crew to come around before we depart, giving you a view of Ploosnar."

Everyone turned toward the window, and silently watched as they flew over the most beautifully bright blue planet there was. Once it was out of range, there was nothing to see but open space. Apparently not too interesting for Bartala.

"Let's toast!" He had a bottle of espidrun and Nalau started handing out glasses while he poured. Surprisingly, even Zri accepted a glass. "Zri, I've never seen you partake of spirits."

"Well Emperor, I do occasionally let my guard down. And with a full crew on this ship and three additional ships behind us, I think it's safe for me to take some down time."

"Here here! To down time and exploration!" Bartala toasted, holding his glass high. They all took sips of the espidrun; it was far too strong to take in full shots. "Wait, four Gaznzulian ships? How much is this going to cost me?"

"Well Emperor, if it makes you feel any better, you won't be billed for my ship. I'm technically on holiday." Zri grinned and sipped his espidrun.

"So there are six ships in our convoy, this one, our two guards, and three more of yours Zri?" Empress Nalau asked rhetorically "Lelelu I think your decision to leave your ship on Ploosnar was brilliant. We'd miss having you here on board Zri's ship with us."

"Thank you Empress. I wouldn't want to miss this fun." She answered, taking a seat on one of the sofas. "So what is the plan once we reach Trella, or do we have a plan?"

There is a variety of couches and chairs in the lounge, the group settled in to chat about the trip.

"I think we should definitely show them the Pink River. Do you remember that forest that grows along the banks of the river M?" Brzko asked.

The Muse of Mischief turned bright red. "Yes, I remember the forest next to the Pink River."

"M are you OK?" Zri asked. "You look like you are overheating."

"She's not hot my friend, she's blushing! She and Brzko must have a history on the banks of the Pink River." Bartala explained. "And I want to hear all about it when we get there!"

"Ha! No chance buddy!" M said, regaining her composure.

"Bartala, have you been to Trella before?" Nalau asked, rescuing M.

"Yes my love. When M and I were young we would *escape* there every time we had angered my father. Like the time we hid all of his bisporks. Remember that M? He thought they had been stolen but we had moved them to a hanger." Bartala said cracking himself up.

"Ummmm I remember YOU hiding his bisporks and me covering for you and then saving your butt by bringing you to Trella until he cooled off." M said, refusing to take responsibility for her old friend's pranks.

"Mah… details. You hid them, I hid them."

"Are all of the rivers pink on Trella?" Nalau asked.

"No, I haven't seen the entire planet but it has many different colors of everything, plants, water, sand." M said. "It doesn't really make sense. It looks like someone chewed up a rainbow and spit it out."

"Ehhh, that doesn't sound appealing." Nalau said letting her disgust show.

"When I was young it was entertaining." M said.

"Are there any structures on the planet?" Nalau asked.

"Not that I've ever seen, have you seen any Brzko?" M asked.

"No, no structures." he answered.

"Since we are escorted by three Gaznzulian ships and two Ploosnarian guard ships, will you land Zri?" Lelelu knew that Gaznzulian protocol prevented a lone ship from landing on a foreign planet.

"Yes, assuming we don't find anything of interest when we scan the planet's surface, we will land. That way we have a base of operations." He answered. Everyone just stared at him. "What, what's wrong?"

M grinned, "You said if we don't find anything of interest when we scan, I assume you meant if we don't find anything of concern?"

"Perhaps the espidrun is having an effect on you Zri." Bartala teased.

"Oh I'm sure that it is, I'm sure that it is." He said finishing off his first drink. He stood and went for the bottle that Bartala had left on the table, he went around the room refilling everyone's glass before filling his own and returning the bottle to the table. He plopped into an overstuffed easy chair and flung his legs up over the arm of the chair taking another sip.

Everyone was still staring at him, Lelelu looked perplexed and turned to M. "Is he always like this at a party?" she asked, teasing him.

"Sometimes he's even more fun! If you're lucky he will show you what a Gaznzulian really looks like." M said.

"Tread carefully M. Remember I know a few of your secrets." Zri said. "Like the day we met, I'm sure you remember that."

"Was that the day you tried to have me eaten?" Bartala asked, smiling.

Nalau giggled, "I have hear this story!"

"Of course I remember Zri, I'm not sure it's interesting enough to share though." M said.

"Then tell us how you rescued Ciic when she was a child." Bartala said. "As long as we're in space we have plenty of time for stories."

"Wait, first I want to hear how you and Bartala met." Nalau spoke up.

Bartala laughed and finished off his second espidrun, "Go ahead M. Let's tell them how we met."

THE DAY THE MUSE OF MISCHIEF STUMBLED ONTO PLOOSNAR

The Muse of Mischief leaned back, kicked off her heels, and put her feet up on the low table in front of her, "Long, long ago, in a land far, far away…"

"Liar, it was not that long ago and it was on Ploosnar." Emperor Bartala said.

"Hey who's telling this story anyway?" He waved his hand and leaned back, settling in next to his beloved Empress. "So anyway…. I was wandering around Trella, escaping from the pretend parents on Earth. If Brzko couldn't get away I used to spend time on…"

"The banks of the Pink River?" Lelelu interrupted.

"Funny, no." M replied smiling, "I used to spend a lot of time on the banks of the Green Lake. It's more of a pond, and it's surrounded by these blue stones that are perfect for skipping. Sometimes you can get them to skip six or seven times."

Nalau interrupted, "Skipping stones?"

"Yeah, if you throw a flat stone with just the right angle you can get it to bounce across the water's surface a few times before it sinks." Nalau just nodded, M thought she was really in for some new experiences on Trella. "The weather is always perfect on Trella, not too hot, not too cold. So after I grew tired of skipping rocks I sat down on a flat boulder that made a great bench, and I start reading a book of short stories I had with me. I never went anywhere without a book when I was young."

"What was it?" Zri asked.

"Sorry?" M didn't understand what he was asking.

"What were you reading?" he clarified.

"Night Shift, it's a collection of horror fiction by an author named Stephen King."

"Hmmm makes sense." Zri said.

"What's that supposed to mean?" M asked.

"You, horror stories as a child, it just makes sense." Zri said.

"Agreed." Bartala piped in.

"Ok, moving on…." M said a little intrigued that her friends were psychoanalyzing her, and getting it right. Brzko was grinning, their friends knew her well.

"I was rereading one of my favorite short stories in the book, it's about an astronaut that is exposed to alien germs or something, and how they begin to transform him into a different being. Anyway, I fell asleep. When I woke up, I noticed that something was sparkling in the rocks on the other side of the pond. I hadn't noticed it there before. In fact I had never seen sparkling rocks on Trella before, so I walked over and bent down to look at it. It looked like a bright blue crystal it didn't look dangerous so I reached for it. The instant I had my hand around it I left Trella and found myself at the top of the palace stairs on Ploosnar. I had startled the palace guards by just arriving, not to mention myself, I had no idea where I was, but I knew I wasn't on Trella anymore. The palace guards assumed I was a threat to

Bartala's father, Emperor Wisssdartai, and attempted to restrain me."

"Attempted?" Lelelu asked.

Bartala couldn't wait for M to answer, he jumped in. "Oh yes! You should have seen it! We were warned of the commotion and being Emperor, my father was kept protected inside the palace, but I ran before they could secure me. I got to the palace entrance and there's M," at this point Bartala stands up to add some animation to his story, "in high heels, striped stockings, and a mini-skirt and of course a derby. She's already knocked four of the guards down and is standing like this…" He bent his knees and lifted his hands in an attempt to mimic her defensive posture. "The remaining guards cannot decide if they want to approach her, they know they will end up on the ground like the first four."

"I don't like to be restrained." M said in her defense.

"I stepped between her and the guards."

"How did you know she wouldn't hurt you?" Nalau asked.

"I just did. I walked right up to her and do you remember what I said M?"

"Of course, you said *Hello friend, I've been waiting for you.*" she answered.

"That's right; I put my arm around her and led her into the palace. The guards were furious with me for having a friend show up unannounced they believed I was really expecting her. We went inside and I hid her in my rooms to wait for everyone to calm down. I went to get my father so that we could try to figure out who she was."

"But I didn't wait for you to return. I'd had enough excitement for one day, I went back to Earth." M interjected.

"Yes, you did that vanishing thing you love to do, and my father thought I had lost my mind and invented pretend friends." Bartala scolded as he picked up the bottle of espidrun and began refilling everyone's glasses before he sat down.

"Well I came back!" M said.

"Yes, you did. You appeared next to me in my rooms the next morning and startled me so badly one of my hearts stopped."

"No it didn't, you're exaggerating! It only skipped a few beats, besides you have two other hearts." she teased.

Everyone laughed at this exchange between the Muse of Mischief and Emperor Bartala. The room grew quiet while they reflected on the story they had just heard.

Lelelu broke the silence, "So Brzko, when did you meet Bartala?"

"It was a few years later, not until I had left the pretend parents on Earth. I knew M had some…." He paused to consider his next word, *"non-Earth* friends that she hung out with when I couldn't get away, but I didn't realize how much exploring she'd done until the first time we went to the Planet of Portals. I was amazed. Not only is your home beautiful Lelelu, the whole concept of the portals is fascinating." Brzko said.

Lelelu had more questions, "Yes, the Planet of Portals is an unusual place. I've never been through a random portal, but I know Trelods that find it addictive. Once they do it they just can't stop, I guess they find it thrilling. The same way a gambler would find a sporting event exciting. So how did you and Zri meet, M?"

Zri answered before she could even open her mouth, "I saved both of their butts from being eaten by a Haplogawa on Chyke 2C95." He said pointing his finger back and forth between M and Bartala.

"What is a Haplogawa?" Nalau asked.

"It's a giant reptile kind of creature that lacks communication skills. Its sole purpose for existence seems to be to eat anything it can swallow." M said casually.

"And it had you and Bartala trapped between it and a fresh lava flow." Zri said.

"I was just about to take us out of there when you grabbed us. I wanted Bartala to get a good look at it first."

"Right, and if you had hesitated at all Bartala would have been eaten."

"Eh, I had other friends."

"Oh thanks M, I appreciate your loyalty!" Bartala said trying to sound hurt.

"Isn't Chyke 2C95 covered in active volcanoes?" Nalau asked.

"Yes, the indigenous population lives in underground caves. Gaznzulians provide security and scanning services for the planet, mapping volcanic activity and making sure they have time to relocate when needed."

"So you just grabbed them off the surface and what, took them to your ship?" Lelelu asked.

"Sort of. I transported down, attempted to grab them both and transport them back aboard. But that one resisted," Zri pointed to M "I was not a commander at that time and my commanding officer was furious. But I couldn't just watch these sentient beings be eaten or cooked in lava. I didn't know M could open an aperture and travel. I thought they needed help. But I was only a science officer at the time, and not authorized to act on my own."

"I thought I was dead, I thought I must have already died when I was grabbed by a Ploosnarian who just appeared. But then on the ship I realized you weren't Ploosnarian, you only appeared that way to me." Bartala said. "Then I wondered if was going to become dinner."

The Muse of Mischief giggled at that idea.

"Of course not, Gaznzulians are an advanced raced. We do not consume anything with a consciousness." Zri said sounding disgusted.

"So how did you finally catch my defiant partner?" Brzko asked.

Zri and M spoke at the same time "He didn't", "I didn't"

M continued, "I kept moving around the planet so he wouldn't have an easy time finding me. I figured Bartala was a goner, eaten, held for ransom, something like that. Anyway, Zri finally caught up with me and transported himself near me, but not too close."

"I said, *I am Gaznzulian, I will not harm you*, and dropped my mental cloak. That did it, she was intrigued enough to stay put and let me explain. I explained that I thought they needed to be saved from the Haplogawa and that her friend was safe on my orbiting ship. Then she demanded to know why I had looked human when she first saw me. I explained that Gaznzulians use reflective mental cloaking to *blend in* with those around them. I guess that answer satisfied her because she disappeared immediately. She went to the ship, retrieved Bartala and reappeared with him."

"I wasn't OK with my pal Bartala being held on someone's ship." M said and shrugged.

"And I appreciated that, especially since you had gotten me into that mess in the first place!" Bartala said. "You and your Haplogawas!"

"Oh come on Bartala, you know it was one of the most exciting things you've ever seen!" M said.

Lelelu interrupted, "Wait, Bartala being eaten by a Haplogawa is not the important thing here. What does a Gaznzulian actually look like?"

Everyone, surprisingly even Bartala was quiet waiting for M to answer. M held Zri's gaze intently, without looking away she answered, "Gaznzulians rarely, if ever, drop their cloak around others. I am honored to have had the experience but it is not something I can share."

The Muse of Mischief was the only one in the room that had seen a Gaznzulian without the mental cloak. Everyone was curious, and wanted to persist in questioning, but at the same time they respected Zri enough to let it go. After everyone had been silent for a few moments, contemplating what M had said, Nalau broke the silence.

"So the three of you explored the Universe, jumping in and out of trouble until you were adults?"

"They did, I had to work." Zri said.

M shot him a challenging look.

"OK, I had some fun too." Zri admitted, grinning. "But that is all the fun I can have today. I'm going to check on ShyUst and then retire for the night. Please alert the crew if you need anything."

"Wait, wait, wait...." M said. "You are attempting to make your exit just when the story becomes entertaining. If you prefer I could tell the stories without you here to defend yourself." she teased.

"Stories? What do you mean stories? I don't know what you're up to M, but I'm going to need another espidrun to survive it."

Bartala was already on his feet with the bottle in hand, refilling everyone's glasses. Surprisingly, even Empress Nalau was keeping up with them.

"So after Zri *rescued* us from Chyke 2C95, Bartala and I returned to Ploosnar by my power. There was no need to inconvenience Zri's commander to take us back to Ploosnar or worse, Earth. A few weeks later I was on Earth and I felt like someone was following me when I was at a mall, which is a huge indoor shopping venue. I could never spot the same person in the crowd. But still, I couldn't shake the feeling. So I went down a long hallway that led to a service area, I passed through a restricted door and hid. Sure enough I was being followed, Zri walked through the door after me."

"I wanted to make sure you made it back to Earth." he said.

"And to find out just what I was, you'd never met someone that could travel like Brzko and I do."

"True."

"So I jumped out of my hiding spot ready to kick his butt, and for the first time in my life I couldn't kick someone's butt. I was too pissed to even be frightened."

"Ha! You were seriously angry. You really thought you could take me down, and I have to admit you were about ten times stronger than you looked but you didn't have as much skill as you do now, and well, I'm a Gaznzulian. We're built for defense." Zri said casually.

"Once I recognized him I was glad to see him. He was projecting the same human cloak he'd used when we met." M continued, "I was curious about Gaznzulians. So I asked him if all Gaznzulians were able to defend themselves like he did."

"You had no fear and I respected how direct you were." Zri said with admiration for his old friend. "I couldn't resist finding a way to help you harness all that strength and energy, teaching you how to defend yourself."

"You trained her to fight?" Brzko asked. "I didn't know you had trained with Zri, but that explains a lot."

"It's true." M said smiling. "He invited me to his home on Gaznzul and I went frequently. Over a period of a few months I trained with him and others on Gaznzul. That's when he developed his fondness for disco music."

Brzko laughed loudly, "Zri, you have a thing for disco music?"

"Yes especially the Bee Gees. I do not understand what the lyrics are about, but I find it soothing. Why is this funny? "Zri asked.

"What is the Bee Gees, and what does their music sound like?" Lelelu asked with genuine curiosity.

Brzko's tablet was already out and unfolded. He scrolled through his music video database and found a video of the Bee Gees singing *How Deep is Your Love* from 1977.

Everyone gathered around the tablet to watch the amazing Bee Gees.

"What are those lights, why are the lights spinning?" Bartala asked. "It nauseates me."

Lelelu answered him with a harsh "Shhhhhhh, I want to hear this."

After the video played through, and everyone was seated again, M continued, "I even took him to a Bee Gees concert."

"What? You took a Gaznzulian to a music performance on Earth? Weren't you concerned that someone would notice him?" Lelelu asked.

"No, I knew I could trust him to keep his "Earth" cloak up while we were at the concert."

Zri laughed lightly, tilted his head back and closed his eyes. A smile spread across his face as he remembered that adventure from long ago.

It was late and they were all tired, the espidrun made them even sleepier. After a little more chatting and well wishing, they all retired for the night.

~~~

The Muse of Mischief and Agent Brzko were up very early the following morning. On the command bridge, ShyUst was showing them the scanning process he was using to look for clues, anything that might lead them to Clyrea X9.

"Is that Trella." Brzko asked "Just coming into range now."

"Yes, that's Trella." ShyUst confirmed. "We should be close enough to start scanning the surface later today."

"How soon will we be able to see the planet?" Brzko asked.

ShyUst paused for a moment, "Possibly late this evening. But we may be able to see the sun now." He moved to the center console to activate the main viewing screen. "Yes, there it is. Do you see that glow?"

There was a faint glow just becoming visible. It looked very distant, surrounded by the blackness of space.

"How can we see the sun already?" Brzko asked.

"Because it's huge, it's one of the largest we've encountered. It lights the entire Trellan Galaxy, even the outlying planets receive enough light to support life." ShyUst explained.

"How many planets are in the Trellan Galaxy?" M asked.

"Over twenty." he answered.

"And they all have life on them?" Brzko asked.

"Our scans have not been detailed enough to answer that with any certainty, but it does seem that many of them *could* support life." ShyUst answered.

"Interesting," M said, "is there a way to scan for the remains of a planet?"

"The remains, I don't understand, why…"

"Because the Suus have found a reference to a planet, possibly in this galaxy, that doesn't seem to exist. Clyrea X9 may hold clues to their origins." Zri answered ShyUst as he approached from behind M and Brzko.

"I see. I'll reconfigure the scanners to detect any unusual matter." ShyUst said, turning to embark on the task immediately.

"What about hidden or cloaked planets?" Brzko asked.

"Interesting idea Brzko. We would need to be able to detect an emission or perhaps a lack of scan data would suggest there is something hidden. I'll have each ship start scanning for different things. If you'll excuse me, I need to visit the ships to configure the scanners." With a slight manipulation of his armband, Zri was gone.

With ShyUst and Zri working hard at scanning the galaxy there was nothing M and Brzko needed to do on the command bridge. "Breakfast?" Brzko asked.

"Hell yeah, sounds good." M headed for the lift. As soon as they stepped out of the lift on the lower level they were hit with the smell. "It smells like pancakes!" M said.

"It sure does, someone's making breakfast." Brzko said as he headed to the community room.

Emperor Bartala was seated at the head of the table, facing the door; Empress Nalau was on his right, Lelelu on his left. The table was filled with plates stacked high with pancakes, there were several different varieties. There were also several small pitchers with a variety of pulverized fruits for topping the pancakes.

"Well, finally out of bed eh?" Bartala teased.

Before M or Brzko could answer Bartala, Lelelu offered an explanation, "I hope you're hungry, I think I made too many pancakes this morning."

"I think we can help you out with that Lelelu." Brzko said, taking a seat at the table.

M slid into the chair next to him, "Wow, they look great Lelelu."

"What have you two been up to this morning?" Empress Nalau asked, knowing that they had not just gotten out of bed as her husband suggested.

"We were up on the command bridge working with Zri and ShyUst, configuring the scanners. There isn't a lot known about this area of the Universe." M said as she helped herself to a variety of pancakes.

"How much longer will it take to get to Trella?" Bartala asked.

"We'll arrive tomorrow. After breakfast I think M and I will go look around and make sure nothing has changed; look for the best place to land." Brzko said.

"Ha! You just want to visit the banks of the Pink River again." Bartala teased.

"What makes you think we haven't already?" Brzko fired back.

The thought of Agent Brzko and the Muse of Mischief being able to "sneak" away from Zri's ship at anytime caught their companions off guard for a moment. The room was silent for just a second. Then the laughter set in, they all shared a hearty laugh.

"What is everyone laughing at?" Zri asked from the doorway.

"It seems our friends have been taking excursions to Trella while the rest of us slept." Bartala said.

"Ah. Aren't you used to that yet Bartala? These two never stay put for long." Zri said.

"I guess I should be used to it by now, I suppose I miss the adventures too. But with responsibilities as an Emperor I can no longer think of only myself."

M disappeared.

"Oh! The mischievous one is up to something." Bartala said.

"This ought to be interesting." Brzko said and went back to eating his pancakes.

M returned, standing behind Bartala with her hands behind her back, everyone was looking at her but Bartala.

"What?" At first Bartala thought they were looking at him. "Oh she's standing right behind me isn't she?"

Nalau giggled and said, "Oh I see why you have so much fun on adventures with these friends!"

M brought her right hand around and presented Nalau with an amazing bright purple flower, the same shade as her outfit. "For you Empress. If you place it in a vase with water it will last for many days."

"Oh! It is lovely, thank you M." She got up and took the flower into the kitchen area to find something to put it in.

M stepped up, alongside Bartala, "And for you," she brought her left hand forward and revealed the contents to him, "one of the blue skipping stones and one of the blue crystals from the same area. I thought you might enjoy looking them over and contemplating them while we travel."

Bartala was clearly pleased. He accepted both items, handling them delicately as if they had great value. The crystal illuminated brightly, turning his face blue. "Thank you M, I will enjoy them. This crystal looks like the ones that line the caves located at the poles of Ploosnar. There is much folklore about them, they are said to have mystical powers and often used for jewelry. I wonder if they are the same."

"Do you have any of the crystals from Ploosnar?" Brzko asked.

"Well not with me, but back at the palace. And…. that does not matter because you can retrieve them." he trailed off. "In my private sitting room there is a chest of drawers near the desk."

"Yes, I've seen it." Brzko said.

"In the bottom drawer there is a small black box, there is a crystal in there. But your arrival in my sitting room would trip the alarm, the palace guard would respond."

Brzko walked over to Bartala, "Then I'll have to take you with me."

"But as Emperor, it is frowned upon for me to travel without palace guards. I am no longer free to jump around the Universe with you and M."

Brzko patiently waited for him to get it, he just looked at Bartala expectantly.

Bartala snapped, "But! I would be going from a place that has palace guards to a place that has palace guards." He stood up, Brzko took his arm and they were gone.

It took them less than a minute to retrieve the box and return. The sat at the table as though they had never left.

"How was home darling?" Nalau asked with a little sarcasm.

Bartala just chuckled. He took the small black box and lifted the lid off. The glow was the same as that from the crystal M had brought.

"They look the same, but we would need to scan them to be sure. I would like to use the scanners on one of my ships, can you take me there?" Bartala asked, looking back and forth between M and Brzko.

"There is no need." Zri interjected. "You can use your arm console - there are temporary transports on both of your escort ships. This allows your guards and my crew to move freely between the ships. I'll show you how to initiate the transport."

Zri, Bartala, and Brzko sat close, looking over Bartala's arm console. Soon the trio was gone, leaving the ladies to clean up.

They returned within a few minutes.

"Woooooooooooooooo!!!! I could get used to that! Zri can I keep this arm console and those temporary transports?" Bartala asked, grinning like a child that had just received a beloved toy.

Zri laughed heartily and clapped him on the back, "Yes, my friend. You may keep them."

"Stop playing with your toys and tell us the results of the scan." M said taking a seat at the table where Nalau and Lelelu were already seated.

Brzko, Zri and Bartala joined them. "They are identical. The crystal you brought from Trella is identical to the one from Ploosnar." Bartala answered.

"They are covalent network crystals, the structures are identical." Brzko added.

"How is that possible? Or if it is possible, what is the likelihood that identical crystals would develop on Ploosnar and Trella?" M asked.

"The Suss may have an answer for that, based on all of the data they've collected and catalogued. But, my instincts tell me that it's highly unlikely. The crystals on Trella may have been placed there on purpose." Brzko said.

"It seems the mystery continues to evolve," Lelelu said "and I just can't resist a mystery! I'll contact Kiik and see if the Suus have any relevant information. Why would crystals native to Ploosnar be purposely left on Trella?"

"It seems that someone wanted the Muse of Mischief and Agent Brzko to find Ploosnar." Nalau said.

"I think you're right my love." Bartala said. "But was it for our benefit or theirs?" He walked over to the sitting area and took a seat on one of the sofas. He still had the crystals in his hand. He placed them on the table in front of him and leaned back. "These are almost the same color as you Lelelu."

With the exception of Zri, the group wandered over and settled into the comfort of the sitting area. Zri excused himself and went back to the command bridge.

The group sat in silence for few minutes, contemplating the crystals.

"Well I guess there's nothing else we can do until we arrive at Trella." Nalau said. "We know how Bartala and Zri met these two, but Lelelu how did you meet them?"

~~~

Lelelu looks to Agent Brzko with a question in her eyes. He nods and says, "Go ahead, and tell the story Lelelu."

She looks back at Empress Nalau and begins, "I grew up on the Planet of Portals the same way most Trelods do, raised by bonded parents receiving education with an emphasis on Universal history and exploration. I took a job as a communications operator for a shuttle company. At first it was exciting, it entitled me to visit a few worlds. But after a while it became boring so I started monitoring the interstellar communications boards for something off of the Planet of Portals. I love my home but I wanted to experience more of the Universe."

Lelelu kicked off her shoes, and drew her legs up under her on the sofa where she was sitting. She was a stunning today, bald with bright blue skin, wearing a simple green dress. This was a relaxed look for her, but she knew there would be no calls to action today.

"I came across an ad for an interstellar communications associate, I responded to the ad and after answering a few preliminary questions, an interview was scheduled. Surprisingly the prospective employer was willing to travel to the Planet of Portals." She turned and looked at Brzko. So did everyone else. "That's when I met the eminent Agent Brzko."

"Had you already heard of him and M?" Nalau asked.

"Yes, but I wasn't sure they were real. There are stories told about them throughout the Universe. As soon as I saw him in the plaza though, I knew who he was. I couldn't believe I was about to meet THE Agent Brzko. As soon as I saw him and realized I was being considered for employment with him and probably the Muse of Mischief I was ecstatic. He was sitting on a bench in the central plaza of Unilond, I approached and said..."

Brzko finished her sentence... "I'm Lelelu and you will not find a better communications associate than me Agent Brzko, hire me and you will not be disappointed. How could I not? That confidence reminded me so much of my beloved Muse of Mischief." He reached over and squeezed M's hand.

"How did you know that he wouldn't be offended but such a direct, confident statement?" Nalau asked.

"I didn't. But I figured if the stores I'd heard about them were true, he would appreciate the direct approach. When I realized what the job was I knew I would do anything to work with these two. I thought they would expose me to experiences I'd not yet had, in places I'd not yet been, and that is so true! The interview alone was like no other experience I'd had."

"How did you interview her Brzko?" Bartala asked.

"We took three short *missions*, the goal was to communicate with each population and obtain a useful commodity. Since all of the portals in Unilond lead to the Glion Galaxy we started in Foskpruchu where they speak in bizarre riddles. Then we went to the moon of the Black Sea Planet and met the League of Mongers. And from there we went to see the traders on Smd. She never lost her cool. She stayed focused on the goal and was always in command of herself."

"What about you? Were you part of the interview?" Bartala asked M.

"No, I was back home while Zri made upgrades to our security and communication systems."

"And you trusted Brzko to hire your assistant?" Nalau asked.

"Of course, I trust him implicitly. If there had been an issue when we met I could have intervened. But we needed assistance, we are constantly asked to help. All of those requests need to be investigated and prioritized. It's a full time job. I prefer to be out doing rather than answering requests." M said.

"So why do you still live on the Planet of Portals? Wouldn't it be easier to live where M and Brzko do?" Nalau asked. Her cheeks blushed just slightly, "Oh right, Earth is infantile, they think they are the only inhabited planet, and you're... blue."

Bartala added what he knew of Earth, "It is an incredibly racist planet my darling. They fear what they are not familiar with and often turn violent toward it. Beings with dark skin are often oppressed and frequently unsafe."

Lelelu nodded at Bartala, as if to confirm what he had just said before she continued. "I can go to Earth, and have several times, but because I'm blue, I have to stay hidden or disguised, and that damages my productivity. Besides, with communications technology and a fast ship, having my base of operations on a different planet doesn't really matter." Lelelu said.

Bartala always straight to the point, asked "Is it true that Trelods remember every experience they have?"

"Yeah, it's true. We have great memories."

"What about bonding and children?" he asked.

"No thank you." Lelelu replied. "I love my life just the way it is. Well bonding maybe, if I ever find one that is compatible."

But there was a look, a brief sparkle in her eye that suggested she had already found *one that is compatible*. M looked at Brzko to see if he had caught it, he had.

Everyone laughed at her direct answer, it sounded so much like something M would have said.

"I felt the same way." Nalau confessed, "Luckily we were able to use a surrogate for our son."

"You two must be excited. Things at the palace will change." Lelelu said.

"Yes! For the better!" Bartala said. He stood and stretched. "Is anyone else hungry?" He asked. "I think it's lunch time."

"Seriously?" Zri said from the doorway. "You just had breakfast!"

"It's hard work being an Emperor, besides my metabolism runs fast, maybe faster than yours."

Zri just smiled and nodded at Bartala. "Right, because you have three hearts. I'm headed to the cargo bay for some training, anyone care to join me?"

M, Brzko, and Lelelu all jumped at the chance for a physical workout. They weren't used to spending an entire day sitting around talking, multiple days of it was taking a toll on them. The three of them headed for the door, leaving Bartala and Nalau to enjoy some time along together.

AN OLD FRIEND ON TRELLA

Another full day on the ship was taking its toll on the Muse of Mischief, Agent Brzko and Lelelu. After working out with Zri and some of his team they were still a little stir crazy. It was easy for Emperor Bartala and Empress Nalau to stay busy. They had administrative duties with regard to overseeing a planet and the roinad empire. There were endless tasks for them, and those were easily completed with basic communication equipment. The other three however, were looking for a way to spend the day.

"Let's just go to Trella and look around." Lelelu suggested.

It was obvious that M liked this idea, but she had a few concerns. "Zri, what do you think? Are you comfortable with the three of us leaving for a while? Or better still, why don't you come with us?"

The group of four was in the cargo bay, post workout, casually sitting on storage containers while chatting and rehydrating.

Zri paused and looked off in the distance, considering this idea. "In a way it makes sense for me to go ahead of everyone and look around. On the other hand if something happens here...." he trailed off.

Agent Brzko jumped in, "We are all in constant contact with your crew and we can have you back in less than a minute."

"Well OK then, give me a few minutes to speak with ShyUst." he headed for the door with a slight spring in his step. He was excited about a brief exploration.

"I'll go tell Bartala we're leaving." M said as she left the room.

She found Bartala and Nalau settled into the common room, both of them engrossed in their duties.

"Hey, we're going to be off the ship for a while. Brzko, Lelelu, Zri and I are going to take a quick trip to Trella. We'll be back in time for dinner." she announced.

"Have a wonderful time, and please be cautious." Nalau said before returning her attention to her work.

"As long as you don't take all of the espidrun." Bartala said without even looking up.

M took a step toward Bartala, ready to lecture him about appreciation or respect, but realized that would only delay the group's departure. Instead she turned and left.

Zri was already back in the cargo hold when she returned. M looked at Brzko and asked, "Green Lake?" He nodded and stepped forward taking Lelelu's arm, they were gone.

M stepped toward Zri, took his arm and they were gone.

She kept a firm grip on his arm for a second after arriving on Trella. He was used to his own Gaznzulian transports but not her apertures; they could make the passenger a little dizzy.

They group stood on the shore, just looking at the water. The lake is the color of emeralds. There was a light breeze, just enough to create small ripples on the water's surface. The ripples reflected the sunlight, creating sparkles. It is not a large lake; one could easily swim across and back. The shores are a combination of sand and flat stones, all bright blue. The area near the lake is clear, at the edge of the clearing is perfectly green grass, and behind that are green trees.

Lelelu broke the silence, "It looks manufactured. Not just because of the fairytale colors but because it's so perfect, so symmetrical. Does everything look like this?"

"You're right I never thought of that when I was a child." M responded. "Yes, I think everything on Trella is *perfect* like this."

"This is where the blue crystals are from?" Zri asked.

"Yes" Brzko answered. "See the sparkle coming from the opposite side of the lake?"

"Interesting. I have some new hive drones. As soon as my ship is in orbit I'll deploy them, I'd like to see the surface of the entire planet."

"Hive drones?" Zri mentioning new technology had sparked Brzko's interest.

"Yes, they are based on the same concept as a Burdohnirc. They function as one unit, combining their power for fast, distant travel. But when they reach their destination they separate into individual units, and cover an exponential amount of territory. Then they rejoin to return. It allows us to send them further from base, and cover much more territory."

"I can't wait to see them in action."

"Is there a place you had in mind for landing? If I'm going to land we'll need someplace with less vegetation."

"M, isn't there a field over that way?" Brzko asked. "It seems like the path here cuts through the trees for a short distance and then ends up in an open area."

M stopped skipping rocks with Lelelu long enough to answer, "It's been a long time but I think so."

"Let's go see." Zri said.

Lelelu chucked the last stone, and it was perfect. "Wow nine skips Lelelu! You killed me on this round." They high-fived each other while both men just looked at them like they'd lost their minds.

"What?" M said defensively when she noticed. "It's not like you two aren't just as competitive."

They both conceded.

"True."

"Well, yeah, you're right."

They headed to the trail with Zri in the lead. After they were through the grassy area, before they even entered the trees, he came to a dead stop.

Brzko was right behind him. "What's wrong?"

Zri was looking down, "Shoe prints from a biped. Someone has been down this trail recently."

M came up alongside him to see what he was looking at. She recognized the prints right away, and she extended her leg and put her boot down right next to one of the prints. When she withdrew it there was an identical print. She giggled.

"Oh, right, when you came to get one of the blue crystals for Bartala."

"Yep." she said.

They continued on for a short distance through the trees. The forest continued on their right but, but in front, to the north of them and to the west, there was a large open area, maybe ten acres.

"What do you think of this area Zri?" Brzko asked. "It's open and flat."

"This looks fine, but I'd like to see what borders it on the other sides."

"Let's go, so we can be back in time for lunch." M stepped into the lead and headed to the right, intent on walking the perimeter of the field.

Zri shook his head, "No wonder you and Bartala get along so well, you're always ready for the next meal."

"What can I say, I love food."

The group finished walking the perimeter quickly. Zri hadn't seen anything to cause him concern about landing his ship here tomorrow. So unless his scanners found something of concern, landing was a go.

"What else do you want to see while we're here?" Brzko asked, looking at Zri and Lelelu.

They looked at each other and smiled, turned back to Brzko and in unison said, "The Pink River."

All four of them laughed. "Let's go." M said "It's over this way." She pointed to the west.

~~~

They group spent a few minutes in the clearing created by the Pink River. Bored, the Muse of Mischief and Lelelu wandered on ahead, heading downstream, while Agent Brzko and Zri were deeply engrossed in a conversation about Zri's new drone technology. Zri was explaining how the controls of his hive drones had been improved when they both heard something.

"Brrrrrrrrrrrrrrzko, Brrrrrrrrrrrrrrzko…….."

"Did you hear that?" He asked looking around.

"Yes, where is it coming from? I cannot detect the origin of the sound." Zri was on full alert. No longer focused on their conversation, he was at full attention, ready to defend himself and Agent Brzko.

"Brrrrrrrrrrrrrzko, Brrrrrrrrrrrrrrzko…….. Do you not remember me? I am Ferocity, I am your Ferocity."

The words hit Brzko. They literally knocked the wind out of him. He plopped down on one of the boulders near him. Zri thought he'd been hit and went to him.

"Where were you hit, do you require medical?" He shook him by the shoulder trying to get a response, "Can you hear me? Agent Brzko?"

"Stand down Zri, stand down. I know this creature. He will not harm us."

Zri was confused and there was no way he could "stand down" as Brzko suggested. Not until he knew what they were dealing with. He stood next to Brzko, surveying the area, looking for anything that may be a threat.

"I remember you Ferocity. Show yourself, please."

The previously sunny day turned dark instantly. Something was blocking the sun. Brzko and Zri both looked up. There was a large winged being drifting down from above them. It had an amazing wingspan, and a long forked tail.

"Is that a Dragon?" Zri asked. "Brzko are you bonded to a Dragon?"

"Yes, I suppose I am."

The winged being landed directly in front of Brzko. He knelt, lowered his head, and placed it in Brzko's lap, "Lord Brzko, you have returned for me."

Brzko reached out and rubbed Ferocity's head, between his eyes. He began to make a sound, similar to the purr of a cat, but much deeper. The sound was so deep it created a vibration that could be felt. "Yes Ferocity I have returned. I, I..." He wasn't quite sure what to say. "It's been a very long time since I've seen you. Have you been here on Trella the whole time?"

Ferocity lifted his head and stood upright. He is a biped, and not much taller than Brzko and Zri, once on the ground with his wings folded behind him he does not seem as large as he had in the air. But he looks as ferocious as his name suggests. At the moment he was the same grayish color as the boulder Brzko was seated on. He has several horns on his head and large claws at the ends of his toes.

"Yes Lord, awaiting your return."

Brzko stood and embraced Ferocity. "I'm happy to see you again Ferocity." He pulled back and turned toward Zri, "This is my friend Zri, Zri this is Ferocity."

Zri stepped up and put his hands on Ferocity's forearms, "Greetings friend. It is a pleasure to meet you, I've heard about Dragons but never have I met one." He was clearly very excited.

Ferocity tilted his head to the side as he looked Zri up and down, "You look like a Dragon to me, but not….." he trailed off. He could sense that something was not as it seemed with Zri's appearance. He inhaled several times in quick succession, sniffing the air around Zri, attempting to identify him.

"I am a Gaznzulian."

"Ohhhh yes, Gaznzulian. We learn of your race as children on Dragona. You are reflective?"

"Essentially, yes."

"Impressive." Ferocity disengaged from the embrace and stepped back to get a better look at Zri. "Fascinating."

"Me? No. But you on the other hand, you do realize that you are a mystery to the Universe. There are stories, but no one seems to know if Dragons really exist. Brzko, why didn't you tell me you were bonded to a Dragon? You could have used his help a few times over the years."

"Ferocity and I used to hang out here on Trella when we were young. It didn't seem like a big deal back then. Ferocity how have your survived alone for all these years?"

"Adolescent Dragons live a solitary life. It is our way, it is how we learn. If we do not survive our youth, we are not strong enough to complete the bonding. It has always been our way."

"So our bonding is not complete?"

"No, for that we must go to Dragona and appear before the Great Assembly."

"Where is Dragona? I've heard tales of the planet but I've never seen a reference to its actual location. I thought it was make believe." Zri asked.

"Only the bonded can know its location. Long ago Dragons were kidnapped and enslaved. We now keep the location of our home world guarded."

Brzko and Zri both nodded, "So how do we travel to Dragona? And when?"

"We will make the journey in my ship. We can make the journey very soon, when you are ready."

Both Brzko and Zri had the feeling that there were things Ferocity was not ready to divulge in front of Zri, in front of a stranger.

"We are here with my partner, the Muse of Mischief and my other friend, Lelelu, you need to meet them."

"As you wish Brrrrrrrrrzko."

"I just need to find out where M is." Brzko said as he reached to activate his earcom link.

"You do not need the device, look inside and ask yourself where she is, ask yourself to feel her." Ferocity said quietly.

"What? I'm not a telepath."

"Are you sure? Use the bond as a link to find her, to ask her where she is."

Zri stayed absolutely silent, just observing.

Brzko was about to protest again, he and M were close, they knew each other very well but could he actually reach out to her with his mind? There was only one way to tell. He closed his eyes and thought of her, tried to picture where she was.

The Muse of Mischief was walking with Lelelu when something came over her. She momentarily lost her balance and startled Lelelu.

"M, are you ok? What's wrong?"

She didn't answer right away. There was something new in her head. She could hear Brzko asking her where she was. It was just like hearing a Suus. She turned and looked at the river to give a visual representation of her answer.

Agent Brzko immediately appeared before her with a being she had never seen before.

They were all caught off guard by the appearance of this new being. Lelelu expressed her surprise by drawing her breath in sharply.

"It worked!" Brzko exclaimed. "You were right Ferocity."

They all heard someone approaching from upstream where Brzko and Zri had been; it was Zri catching up with Brzko and Ferocity.

M turned back to Brzko, "What just happened and who is our new friend?" She was thinking that somehow this creature that looked like a mythical Dragon had facilitated Brzko's telepathic ability.

"This is Ferocity, my Dragon. Ferocity, I present the Muse of Mischief."

Ferocity stepped forward and bowed in front of M, "Your Highness. I am at your service."

"Hello Ferocity, I'm pleased to meet you. I didn't know Brzko had a Dragon. Did you somehow facilitate his ability to contact me telepathically?"

Ferocity paused, allowing Brzko a chance to answer. "No, he just told me that I could because I was bonded with you, I tried it and it worked. I'm still a little surprised myself."

"As am I!" M said.

"Ferocity, I'd like you meet Lelelu, she is a friend and significant member of our team."

Ferocity turned to Lelelu, "Lelelu, it is my honor."

"You three must have some things to discuss why don't you take a walk? Zri and I can hang out here for while, right Zri?"

"Of course, you can teach me how to skip rocks."

M turned just in time to see him looking at Lelelu; he had the same twinkle in his eye that she had seen in Lelelu the night before. Could they be... Those thoughts would have to wait.

"Thanks Lelelu, that's a good idea." M said.

Brzko added. "We'll catch up with you later. Call us if you need anything."

He headed up the trail, back the way Zri had come. M was walking next to him and Ferocity was just a step behind. The trio walked in silence for few minutes, they paused where there was a deep bend in the river.

M could wait no longer, "So when did you two meet?"

"I've been thinking about that, trying to recall. It was the first time I came to Trella."

"When you were a child?"

"Yes, and so was Ferocity, well not a child but whatever you call young Dragon. I think he was here every time I came to Trella alone. And it turns out he never left, he's been waiting for me to return." Brzko turned toward Ferocity, as did M.

"How did you survive alone for so long Ferocity? And why didn't I ever see you here?"

"You did not see me because I was not meant for you. Adolescent Dragons are solitary creatures. It is how we become strong. Only those that survive are worthy of being bonded. I have survived. I am ready to complete the bond with Agent Brzko if he will have me."

"What exactly does that mean?" Brzko asked.

"Dragons are creatures of servitude. We always have been. However, unlike slaves, we choose whom we serve. Only those that are worthy are able to bond with a Dragon. Once bonded my purpose becomes to protect you, to support you, to care for you."

Brzko realized that Ferocity was no longer grey; he had become more of a brownish color, the color of the sand they were standing on. "You've changed color since I first saw you."

Ferocity smiled, with his large open nostrils and jagged horns jutting out of forehead, it was difficult to see pulling his lips back and baring his teeth as a friendly look. But his eyes, his golden eyes displayed exactly how he was feeling, and they sparkled with joy. When he blinked there was a second, inner eyelid, clear, that covered the eye from front to back; rather than top to bottom.

"You are still just as observant and inquisitive as you were as a child. Yes, my color has changed, now that I am fully grown it changes to adapt to my surroundings. It is naturally passive, but I can also control it - amplify it." He sat down on the sand, with his legs drawn up, he wrapped his wings around him and changed his color to exactly that of the sand he was sitting on. His eyes were the only thing that stood out, once closed he blended in so well that he was almost invisible. He stood back up. "It is useful when I do not want to be seen."

"That's impressive. And I know you can fly, I've seen that. And you knew I could contact M telepathically. How did you know that?"

"Because I see both of you for who and what you are. Your visions of yourselves are veiled by your own limited expectations."

"Do you know what we are?" M asked.

"No, not for sure. There are stories on Dragona about beings like you, beings that can travel through their own apertures."

It was M's turn to ask some questions. "So how do you travel through the Universe? You breathe so surely you don't fly through space."

"Dragons use ships to travel. Our ships are somewhat sentient. They are small and very fast and cloaked. This is why scanners did not detect it."

"A sentient ship? Oh I'd like to see that!" Brzko said, excited about the idea of new technology.

Instantly an image appeared in both his and M's mind. It was a ship with a small center chamber and a large pointed wing on each side. It looked like a fighter of some kind. It was sitting in an open field, near a large rocky outcropping, and then it just blended into its surroundings and seemed to disappear.

"You're telepathic?" M asked.

"Yes, slightly. Once bonded it will be stronger between Brzko and me. And because he is bonded to you, I can also communicate with you."

"Speaking of bonding you said this would be completed on Dragona in front of a Great Assembly and that it would happen when I was ready. What did you mean?"

"A bond cannot be undone. A Lord can shun his Dragon, force him to live in exile, but the Dragon cannot bond with another, nor can he return to Dragona. This would force the Dragon to live in eternal solitude. The bond should not be completed if the commitment is not genuine."

"What responsibilities do I have? I mean, am I responsible for your, housing, sustenance, things like that? And what do you eat? You've been alone on Trella for more than a decade and I've never seen any creatures large enough to qualify as a food source here."

"A Bond does not need to provide housing or sustenance, although some do. Some want their Dragons under their roof, others just want them available. As for sustenance, Dragons evolved to survive on a diet of plant foods, just as you do."

They were silent for a few moments, reflecting on the things they had just learned.

"I have another question, how did you choose Brzko? What brought you to Trella to meet him all those years ago?"

"Dragons are selected in a variety of ways. Someone made a deal with my father, at the appropriate time I was sent to Trella. I do not know who made the arrangements. It is an honor to be chosen to serve one such as you. To question it would be disrespectful. You need time to think Lord Brzko. I will return to my ship. You have seen it so you can now find it, or reach for me with your mind. I will hear you." He bowed to Brzko and then spread his enormous wings and flew up, past the trees. They watched until he was out of sight.

Brzko plopped down, sitting on the sand. "I, wow, um...."

"A little speechless huh? I guess it's not every day that you find out you're bonded to a Dragon!"

"So you think I should proceed with the bonding?"

"I think it's an honor to have been selected to bond with a Dragon, I think it would be foolish not to accept such an honor. If we can find out who arranged for you to have a Dragon, we may find more clues to our origins."

"But this will change things M this could create some big changes."

M stood in front of Brzko, with her hands on her hips she looked down at him and asked, "And your point is....?

Brzko reached up as though he wanted a hand up, but instead, when she took his hand, he pulled first. He pulled her down on top of him, making her giggle like a schoolgirl. "I'm crazy about you M, you make everything better."

"I love you too Brzko. Let's get our friends and go back to the ship, I'm sure they have a lot of questions for us."

~~~

The outing to Trella had been just what they needed, even though it was more than they expected. The Muse of Mischief and Agent Brzko had retired to their room as soon as they returned. There was never a doubt that Brzko would accept the honor of being bonded to a Dragon, but they still wanted a little time alone to come to terms with it, to digest it. He went back to Trella to speak to Ferocity, to accept the offer of bonding. And M joined the others in the community room.

Lelelu had been reviewing messages, sifting through them to see if anything needed M or Brzko's attention.

M plopped down on the sofa next to her, "Anything interesting?"

"Yes and no. Bivoor checked in, everything with the hives seems to be fine. There are still no signs of aberidus. And the Rogsaars are readjusting to life on Myaad. Several of them are already planning exploration missions. I guess adventure is in their DNA. There is also a message from G'ist. He and Rogsaar are expecting their DNA was successfully combined."

"Fantastic! The first Xinood Myaad cross."

Empress Nalau joined them, she squealed with delight, "Ohhhhhh!!! That is wonderful news! Is there anything we can do for them? Do they need anything?"

"I don't think so, at least not yet." Lelelu answered. "I think they are keeping a low profile. Not everyone supports the idea of different species joining to create offspring."

"An antiquated barbaric belief. Are we talking about Earth again?" Emperor Bartala asked, taking a seat next to his wife.

"What happened on Earth?" Brzko asked from the doorway.

"Nothing, well nothing we know of. Lelelu was just telling us that she received a message from G'ist. They were successful, he and Rogsaar are expecting." M answered.

"Exciting news!" Brzko said. "I have some additional news for you. Unless M and Lelelu already told you?"

Bartala turned to Brzko, standing in the doorway. "Told us what? What has happened Brzko?"

"I have been reunited with an old friend of mine on Trella, his name is Ferocity."

"Wait, I thought there weren't any beings on Trella." Nalau said, "I'm confused."

"It has been so long, and I was just a child when I last saw him, I forgot that I used to hang out with a Dragon whenever I was there alone."

"A Dragon?" Bartala said waving his hand dismissively. "Stop Brzko, we have not had enough espidrun to believe tall tales yet. In fact we have yet to open a bottle."

"I kid you not Emperor. Would you like to meet him?"

Bartala almost gave himself whiplash turning toward Brzko, still casually leaning in the doorway. Nalau jumped to her feet. "You're not kidding. And the others aren't saying anything, it must be real Bartala." He jumped to his feet.

"Yes. Yes, of course we would like to meet a Dragon! Is he here?" Bartala said.

Brzko stepped through the doorway; Zri followed him into the room.

"No, you can meet him as soon as we get to Trella." Brzko said taking his usual seat next to M.

"Did you begin today's story hour without us?" They all turned and looked toward Zri still standing near the doorway. He was uncharacteristically outgoing on this trip.

Everyone just stared at him. "What? Oh, you two want more information about Brzko's new friend."

Their attention turned to Brzko when he spoke. "Dragons are real, I have one, I will soon be bonded to him, and you can meet him when we land on Trella tomorrow. Now who's pouring?"

M couldn't help it, she suffered a fit of laughter, Lelelu and Zri joined her. "Oh that's just cruel Brzko. I love you but, c'mon you can't leave them hanging like that."

Empress Nalau jumped up to retrieve a fresh bottle of espidrun and glasses, "I'll pour Brzko. But please give a little more detail before we have... *story hour* as Zri called it."

"OK, OK, here's what we know so far. Dragons are real, not mythical and they become bonded to individuals they deem worthy. My Dragon's name is Ferocity. I used to see him when I visited Trella as a child. But that was so long ago that I had forgotten all about it. Anyway, he's a little taller than me; he has horns and large wings. He looks frightening but is actually very gentle. You'll meet him tomorrow when we land. I still have a lot to figure out, so that's all I can tell you right now."

Nalau had finished filling everyone's glass with espidrun by the time Brzko finished his explanation. She sat down next to Bartala, took a sip of espidrun. After a moment she said, "OK, who's telling stories of their past tonight?"

Before anyone could begin a story, Bartala offered a toast, "To friends and story hours, may we always have time for both!"

Everyone agreed and drank. Zri plopped into his usual chair and swung his legs up over the arm. Everyone stared at him.

"What? What is wrong? Why are you all looking at me?

"We just aren't used to seeing you relax, ever." Bartala said.

"I used to relax a lot when I was young." He smiled across the room at M.

She laughed out loud, and even though the group was looking back and forth between her and Zri, hoping for an explanation, she offered none.

"So what did I miss about G'ist and Rogsaar?" Zri asked.

"They are expecting. And I was explaining that they are going to keep a low profile, as not everyone approves of interspecies reproduction." Lelelu explained.

"True. There is no shortage of feeble minds in the Universe. Will you please send them a message for me? Tell them that Gaznzul is willing to provide them with complimentary security services. We can help secure their dwelling or keep a ship in orbit around Xinood 5, provide an escort for their ship, whatever they need."

"I'm happy to convey that message to them, thank you Zri."

After a few moments of silence, Bartala spoke up, "It's time you to tell us how you saved Ciic. Just how did the leader of Suus become indebted to you?"

"Yessssss," Zri said "This is a great story because Gaznzul saved the day!"

Everyone got a kick out of Zri's exuberance.

Brzko started off...

"Lelelu had us travel to ancient Ireland. She had received a request for help from...?" he looked at Lelelu, waiting for her to fill in the blank.

"The initial message was anonymous; it appeared to be from someone that served the Naan family. But we now know that it was actually originated in Ireland... Earth. She clarified.

Brzko continued, "We were waiting for an Irish Faerie, I couldn't imagine why a powerful being like this would need from me and M. Irish Faeries have the ability to travel between this world and Otherworld, sometimes friendly, sometimes not, but always powerful."

"Otherworld? Is that a planet?" Bartala inquired.

"Sort of, it's ancient mythology, the name translates as other Earth. Many cultures describe a place like this, usually containing beasts or odd creatures. The area that is Ireland was heavily influenced by a group called the Celtic. They described Otherworld as an island off the coast, with creatures that were red and white." Brzko paused to sip his espidrun and continued. "It was cold and damp while we waited for the Faerie in the early morning, before it was light. Standing still gave strength to the damp cold so we started walking around the stone cairn where we were meeting the Faerie. We were both a little on edge; Hag's have a bad reputation."

"Hags?" Nalau asked.

"Ancient beings thought of as witches or sorceresses." M answered.

Brzko continued, "The place seemed to have a lot of energy, there are many stories about the area. Some believe that the hills are haunted! It is said that Ireland was ruled by a witch sitting upon the Hag's Bench. While smoking her pipe she doled out her demands, those that didn't comply had spells cast upon them. The tombs were created by the witch when she was flying over the hills dropping stones to make the cairns. She fell and broke her neck, ended up buried under a pile of stones. No one knows for sure, but some say the tombs are actually doorways to Otherworld.

Anyway, we walked around the huge stone structures. The largest one had a single opening with a huge flat stone on the Northern side, that's the stone that's called the Hag's Bench. We couldn't shake the cold so we kept walking around the ancient burial chamber. All of sudden I see this woman where she hadn't been before. It stopped me in my tracks.

She was standing on the stone, and she was stunningly beautiful. She wore a long white gown with so many layers it seemed to be alive in the breeze. There was a golden rope tied around her waist. It looked like stone in the center of her headband was moving, the color seemed fluid. She looked like the very definition of femininity. Yet… she seemed to exude so much power that it could be felt in the air. It was like being near lightning strikes in an electrical storm.

You may call me Mahb. She says with so much authority that we immediately knelt and averted our eyes.

I am the High Queen of the Daoine Sidhe, and Supreme Ruler of the light realm of the Otherworld. Do you know why I have summoned you here?

We did not know why she had asked to see us, and told her that.

She asked what we knew about Changelings."

"Changelings? What is a Changeling?" Bartala asked.

"Irish folklore says that Changelings of that time were Faeries, sometimes children, sometimes old. Faeries took human children to Otherworld and left a changeling in the child's place." Brzko explained.

"A common story in many cultures. But they are usually just stories meant to frighten children. Are Irish Changelings real?" Nalau asked.

"It seems they are, or were. Mahb told us that one of the stolen human children was recently brought to her by a Faerie under her rule. But that the Faerie had been tricked because the child was not human and that if the child stayed in Otherworld she would destroy them all. We didn't want to ask Mahb any questions because she clearly lacked patience and had a lot of power. A bad combination. Even though there is no physical place or time that can hold me and M, we knew there was a good chance that this creature could hurt us. And truthfully we were curious, what kind of child could frighten the ruler of Otherworld and how could she be linked to Suus? She told us she needed us to take the child back to wherever she was really from.

I asked her if she knew where that was and she lost it! She turned on me with vicious speed and yelled *If I knew THAT I would have had her delivered there by a faerie.* This Queen seriously hated men.

We asked where the child's human parents were. She said that the Changeling that had been left with them killed them and fled. She told us she would go and get the child from Otherworld and then we were to leave her time and place immediately. In exchange she would grant us one favor. All we have to do is return to the Mountain of the Hags and summon her."

"So when was this? I mean what century was this Mahb creature living in?" Zri asked.

"It was what Earth defines as about 900 years BC - so it was about 3,000 years ago." Brzko answered.

"Are you ever concerned that you'll get stuck in a different time? There are children's stories about time jumpers getting stuck. Or worse, changing something in history and then returning to the present time and finding things have been changed. How do you know you aren't making changes?" Bartala asked as he got up to refill everyone's glasses.

"History can't really be changed." Brzko explained. "It will always take care of itself. If we are in the past, we are just observers. We can interact but nothing significant can be changed because it already happened. The worst you can do is create a new timeline. There is not a single timeline in a single Universe, timelines split into different possibilities."

Bartala wasn't quite satisfied yet, "Can you take a passenger, like you do when you open an aperture and travel?"

"No, we've tried a few times. Lelelu has been kind enough to try, but it just doesn't work." Bartala nodded, acknowledging Brzko's answer.

Brzko continued, "So she disappears to get the child, and we wait in silence. We kept our mouths shut because someone may have been listening. We circled the cairn one more time while we waited. Even after sunrise the Mountain of the Hags has its own eerie energy. There are definitely some secrets there, including exceptional symbols engraved in the stones. I don't think their meanings are fully understood to this day.

By the time we got back to the Northwest side of the cairn, Mahb had returned. She was sitting on the Hag's chair, with the child below her, she was holding the child in place with a very heavy hand on her shoulder, and her fingers were digging into the child. Which was odd, why didn't she just use her magic to hold the child in place. We realized there must be something really unusual about this *child*.

Why must you keep me waiting? She yells when she sees us.

I bowed and apologized, referring to her as *Your Majesty*. I told her we were savoring the beauty of the place before we had to leave. She was mad, but my charm was just enough to keep her from lashing out at us again. She looks at me and says *Remember our agreement, you will remove this vile creature from this place and time and you will do so immediately.* She shoved the child toward us and disappeared.

The child looked like a young human girl, a little more than a meter in height with long, smooth black hair, and dark eyes. They were black, the darkest eyes I had ever seen. But that was before I met Rogsaar. We introduced ourselves and asked her name, she just stared at us. We didn't want to piss Mahb off so we decided to leave right away. We don't usually take beings to our home but we didn't know where else to go, se we took her there."

"Wait, how did you get her from a historical time to present day?" Zri asked as he turned to the side and kicked his legs up over the arm of the chair, after pouring another round of espidrun for everyone.

M smiled at him, she really enjoyed seeing her old friend relax and enjoy himself. It had been far too long. "We weren't sure we could do it at the time. But we think it's because she wasn't from that time, and we were essentially bringing her back to *her* time."

"How did she get to a different time?" Nalau asked.

"Probably with either a hired timeship or a time portal. There are portals on the Planet of Portals that lead to different times." Lelelu answered. "The problem with using them is returning. All Portals are one way. M and Brzko are the only beings we know of that can move through time on their own. These Portals were secured long ago, but with the right influence the Portal Authority could be swayed to provide access. And the ruling family of Suus could definitely have the right influence. I think that's more likely than a hired timeship."

Brzko paused to sip his espidrun and let Lelelu's answer sink in. It was new information for them, the time Portals on the Planet of Portals were not well known. "When we get back to our home the *child* wouldn't answer our questions about who she was or where she was from. But she really stunk! I mean if you got close she smelled like carrion that had been rotting in the sun for days."

Brzko's expression was priceless as he remembered the smell. Surprisingly no one interrupted, so he continued with the story.

"So you've probably figured out that in order to look human Ciic was put into some kind of *shell*, the shell had begun to deteriorate as she approached maturity. We'd been home for a few hours and were trying to decide how to figure out what kind of being this was and where it was from when she finally *spoke*. It gave us a terrible shock when her telepathy reached us. Telepaths were not new to us, but she looked human. She told us exactly who she was and that she was next in line in the Naan family to rule the planet Suus. She explained that the Viiv family was attempting to overthrow the Naan so she was hidden in ancient Ireland until she was old enough to take the throne. She said if Mahb had figured out that she was to be the ruler of a planet, she would not have let her go without a ransom. Ciic said that Mahb had powers we *could not imagine*, it almost seemed like she was telling us that Mahb is not of Earth. Which could explain how she was able to send the original message, and why the Suus picked an ancient Earth culture to hide Ciic.

We considered having Lelelu contact the Naan family and let them know where she was and what had happened. But Ciic didn't think the privacy of the communication channels on Suus could be guaranteed. Our next option was to travel there, but that would take a little preparation and it was late. So we decided to wait until the morning. We set Ciic up in the spare room but she didn't require sleep so she started watching a science fiction show called Star Trek: Next Generation."

"Oh? What is that is it better than Babylon 5? What are the hairstyles like?" Bartala asked.

Everyone laughed, at first he couldn't" figure out why, but then he joined in. "Oh I see yes, that is humorous. But you see this is validation. If a being like Ciic watched Earth science fiction then perhaps it is not so foolish an endeavor for me!" He dramatically finished off his espidrun, setting the glass on the table; he leaned back and settled in next to Nalau.

"It's not foolish at all my friend." Zri said as he stood up and retrieved the bottle. Knowing another round was to be poured; those that had not finished the current round did so. "I too have seen much Earth science fiction and it is quite entertaining. It is fascinating to see what a primitive species thinks the Universe may be like. They are so arrogant!"

Bartala nodded enthusiastically, he was pleased to have someone on his side.

"Zri, you've been watching Earth science fiction?" M said a little shocked.

"Hey, you are not my only source for goods from Earth."

"I realize that, but what I'm wondering what is your favorite production is?" she teased back.

"Another day my friend, I will tell you on another day." He smiled and sat back down after refilling everyone's glasses, legs dangling over the arm of the chair.

M picked up the story giving Brzko time to catch up with the espidrun, "We never had a chance to decide what to do with Ciic. We were awakened by an intruder a few hours later. A Viiv had used a black market code jammer, probably purchased on the Black Sea Planet, to get through our security system. They jam the signals just long enough to transport through a system, but it immediately triggers the security alarms. So within seconds Zri and his team were there."

She paused to see if he wanted to finish the story. "When we arrived we found the Viiv holding Ciic, who still looked like a small human, by the neck. She was amazingly calm, just patiently waiting to see what would happen. She was intelligent enough to know that if she struggled, it would have made rescue that much more difficult. There was a brief dialogue, I demanded that he release the child, he demanded his family had a right to the throne on Suus. He would not succumb, there was an opportunity to neutralize him without harming Ciic and he was taken out. The team made sure there were no other breaches, updated the security system firmware so that style of jammer would never work again and prepared to leave. M and Brzko explained who Ciic was and why the Viiv wanted to kill her. I offered to take her and hide her until her ascent to the throne. And that's it. She was on Gaznzul for less than 200 rotations before she shed the human cloak and emerged as a mature Suus. She returned home, took the throne, and married Muum."

"No wonder she feels indebted to you three, without you she would have never lived long enough to take the throne." Nalau said.

Without meaning to, the three of them answered at the same time, "It's what we do."

This made everyone laugh. When the laughter subsided Bartala spoke up. "What's for dinner? I'm hungry." This created another round of laughter.

TOUCHDOWN ON TRELLA

The next morning, the surface sans did not divulge anything concerning. The Gaznzulian ship touched down effortlessly in the field they had surveyed the day before. By the time the Muse of Mischief got to the community room Lelelu, Emperor Bartala, and Empress Nalau were standing in a group in front of the observation window. They were so interested in the view that they didn't hear her come in. She just couldn't resist - with a thought she placed herself outside the window, looking back at them and started waving.

Their shock only lasted for few seconds, but it was priceless. She came back inside.

"Soooo, have you seen anything interesting yet?" she asked from behind her friends.

"You are truly mischievous!" Emperor Bartala announced, laughing.

"Well d'uh!!!!" she exclaimed. "I am the Muse of Mischief. Jeez, I thought you got that by now. Are you ready to go meet Ferocity and do some exploring?"

"Yes!" Bartala said.

"Do we need to bring anything with us?" Nalau asked.

"I don't think so Nalau, I don't expect to be gone for very long on this first trip. Two of your palace guards and at least one of Zri's crew will be with you two at all times, just in case any issues should arise. And remember, those arm consoles can return you to this ship instantly. We'll be exiting through the door in the cargo hold area, let's go."

Lelelu caught up with M as she walked toward the cargo hold, "Are Zri and Agent Brzko already out exploring?"

"Yes, surprisingly they didn't wait for the ship to land. Zri let ShyUst handle the landing. Brzko wanted a chance to speak with Ferocity before we all arrive."

As the group walked down the ramp, two palace guards and one of Zri's crew followed them. Zri and Brzko were standing a short distance from the ramp. "Where's Ferocity?" M asked.

Neither of them answered, they just looked up. Everyone followed the direction of their gaze. Ferocity was flying far above their heads. He was beautiful from this angle. His long jagged wings stretched wide and his forked tail extending out behind him.

Brzko projected his thoughts to Ferocity, "*The others have arrived, please come down.*" He could feel Ferocity's affirmation. He immediately began to descend, landing a few steps behind Brzko. He folded his wings and stepped forward, Brzko began the introductions. Beyond hello, no one spoke.

"Bartala are you actually speechless?" M asked. "I have never known you to be at a loss for words!"

He managed to pull his gaze from Ferocity and look at M. "Yes, I think I am speechless. I have so many questions but finding out that the mythical Dragon is real? I don't know what to say."

254

"No need to say anything, we're here to explore and Ferocity is one of us. We'll all get to know him in time." She could feel Ferocity's gratitude for taking the group's focus from him. "So what do you guys want to see first?"

"Pink River!" Bartala and Nalau said in unison, and then looked at each other and laughed.

The group took off in the direction of the Pink River. They walked quietly for a while, taking in the perfection of the grassy field and impending forest.

Bartala broke the silence, "I noticed you don't wear your striped stockings on Trella, is this your explorer outfit?"

His attempt to catch her off guard did not work. She was ready for this, knew it was coming. "Yes, actually. Pants and boots will make it much easier for me to throw your ugly butt into the Pink River today. Do you remember the last time we were on Trella?"

"Oh no! We were just children then, you wouldn't dare!"

"I wouldn't trust her if I were you Bartala. She's been known to toss more than one friend into the rivers on Trella." Brzko teased with Ferocity walking along beside him.

M paused, and turned to look at Bartala and Nalau. They were of course stunning in their own exploration garb. Nalau was in ankle length pants that were a nice shade of beige and a white blouse. Bartala was almost identical except he was wearing long shorts. "No, I probably wouldn't. But only because it would mess up that Londo hair of yours!"

Nalau covered her mouth, trying to stifle a laugh. It didn't work, she let it out. "Oh Bartala, the image of you dripping wet with that hair is quite hilarious!"

Her comment left him quiet, they continued on. At the edge of the field they approached a thick forest. One of

Bartala's guards felt the need to take the lead. The forest here is made up of incredibly tall trees that look like pine trees, they have segmented branches that are covered in needles. Unlike the conifers of Earth, the needles on these trees move with the breeze. They make a slight rustling noise as they move. The forest floor is covered with small clusters of wildflowers in every color. Even though the forest seems thick, it is not dark, not the least bit intimidating.

A short distance down the trail, Nalau stopped to survey her surroundings, "Ploosnar is the most beautiful place I've seen but this, this is absolutely stunning. It's so perfect that it doesn't look real." She looked in each direction, absorbing the beauty. The others, except for the guards, did the same, silently. After a few minutes they moved on. After ten minutes or so, they were able to see a clearing up ahead, at the edge of the forest.

The forest gives way to a small grassy area, which gives way to sandy shores. The sand is well compacted rather than being the soft kind that swallows shoes. There is a gentle slope leading from the edge of the grass to the water. The river is about four meters across with some current to it, but not so much as to make it look dangerous. The water isn't just tinted pink - it is literally the color of cotton candy.

"Whoa! I didn't expect the color to be this bold. I thought it might be tinted pink. Can I touch it?" Lelelu asked.

"I guess so. I did when I was young and was not hurt. Ferocity, you've been living here for a long time, do you know if we would find any of the waters on Trella dangerous?" M asked.

Ferocity was standing next to Brzko, not quite as detached as the guards, but certainly not comfortable yet with socializing. "I have not encountered anything indigenous to this planet that would harm you."

Lelelu walked to the edge of the stream, knelt down cupping her hands, and scooped up some water. It was still pink in her bright blue hands. She was in awe, scooping up several more handfuls, taking in the amazing color.

Bartala and Nalau were pretty much speechless. Bartala knelt next to Lelelu and joined her in the closer inspection of the water. Nalau began walking upstream, at the water's edge. She passed a large tree with smooth bark and deeply lobed leaves on the river bank. The trunk curved so that all of the branches lean out over the water's surface. She paused when she got to the tree and looked out over the water. Something piqued her interest.

"Come and look at this."

When they were standing alongside her she pointed to the opposite side of the river, "Look at that stream over there, flowing into the river, it's bright blue and where the waters mix its lavender for just a bit before becoming pink."

"I see, it's beautiful isn't it. It's like a fairytale." M said.

"It's even more beautiful than I remember," Brzko said to M. He put his lips close to her ear and so that only she could hear, "So why does it feel creepy now?"

M didn't say a word. She just turned to him and expressed agreement with her mind.

Nalau was silent, just taking it in. Bartala and Lelelu had come to look at the lavender water. As usual, Bartala broke the silence, "What is the wildlife like? I seem to remember some birds when I was here before."

"Yes, sure. There are birds. I don't remember paying much attention to them when I was young. I've also seen fish, frogs, and lizards. But I don't remember any mammals." M gave them a little more time to soak up the beauty of the Pink River and then made a suggestion. "If you're up for more exploring we could walk downriver for a while. The banks are easy to navigate."

They continued on, strolling downriver alongside the Pink River. After a while they came to a wide open area, their path was impeded by another river that flows into the Pink River. This one is green, and about the same size the Pink River. They all went down to the very tip of the bank where the rivers converge. Although neither river seems to qualify as having rapids, the sound of the confluence is loud. Bartala dropped down and just sat, it was so sudden that they were all startled.

"Darling, are you ok, what is wrong?" Nalau asked kneeling next to him.

"Nothing is wrong my love, nothing. I just, I have never seen such beauty. This is amazing, and the sound...." he trailed off and looked back at the water. Nalau sat down next to him, they sat arm in arm, absorbing the beauty of the rivers.

M looked at Brzko and smiled, they were both entertained to see Bartala drop his gruff, sarcastic exterior and just allow himself to exist in a beautiful moment. They stepped back to give them some time alone.

"We should have brought lunch." Lelelu said to M. "This place is perfect for a picnic. We might be able to sneak back to the ship before they even notice."

M turned to Brzko and Ferocity, "How about you two, are you interested in lunch?"

"Maybe later." Brzko said. "Zri and I would like to take the hive drones for a spin. Zri, if you are ready we can return to your ship and start mapping."

"Yes. I will meet you there." Zri pressed the button on his armband that took him back to his ship.

Brzko turned to M, "Enjoy the picnic, call if you need anything." He kissed her cheek. He reached for Ferocity with his mind, "*Please meet me and Zri at the ship. It will take us a few minutes to unpack the drones.*"

He immediately took flight.

Brzko also left.

"Looks like it just us Lelelu. Are you ready?" M said. She looked for their Gaznzulian guard to see if he was near, and of course he was, he nodded to her, showing that he understood the situation precisely. M and Lelelu were going to disappear for a moment and he and the other guards were to stay put with the Emperor and Empress.

M waited for Lelelu to activate her transporter before she left. It only took a few minutes to load some fruit, nuts, and a few other snacks into a large bag. Lelelu went to a storage bin and took out a large tablecloth.

"We can use this to sit on. Are you ready?"

"Yep." M took her arm and they were back on the river bank. The Gaznzulian transporter could not return her to the riverbank.

Bartala and Nalau hadn't even noticed that they were gone. M and Lelelu laid out the picnic, once it was ready M called to them. "Hey you two lovebirds, want some lunch?"

~~~

The Muse of Mischief was in desperate need of a shower. After two days of casual walks her body craved some exertion. While Agent Brzko was out with Ferocity, she had the perfect chance for some sparing with Zri.

"This reminded me of old times Zri, back on Gaznzul when we were both young and invincible."

"Speak for yourself M, I still am." Zri teased, nudging her with his shoulder and handing her a towel. "And you're a little more unpredictable now, a better opponent. I like that."

"Well I've accumulated some experience over the years." She said dabbing her sweaty face with the towel. "Thank you for this trip Zri, it's really meant a lot to our friends and I have seriously enjoyed seeing the real you. The one I got to know long ago. You don't often let your guard down."

"No, I can't. My work is serious, as you know for yourself, being responsible for the safety of others requires a serious commitment. But I have enjoyed this time with you and your friends, our friends. And if we hadn't come Brzko may have never reunited with Ferocity. A Dragon? I didn't believe they were real. Hmmmm this is going to add an interesting dynamic to your work."

"Hell yeah it is. How many crime fighting, planet hopping, time traveling, superheroes do you know that have a Dragon?"

"Just as feisty as the day I saved you from the Haplogawa! Go take a shower, you stink." Zri said shoving her toward the door.

By the time M got out of the shower, Brzko had returned. He was sitting at the small table in their room, waiting for her.

"What's wrong Brzko?"

"There's nothing wrong, what makes you think that?"

"Because you have that I have to tell M something she's not going to like look, and I can feel it."

"I can't hide anything from you, can I?" She didn't respond, just waited for him to continue. "I'm going to Dragona tomorrow to complete the bonding."

"And you thought that would upset me? C'mon now, you know me better than that. I think it would be foolish not to complete the bonding, and it's something you have to do alone."

"You're right, and I knew you wouldn't be upset. I guess I'm just a little apprehensive about being away from the group. This has been a great trip but I feel responsible for our friends. I don't want them to feel abandoned."

"This has been a great trip, hasn't it? Don't worry about us; you know I can take care of me and the others. But I also have Zri and his team AND palace guards. We're good."

"You're right, there's no reason to worry."

"How long will you be gone?"

"A few hours, we'll return before nightfall."

"So has Ferocity answered all of your questions? Are you completely convinced that there is nothing being hidden from you, everything is as it seems? How will you get to Dragona without knowing its actual location?"

"Ferocity's ship is large enough for both of us. Zri and I toured the ship and Zri ran some scans to confirm that it is in good shape with adequate technology. The only thing I can't figure out is where he will live. He'd be difficult to hide on Earth, but I need him close if he's going to be helpful."

"Good. I'm glad you had Zri check out his ship. I see two choices for Ferocity- Ploosnar under Bartala's protection or the

Planet of Portals under Lelelu's protection. Because Bartala reigns over the entire planet, I think that is the safer choice."

"You're right M. Do you think he'll approve?"

"Yep. Once we ask, I don't think he'd let you change your mind. I suspect he'll want Ferocity to live at the Palace. It's the best way to ensure his safety. Will Ferocity be OK with that?"

"I'm sure he will, as long as his existence can stay confidential from the general population."

"That shouldn't be a problem, his palace is huge. We can go talk to him after you tell me about the new drones."

"Oh M! They are kick ass! So they start out larger than what we have now, but then they divide into individuals and cover exponentially more terrain. Traveling as one unit is more efficient so they have a broader range. When they detach they look like a swarm of huge bees. The controls are pretty much the same. I've already asked Zri for a set."

"A set, as in one hive drone that breaks up into a set of small drones or a set as in one hive drone for me and one for you?" M asked with her hands on her hips, ready to scold him.

"Really? A set as in one for you one for me of course. They will be waiting for us when we get home."

"Great! I can't wait to take them out for a spin! They sound like a great addition to our inventory. Are you ready to talk to Bartala?"

"Yep, let's go find him before he breaks out the espidrun."

~~~

"Tomorrow is scheduled to be our final day on the fairytale planet of Trella. But... I won't be here in the morning. Ferocity and I are going to Dragona to complete the bonding." Agent Brzko paused, waiting for their reactions.

"Ahhhh this is why you have asked if he could live on Ploosnar. I thought that might be the case. Congratulations!" Emperor Bartala lifted his glass toward Brzko and Ferocity.

Everyone joined him. Ferocity was seated on a tall stool near Brzko, this was his first attendance at a social gathering inside Zri's ship and he looked uncomfortable. With his long snout and protruding horns it was difficult to say what made him look uncomfortable, maybe it was just that his discomfort could be sensed.

"Don't worry Ferocity; they aren't a bad bunch of beings. They just take a little getting used to." Zri assured him taking his usual seat and dangling his legs over the side of the chair.

Ferocity only nodded in acknowledgement. He would need time to get used to the odd bunch.

"We will leave Trella in the morning and return by midday. We will return in time to leave Trella tomorrow night as scheduled."

"Will you go alone?" Lelelu seemed slightly alarmed.

"Yes." Brzko answered, he looked to Ferocity, waiting for him to offer more of an explanation.

"Many generations in the past Dragona was invaded and Dragons were enslaved. Dragons serve with honor but we do not accept dominance. The attempt almost killed us off, but our ancestors finally won our freedom and killed of the enslavers. Since that time we have kept the location of Dragona to ourselves. Only a Dragon ship can enter Dragona space and the only outsiders that may travel there are those to be bonded." Everyone was silent, contemplating what Ferocity had just shared.

"It saddens me to know that the Muse of Mischief will not attend this momentous event with you Brzko, but we wish you the best." Bartala stood and lifted his glass, the group followed his example. "To Ferocity, welcome to... us!"

Brzko could feel Ferocity's discomfort at being the center of attention; he sat down and redirected everyone. "Who is telling tonight's story? It's time for the telling" Captain Walker." He said mimicking a line in a Mad Max movie.

The Muse of Mischief could not hold her laughter; she was in mid sip of espidrun and spit it across the room, some of it landed on Zri.

"Oh! Thank you M but I already bathed today!" he said trying to sound disgusted. This got the whole group laughing.

"Wait who is Captain Walker?" Lelelu asked.

"He's a character in an apocalyptic Earth movie, Mad Max I think." M said.

"It sounds, well, not good. I don't see how apocalyptic themes would be entertainment, but Earth is odd. How about a happy story? I'd like to know how Bartala and Nalau met." She looked across the room at them, waiting for a response.

"Shall we tell them how we met my darling?"

"Yes, of course. You begin and I'll correct you along the way." she teased.

"Oh I see M really is rubbing off on you! Next you will be reminding me that you are female, not feeble." he said refilling their glasses and passing the bottle to M on his left. "I had seen Nalau several times before I actually met her. Her father was a liaison to my father; he represented the roinad shipping pilots. They frequently met at the palace and Nalau would sometimes accompany him. I never took an interest in the roinad empire; I knew I would have to run it one day, but I didn't see any reason to give up my freedom before I had to. So I never volunteered to attend any meetings."

"And you were having too much fun with me." M said.

"That is true my friend. I remember the day I fell in love with Nalau, it was the first time she spoke to me."

"What? I didn't know you felt that way. You came off as cold and unreachable the first time we spoke."

"Mmmm of course my darling. I was the Emperor's son, I had to play hard to get." Bartala chuckled and patted her hand. "She had left the meeting in my father's sitting room to find the restroom, but she got lost on the way back. I came upon her gazing at the statues of my ancestors. She was stunning - a long pink gown with a tight waist and billowing skirts, her long dark hair was perfectly straight and smooth hanging almost down to her waist. It was such a contrast to the pink of her gown. I made a sound so that she would hear me. I did not want to startle her; she turned toward me and said *Good afternoon, would you think me rude if I asked you who this statue represented?*"

"This was in the creepy hallway?" Lelelu asked "You were in the creepy hallway?"

All three of the ladies laughed out loud. Nalau could not answer. She only nodded her head to confirm that it was indeed the creepy hallway.

"Creepy hallway? You three call the hallway with statues of my ancestors the creepy hallway? I am insulted."

"No you're not." M said. "I can see you attempting to hide a smile."

He laughed, "You are right I understand why it may seem creepy, the statues are very lifelike. The statue Nalau asked about is a representation of my grandmother, my mother's mother."

"The dress she is wearing was unlike anything I had seen before." Nalau explained. "It had a magnificent high collar and lace sleeves."

"I tortured her by escorting her down the hallway and back, my hand on her arm, naming all of the statues. I was really just trying to find any excuse I could to prolong our conversation. I knew she was lost, she was captive."

"Oh you are terrible, keeping poor defenseless me against my will." she teased.

"Mmmm yes, against your will. I think you were quite charmed that day. Perhaps it was the dress I had made for you. After that day you never let your father never come to the palace alone."

"You had a dress made for her? That's intriguing." Brzko said, standing to retrieve the espidrun bottle.

"Yes he did! My darling Bartala contacted the original designer that had made his grandmother's dress and asked him to make an identical one for me. Even though he was retired, he was kind enough to make the dress for me." Nalau was beaming.

"It is difficult to say no to the Emperor's son, and... he was well compensated for taking a break from his retirement."

"So that was it for you two? You've been together ever since?" Lelelu asked.

"Yes." they said in unison.

Bartala continued, "The joining ceremony was really just a formality, we knew we would always be together."

"So if Nalau had not gotten turned around in the palace, you may never have ended up together." Lelelu summarized.

"And Nalau married into the position of Empress. But what about your parents, which one of them carried the line of the monarchy?"

"My mother, it was my father that married into the family."

"Interesting, so is it the first born child that ascends to the throne then, regardless of sex?" Zri asked.

"No. First we do not have a *throne*, as Emperor I consider myself to be a regular Ploosnarian. But I have the responsibility of running the roinad empire and that added responsibility entitles me to the amenities of the palace. The position passes to the most capable offspring, birth order and sex are not considered. However, Ploosnarians rarely produce more than one offspring."

"Do you know what you will name your son yet?" M asked.

Nalau's face changed as soon as she heard the question. "Well it won't be Haplogawa as you suggested."

"Darling I was kidding. It was a joke, really my love I would never... Thank you M. You've gotten me in trouble again."

Nalau nudged him with her shoulder, "You're not the only one that can joke my dear Bartala. I know you would not name our son after a giant lizard that almost ate you once."

The way she phrased it made them all laugh. Even Ferocity looked as though he enjoyed the jest.

THE BONDING

The Muse of Mischief and Agent Brzko were up well before first light the next morning. The anticipation of Brzko's trip to Dragona prevented either of them from sleeping well.

"Don't worry M, I'll be fine. Zri has given Ferocity's ship a once over and confirmed its flight worthy. If there is any trouble I can return here."

"I know, and we often travel alone. But it's usually to places that we've both been, so we could catch up with each other if we needed to. I completely understand why they keep their home secluded, but I don't like not knowing where Dragona is."

"But I don't need to know where it is to leave if I need to. Do you have any sense that Ferocity is not what he seems?"

"Nope, none at all. So you're right that there's no reason to worry. Maybe I'm just wishing I could watch this ceremony."

"I think you can, close your eyes."

M complied with his request. It was foggy at first but she began to see herself through Brzko's eyes. He was somehow sharing his image with her. She opened her eyes and the image was gone. She was once again looking at Brzko.

"I knew I could send you the *idea* of where I am, a single image, but we can actually just watch events unfold through the other's eyes? I didn't know we could do that."

"Neither did I. But remember Ferocity said that we were limiting ourselves with our expectations of ourselves. And we've been learning to use telepathy, so I figured we should be able to use visual telepathy too."

"Huh, I wonder how close we have to be, and I wonder if we can just tap into each other anytime we want to."

"We shall see my love, we shall see." Brzko held his beloved Muse of Mischief for a few minutes. "I'll be in contact when I can M, I love you."

"Bye Brzko, be careful."

Brzko left Zri's ship, arriving near Ferocity's ship. The doorway in the back was open and the ramp extended. Brzko stopped at the bottom of the ramp and paused, waiting for Ferocity to notice his arrival.

"Welcome Lord Brzko. Enter as you please."

"Thank you Ferocity."

The inside of Ferocity's ship is simple yet comfortable. There is a command center in the front, where the controls are located. A small room in the back provides for Ferocity's living quarters. It is really just a small room that provides him shelter from the elements. Dragons don't need much more than that.

"Are you ready to go?" Brzko asked, after he'd had a look around.

"Yes, preflight is done. You may sit here." Ferocity motioned to a high backed chair, in front of the consoles, facing the front window. Next to it was high stool. Brzko took his seat and looked at the stool.

"I guess wings get in the way with chairs."

"As does a tail Lord Brzko, are you ready to depart?"

"Yes, how long will it take to get to Dragona?"

"Less than an Earth hour."

Brzko could feel the ship ascend, within seconds they were well beyond the atmosphere, already in space. He reached out to M. *"Can you feel me M?"*

She responded immediately, *"Yes, wow. You're already beyond the atmosphere, not wasting any time I see."*

Brzko was relieved to know that she was still able to *hear* him.

"Initiating jump drive." As Ferocity made this statement a safety belt emerged from the edges of Brzko's seat and connected in the center of his lap. While he appreciated the safety aspect of the belt, the automation of the action was uncomfortable. He wondered what else was automated on a sentient ship.

"Jump drive? I thought that was only theory, Dragons actually possess the technology?"

"Yes. We must be able to quickly move throughout the Universe. It is the only way we can keep up with our bonds."

The ship had a slight vibration, the view out the windows was as though they were racing through a star filled tunnel; occasionally the hint of other colors was visible. After only a few minutes the ship seemed to come to almost a dead stop. It hadn't stopped, it just seemed that way when it slowed down after traveling at jump speed. They had arrived.

Brzko was so taken with what he saw out the window that he didn't realize the safety belt had automatically withdrawn. He was looking at a huge red and black planet. He reached for M.

"Yes, Brzko, I can see it. Wow!"

"Ferocity, this is beautiful, it's so vibrant."

"Yes. Dragona is like no other place. We will maintain our orbit until we are summoned."

"What do I need to do to prepare for the ceremony Ferocity?"

"No preparation is needed. We will land and be escorted to the great hall, an oath will be read. If you choose to do so, you will affirm the oath. After that I am bonded to you."

"Ferocity, before I can affirm anything, I need to know that you take this action freely. That it is entirely of your free will that you will be bonded to me."

To Brzko's surprise, Ferocity knelt in front of him and bowed his head. "Lord Brzko, it will be an honor to be bonded to you. By my free will I accept this bond." An inconsistent ticking sound began coming from the main control panel. Ferocity stood and stepped back, "We have been summoned."

"Is that sound an alert that you have received a message, or is that the actual message."

"It is the message. Dragons use an ancient language for all off planet communications. If we are overheard it only sounds like space static to other listeners. Please take your seat."

The both took their seats, the ship began to descend. As they dropped through the atmosphere Brzko got a good look at Dragona. It was likely to be the only time he saw Ferocity's home. They dropped out of space over what appeared to be a bright red sea. The water on Dragona is amazingly vibrant, as land came into view he could see huge waves crashing against a black rocky coastline.

"*M?*"

"*Speechless, Brzko. Wow.*"

The land they flew over was made up of huge black boulders, a few small red streams cut through them, leading to the larger body of water they had first flown over. Up ahead Brzko could see a huge structure. It looked like a big, black castle. There is a large raised platform on what looks like an island, large enough to land the ship. A raised walkway leads over the water from there to the great castle.

Ferocity sat the ship down with the rear entrance facing the castle and opened the door and extended the ramp. "You will follow me into the great hall, when we emerge it is I who will follow you, until the end." Ferocity headed down the ramp and Brzko fell in step behind him.

The smell was amazing. Dragona has a strong ocean like smell, the smell of saltwater. As they neared the raised walkway Brzko realized the edges, on both sides, were lined with Dragons. They were so still that he first assumed they were part of the stone. Ferocity stopped before entering the walkway, he extended his wings, leaned forward, and roared. It was the battle cry of a Dragon, a narrow stream of bright red fire shot from Ferocity, it only lasted a second. He stood and began walking again.

As they progressed down the walkway each Dragon they passed took flight and began circling above them. Their wings were creating a strong wind from all directions at once. Brzko's long coat fluttered out behind him. He removed his derby and carried it. By the time they were halfway down the walkway there were well over a hundred dragons in flight. The sky had turned dark because the light was blocked by their vast wings.

"*M?*"

"*Uh-huh, still with you.*"

Ferocity stopped at the door, he raised both of his hands, made fists and banged one fist on each door. They opened. He stepped through the doorway and stopped. The doors closed. They were in a huge stone room, the ceiling so high that it couldn't be seen. The walls were lined with a single file line of Dragons; each wore a medallion on red chord. Above each was a sconce with a bright red flame. The Dragon in front of them was on a stone platform holding a scepter topped with a glowing red orb. Once the doors were closed they walked to the center of the room and stopped.

The Dragons all began ticking, speaking a language that Brzko could not understand. It became very loud. The scepter was raised and gently brought to the floor. There was instant silence.

"As we have for millennia, Dragons bond to those that are worthy, those that are a positive force. Before us stands Ferocity, he comes here to complete his bonding to such a being. Ferocity, present the Bond." The Dragon again raised the scepter and brought it to the floor.

Ferocity turned toward Agent Brzko, standing to his right, a half step behind him. "I present Agent Brzko, a being of unknown origins. He is a being of light, a representation of that which is good. He is a protector of those that cannot protect themselves. I willingly accept the bond."

"Agent Brzko, you have been found worthy of a bond, if you are to accept Ferocity as your bonded Dragon for all of time, knowing that only death can break this bond, you will step forward and kneel before the Great Assembly."

Brzko stepped forward and knelt, lowering his head. Ferocity knelt beside him. The scepter was extended toward them, a bolt of red light jumped from the scepter. It split and completely enclosed Brzko and Ferocity. Visions began to appear in Brzko's mind, he was seeing through Ferocity's eyes, seeing his life up to this point. Just when he thought he could take no more the vision ceased, the light was gone.

"Stand!" The Dragon commanded and they stood. "You are now Agent Brzko and his bonded Dragon Ferocity."

The Dragons began ticking again then all at once they ceased, and were no longer visible. At first Brzko thought they had disappeared, but then he realized they had probably changed their appearance to blend in. He knew it was time to leave so he began walking toward the door. His Dragon followed.

"*M?*"

"*OK, this time I really am speechless.*" Brzko had a huge smile as he opened the doors, placed his derby back on his head, and headed down the walkway. The Dragons were gone. Other than Ferocity, he would probably never to see another.

When they got to the ramp of Ferocity's ship Brzko turned to him, "Let's get back to Trella Ferocity. I want to see M."

"As you wish Lord Brzko."

The return trip to Trella was just as fast as the trip to Dragona. They traveled in silence most of the way, Brzko had been given a glimpse of Ferocity's life leading up to the present. He needed time to let it sink in, to absorb it. He wasn't willing to devalue it by commenting before he was ready.

"When we get there I'd like to land near Zri's ship. I'd like you to be with me on his ship when we return to Ploosnar; we can transport your ship in one of the cargo holds of the other Gaznzulian ships."

"As you wish Lord Brzko."

M was waiting on the ramp of Zri's ship when they landed. As usual, Brzko didn't wait for the door to open. He appeared next to M, took her in his arms, leaned her back, and kissed her.

The rest of the group was gathered at the top of the ramp to welcome them back. Empress Nalau turned to Emperor Bartala, "Why don't you ever kiss me like that?"

Bartala opened his mouth to respond, but couldn't think of anything to say. Luckily for him Ferocity arrived at the ramp and everyone's attention turned toward him.

M was of course the first to greet him. After that Zri approached him.

"Ferocity, I have some things for you. I want to make sure that you have a com link to us at all times. I know that one of our usual earcom links will not work for you, so I had this made." He had a small device, the size of a vitamin capsule, in his outstretched hand. "It's subcutaneous, similar to the one I wear. If you want to give it a try we can…"

Ferocity exposed his teeth and nodded his head a few times. "This pleases me Zri. I will try your device. Is it ready now?"

"Was that a Dragon smile Ferocity?" Brzko asked.

"Yes Lord Brzko. Zri has made your Dragon smile." He turned from looking at Brzko back to Zri, "You said things, plural."

Zri chuckled, "Yes I did. It seems you enjoy technology as much as Brzko. Here, wear this on your arm, I think it's large enough. It will provide you with the ability to transport to my ship. With your permission we can install a receiver on your ship as well, then you can transport between the two. Follow me, I'll show you how to use these, and a few other things I have for you. Brzko said you'd be returning to Ploosnar with us, we've prepared quarters for you." He turned and walked back into the cargo hold, Ferocity followed.

As they passed Bartala he called to them, "Hey don't take too long with your toys. The rest of us are ready for the last picnic on Trella, it's lunch time!"

Zri called back over his shoulder, "It's always lunch time for you Emperor!"

THE LAST PICNIC ON TRELLA

The group emerged from the forest, enjoying their final outing on Trella. They were all there, even Ferocity.

"This is stunning; the blue water is so bright!" Empress Nalau exclaimed as she approached the edge of the water.

The banks of the river were fairly flat so she was able to stand right at the edge. Emperor Bartala joined her.

"Hey Lelelu if you went swimming in here no one would see anything but your eyes!" he teased.

"You're just jealous because you have boring colorless skin." She fired back as they stood at the water's edge. Looking down at the water near her shoes she said, "I enjoy a good swim as much as any Trelod, but those little purple fish look carnivorous! You go first Bartala."

There was a school of small heavily finned fish swimming about near the surface. They were more fin than fish.

"Hmmm no. My hair would be ruined." Lelelu turned and looked at him, they laughed at the idea of Bartala's hair getting wet.

"Let's go eat." She said as they walked over to where the other's had gathered.

The group used the boulders near the river's edge as seats and settled in to chat and tell stories as they had during much of this trip.

"Break it out Lelelu. I know you brought a bottle of espidrun and disposable cups in your pack." Bartala teased.

"I guess I can't hide anything from you Bartala." she answered.

"Actually I was just hoping; I had no idea!"

They all laughed while Lelelu handed each of them a flat disc that popped up into a small glass, then she went back around and poured a little espidrun in each glass.

"Just a little though. We have a long walk back to the ship and I'm not carrying anyone, especially you Ferocity." She teased.

"You have nothing to fear Lelelu. Dragons do not feel the effects of alcohol." he said.

Bartala drew his breath in dramatically, "Oh that is awful! Always sober, I cannot imagine." he said shaking his head. He stood up and held his glass high, the others followed his example "To good friends, new and old, and the adventures we have had, may the memories last a lifetime. We did not solve the mystery of the blue crystals but we gained a new friend."

They all mimicked him and sipped their drinks before sitting back down.

"This really has been the most fun I have ever had." Nalau said. "But I look forward to returning to Ploosnar tomorrow. I am a little homesick."

"As am I my love, as am I." Bartala said.

There was a commotion at the edge of the clearing. The guards seemed to be engaging with someone, Bartala's guards immediately surrounded him and the Empress. Zri, M, and Brzko ran over to the commotion. Ferocity took flight to survey the surroundings from above. Zri arrived first. He had his back to them, facing two beings that were restrained by the Gaznzulians.

When M got close enough to see around Zri she stopped dead in her tracks. She grabbed Brzko's armed and looked at him to see if he saw what she did. They stood there for what seemed to be a long time. Lelelu came up behind them.

"They look just like you two. Do you know them?"

The male was tall and dark; he was built just like Agent Brzko. The female tall with long light brown hair, she looked fit but not threatening. She looked like the Muse of Mischief. The male leaned forward, clearly wanting to step toward them but prevented from doing so by the presence of the Gaznzulians.

"Please... We are not here to harm you. We have been searching for you Muse of Mischief and Agent Brzko. We can tell you about Clyrea X9, about what you are."

Zri turned and looked at the Muse of Mischief over his shoulder, the question in his eyes was clear, "*Were these strangers a threat to his oldest friend or did they really have information about her origins?*"

They all heard Ferocity's voice in their minds, "They are cloaked. They are not what they seem. You must escape now."

The Emperor's guards did not waste a second; they immediately activated the emergency transports on Bartala and Nalau's wristbands, and then their own.

M turned to Lelelu, "GO!" She complied, activating her own transporter.

Gaznzulians from the orbiting ships transported to the surface and surrounded the imposters.

M approached the imposters, "Who are you?"

The one that appeared female answered. "We are you from another time, from another dimension."

"Then why are you cloaked? I can tell that your appearance is false. Who are you and what do you want?"

"We want only to know you."

While M had their attention, Brzko spoke quietly to Zri and his team through his ear com. "Transport them to a cell on one of your ships."

Zri made no indication that he had heard Brzko; neither did the four Gaznzulians who surrounded the imposters. With perfect choreography the Gaznzulians made physical contact with the imposters, each grabbing the arm of an imposter at the same time they activated their transports.

The imposters realized they had been captured and shrieked, it was a horrid high pitched sound. In the last second they were visible, their shapes changed. They were bulky with elongated heads and large eyes, long appendages, covered in tentacles hung down from the front of their faces.

M and Brzko were left standing with Zri and two other Gaznzulians. Ferocity landed and joined them.

Zri turned to him, "Thank you Ferocity. Your quick action may have saved our friends. How did you know they were cloaked?"

"VReoria have a death smell. They are safely aboard your ship?"

"Yes, they are secure. Have you seen those beings before?"

"They are VReoria, they are the enslavers. If they cannot enslave a species they exterminate them."

"Why would they be trying to get to us?" M asked, really just thinking to herself. "Unless… could they be responsible for the demise of Clyrea X9?"

"Let's get out of here. There may be more of them." Zri said. "Everyone transport back to the ship now, I want to get off this planet."

Zri's ship was secured, the ramp was closed, and the observation window was covered. As he was heading for the command deck and remembered they had not yet installed the transporter on Ferocity's ship. "Brzko, can you take Ferocity to his ship? The transporter is not installed yet and I don't want to open the door."

Before Brzko could answer, Ferocity did. "There is no need, my ship is sentient. She will go where I tell her to." As if to prove his point his ship ascended, joining the other ships in orbit.

"ShyUst, get us out of here." Zri said on his way out of the cargo bay.

Lelelu, Bartala, and Nalau stayed out of the way in the common room. They knew they would be called upon if they were needed.

M, Brzko, and Ferocity joined Zri and his crew on the command deck.

"Why didn't we detect them before we saw them? Do they have a ship in orbit?" Zri was very agitated.

"We have not detected any ships, sir." ShyUst said.

To everyone's surprise Ferocity had the explanation, "They have the ability to transport great distances from their ships. Their ship is likely beyond sensor range."

Everyone turned and looked at him, they waited for more. "We thought we had exterminated the VReoria, they have not been seen for a very long time. They cannot be allowed to live, they will attempt to return to Dragona and exterminate us. And if they are after you Lord Brzko, they will not stop."

"How do we find their ship, what do we scan for?" ShyUst asked. "And how can we make sure they don't follow us."

"We wait."

"Wait? Really Ferocity? Wait for them to get close and then hope that we can escape them?" Brzko asked.

"No, we wait for the Dragons, they are coming. When they arrive we may leave without being followed."

"How long?" Zri asked.

"Minutes."

"ShyUst as soon as Ferocity gives the word depart. I'm going to go speak to our *guests* and…"

"They are dead."

This shocked everyone, they stared and Ferocity waiting for an explanation.

"VReoria will not be taken captive. By now they will have activated the death gland."

Zri disappeared, transporting to the bridge of the ship with the prisoners. He returned in less than a minute. "He's right, they're dead."

Ships began dropping out of jump all around them. Each time a ship drop out of jump there was a brief flash and the Gaznzulian scanner alerting them to the sudden appearance of an unexpected ship. There were already more than thirty of them, more were on the way.

"It is time for us to depart."

Zri turned toward ShyUst, "Alert the other ships we are leaving. Ferocity, is your ship secure?"

"Yes it is in the cargo hold as you instructed."

Zri took his place in the command chair, watching the data stream that reported their position. ShyUst took his position, standing behind his commander. Zri would not be relaxing anytime soon, not until he was assured that his passengers were safe.

M projected to Brzko and Ferocity as she headed to the lift, *"Zri has everything under control, let's go. We need to update the others."*

They followed her down to the common room to bring the others up to speed. The trip home would surely not be as jovial.

THE TRIP HOME

The attempted capture of the Muse of Mischief and Agent Brzko by the VReoria had surprised everyone. But they were prepared and had reacted properly, and everyone was fine. It certainly wasn't the first time M and Brzko found themselves in danger. Even Emperor Bartala and Empress Nalau seemed to be fine. They were happy to be heading home - they expected to arrive the next morning. The only one that wasn't OK was Zri.

Neither M nor Brzko could sleep knowing that Zri was probably still beating himself up for the encounter with the VReoria. They found him in the common room staring out the window.

"Did you manage to get any sleep?" Brzko asked as they entered the room.

"No, I didn't see the point in trying."

"Zri how long ago was it that the Brusher was hunting for me and Brzko?" M asked.

"It was a few days before we left for Trella."

"And in the last five years, how times has someone been chasing or stalking me or Brzko?"

"Uhhh, at least ten, maybe fifteen that I know of. Why?" He pulled his gaze from the window and looked at her. He didn't see what she was up to yet.

"So isn't it fair to say that this is all in a day's work, and you're really just upset because you think that you alone were responsible for everyone's safety on this trip. But everyone on this ship, maybe with the exception of Ferocity, knows what Brzko and I do, and knows that we are constantly faced with danger. And everyone here is smart enough to know that being with us, could put them near that danger. But they also know that being with us is one of the safest places to be. Get past this Zri, get past it and help us work on where we go from here. Don't let this ruin the fine memories we all have from this trip. This trip was like nothing we've done before, and I expect to do it again." Brzko touched her arm, concerned that she was pushing him too hard.

Zri was silent for what seemed like a long time, contemplating what his friend was telling him. "M, would you please do me a favor and stay out of my head. I really hate it when you do that, when you use logic to make me accept things I cannot change." He was softening.

"If we had not gone to Trella, Brzko would not have been reunited with Ferocity, true?"

"Yes." he affirmed.

"If we had not gone to Trella, Brzko and I may have encountered the VReoria while alone, or worse in a highly populated area without the ability to call upon Dragona to… shall we say neutralize them, true?"

"Yes." he affirmed.

"And you took the proper precautions, everyone was prepared, and handled the situation flawlessly, true?"

288

"Yes." he affirmed. She was breaking through.

"And if we had not gone to Trella, you would not have figured out that you have a taste for espidrun, nor would you have given yourself permission to relax and hang out with old friends and get to know new ones, true?"

"Yes." He affirmed, this time he smiled.

The Muse of Mischief took hold of Agent Brzko with one arm, and Zri the Gaznzulian Commander with the other, "Then let's go get a bottle of espidrun, and tonight we will be nothing more than old friends."

Afterward

I hope you've had as much fun as I have, but the story is far from over. The Muse of Mischief and Agent Brzko have much more work to do. What are they? And where are they from? Will they stay on Earth, or tire of its infantile nature?

You'll have to wait to find out, but not long. Volume two is well underway. To be notified of its release you can follow my Amazon page at:

amazon.com/author/catrinabriscoe

There, you will also find a few of my photography books, and even a children's book.

Thank you for joining M and Brzko on their amusing journey, led by the Universe's favorite **Superheroine**. She might be female, but she's certainly not feeble!

See you soon,

Catrina

THE MUSE OF MISCHIEF

The Muse of Mischief is a modern day superheroine. Hidden on Earth as a child to be raised by humans, she travels the Universe with her loyal companion Agent Brzko and a team of crime fighting aliens to vanquish the villains, all the while trying to find out just what she is and where she's from. She has superhuman strength and the ability to travel through space and time. As an energetic advocate for all beings, she has been serving the Universe since she was young. She may be female, but she's not feeble.

AGENT BRZKO

Agent Brzko is a superhero like no other. Equal to the Muse of Mischief in every way, he was also hidden on Earth to be raised by humans. He unexpectedly met the Muse of Mischief as an adolescent and they have been together ever since. He also has superhuman strength and the ability to travel through space and time, but he also has the ability to project calmness to those around him. After being recently bonded to a dragon, Brzko has learned that he has powers he previously didn't know about. He is determined, dynamic, and debonair.

EMPEROR BARTALA

Bartala is the Muse of Mischief's oldest friend and the Emperor of Ploosnar. They met by chance when they were young. As Emperor, his main responsibility is running the roinad empire of Ploosnar. He is a quick-witted jokester that can actually keep up with the Muse of Mischief's high jinks. Physically Ploosnarians look very much like humans but they all have bright blue eyes and three hearts. Bartala is kind and giving, often using to assets of Ploosnar to aid the Muse of Mischief and Agent Brzko in their endeavors. Sometimes, he even gets to tag along.

EMPRESS NALAU

Nalau is Emperor Bartala's wife. She is truly a beautiful creature inside and out, always convivial and selfless. Her role as Empress of Ploosnar is one of diplomatic generosity. Always handling herself with grace, she is truly a vision of feminine beauty devoted to her people.

LELELU

Lelelu is a Trelod, native to the Planet of Portals. Trelods have bright blue skin and no hair. They have fantastic memories, some even claim to be able to recount every moment of their lives. This exceptional memory makes her the perfect personal assistant to the Muse of Mischief and Agent Brzko. Lelelu is an amazing detective because she is objective, patient, and persistent.

ZRI

Zri is from Gaznzul. Gaznzulians are agamic beings. They are reflective and rarely show their true selves. To Humans they look Human, to Trelods they look Trelod. They provide a variety of security services throughout the Universe. Gaznzulians have the highest integrity and the best technology. The Muse of Mischief is one of the few to have seen a Gaznzulian without their reflection. Zri is tireless, loyal, and selfless.

FEROCITY

Ferocity is a Dragon bonded to Agent Brzko. He is a flying biped with golden eyes and telepathic abilities. All Dragons have the ability to breathe fire, but he can also breathe cold. His ship is sentient and has the ability to travel at jump speeds. When he's not on assignment with Agent Brzko he stays under the protection of Emperor Bartala on Ploosnar as he cannot live on Earth with Agent Brzko. Ferocity is a courageous member of the team.

GLOSSARY

Aberidus - a respiratory disease resulting from the inhalation of spores that reside in soil.

Bispork - a species of four-legged rideable beings with the ability to speak. They resemble small dinosaurs with humps; they run very fast and enjoy transporting riders. Because they can speak they are treated like beloved pets.

Bivoor - one of the three beings from Myaad, they are asexual. Bivoors are responsible for the administration work in their society. They look like all Myaads with pale skin, messy white hair and black eyes. They tend to be shorter and more petite than Dumeers and Rogsaars.

Black Sea Planet - a dangerous planet covered entirely in water. The native inhabitants are aquatic, but many nefarious beings now inhabit the planet on floating structures, making it dangerous.

Burdohnirc - aquatic creatures from Drolla O0. They are comprised of numerous small creatures that rummage and feed on their own, but they are connected and actually a single being. They are colorful with long flowing fins.

Cazoova - a planet of entertainment. Cazoovians are hoofed animals that race, similar to the horse races on Earth. The planet is ruled by a governing council that attempts to ensure the Cazoovians are not exploited.

Chyke 2C95 - a planet that is covered in active volcanoes. Because of the lava and the Haplogawas, the surface of the planet is uninhabitable. The occupants live in underground lava caves.

Ciic - the current leader of the planet Suus.

Clyrea X9 - possibly a planet where beings like the Muse of Mischief and Agent Brzko may have originated. The exact location of the planet is not known.

Drolla O0 - a planet where foods such as niptdyn is grown. They also produce products like espidrun. Markets and trading centers for everything they produce are located on Smd, one the planet's moons.

Dumeers - one of the three beings from Myaad, they are asexual. Dumeers are responsible for tangible operations (i.e. housing, food production, etc.) in their society. They look like all Myaads with pale skin, messy white hair and black eyes. They tend to be stocky and more muscular than Bivoors and Rogsaars.

Earth - an infantile planet where the Muse of Mischief and Agent Brzko were hidden as children. Although some Earthlings suspect that they are not alone in the Universe, Earthlings in general incorrectly think that they are the center of the Universe. The planet is not considered safe. There are numerous cultural problems such as famine, disease, violence, and oppression.

Espidrun - a liquor made from fermented niptdyn on Drolla O0. It is hot pink in color and lets off blue steam when it's poured. Espidrun is marketed in beautiful bottles made of heated titanium.

Foskpruchu - a planet in the Glion Galaxy where they speak in confusing parables and riddles.

G'ist - a Xinood. Like all Xinoods his skin and hair is as black as obsidian, his eyes are bright green. Except when angry, then they turn bright red. G'ist is in a relationship with the Rogsaar that was stranded on Xinood 5.

Gaznzul - a small planet with a population of agamic beings. Gaznzulians are intelligent and loyal, they have the utmost integrity. Their mastery of technological gadgets has helped them to become the most highly sought after security service providers in the Universe. They are reflective. To Ploosnarians they look Ploosnarian, to Sarfets they look Sarfet. Very few beings ever see a Gaznzulian without their reflection.

Glion Galaxy - a peaceful galaxy with many planets. One way to reach it is via the portals on the Planet of Portals.

Haplogawa - a very large bipedal lizard that inhabits the surface of Chyke C295. They have large mouths, sharp teeth, and eat anything they can get a hold of.

Kiik -the lead researcher on the planet Suus.

Kilome - a designer working at Schatorren Designs on Ploosnar. He his half Ploosnarian and half Sarfet. He is the Muse of Mischief's favorite fashion designer.

League of Mongers - a group of interplanetary exploiters, criminals.

Lecur - a small community east of the palace on Ploosnar. Previously roinad was processed here but recently it was used as a gathering place for the abandoned Rogsaars.

Leel - white flowers with nebulas at the center of each. From Suus, they grow on vines and have a pleasant smell.

Lusimis - a paste made from legumes. It's a delicacy on Ploosnar.

Mahb - the leader of Otherworld in ancient Ireland. She resides in Sidhe with other Irish Faeries but has the ability to travel between Earth and Otherworld. The extent of her power is unknown.

Muum - Ciic's husband.

Myaad - a planet with no surface water. There are three types of beings on Myaad, Bivoors, Dumeers, and Rogsaars. They are parthenogenetic breeders that use hives to incubate their young. Each type of being is physically identical to the others in their group. However, they are individuals due to independent thought and life experiences. Recently the disease aberidus decimated their population. All Myaads have pale skin, white hair and black eyes. Bivoors function as administrators; Dumeers function as operation specialists, and Rogsaars function as explorers.

Naan - the ruling family on the planet Suus.

Nekmid - a liquor that is colorless. It takes like spicy teriyaki sauce and is very potent. It is available throughout the Universe.

Niptdyn - a delicious fungus grown on Drolla O0, available in the markets on Smd. It is fermented to make the liquor espidrun.

Planet of Portals - a planet with small communities, each containing different types of portals. Some lead to random places; some lead to specific places. All portals are one way. The portals are often used by desperate beings or criminals. There are a few restricted portals that lead to different times. Trelods are the native species on the planet.

Ploosnar - a planet with three suns and the only planet where roinad is mined. Ploosnarians are humanoids that have three hearts and bright blue eyes. All citizens benefit from the roinad empire, they want for nothing. Because of the roinad all plant life on the planet is blue. There is virtually no crime here; Ploosnarians are honorable and hard working. Emperor Bartala is responsible for running the roinad empire.

Pragma - a cross between grass and fruit that looks like a long, slimy blade of grass. It is considered a delicacy on Ploosnar with both a sweet and savory flavor.

Prujelst - a small bird on the Planet of Portals. Where one is said to have *prujelst bumps* when cold or creeped out.

Rogsaar - one of the three beings from Myaad, they are asexual. Rogsaars are the explorers of Myaad; responsible for establishing trade partnerships for supplies and knowledge. When there was an outbreak of aberidus on Myaad they were all stranded on other planets in the Universe and left to survive on their own. They look like all Myaads with pale skin, messy white hair and black eyes. They are larger than Bivoors and strong, but not as muscular Dumeers.

Roinad - a regenerating element mined exclusively on Ploosnar. It's bright blue and used in everything from atmospheric filters to fabrics. The mining methods used are considered sustainable. All Ploosnarians receive a portion of the profits from roinad.

Sarfets - native to Drolla O0, they are empathic humanoids with angled noses and flared nostrils. Because Drolla O0 produces and markets many products, most Sarfets work as producers or traders.

Schatorren - a Ploosnarian fashion designer and tailor. He is the founder of Schatorren Designs, the favorite designer of Empress Nalau.

Scorchbrooke, Oregon - established around 1857, it is now a ghost town between Pendleton and Hardman, Oregon. Rogsaar was stranded here when there was an outbreak of aberidus on Myaad.

ShyUst - a Gaznzulian, he is second in command to Zri.

Smd - a moon of Drolla O0, is home to many trading posts and retail markets.

Suus - a planet of advanced beings. The Suus are tall with green skin, four arms, and tails. They do not have mouths. They communicate through telepathy and feed on vapors. They have devoted themselves to cataloging everything they can into a massive database. They also frequently assist in benevolent efforts throughout the Universe.

Sw'dell - a sea dwelling creature that looks like a hermit crab. Their shells look as though they are made of glass.

Trelods - are native to the Planet of Portals. They have bright blue skin, no hair and frequently integrate into other cultures. They have phenomenal memories, some claim to be able to remember every moment of their lives. Lelelu is a Trelod.

Unilond - a city on the Planet of Portals. All of the portals here lead to places in the Glion Galaxy. This is where Agent Brzko first interviewed Lelelu.

Vassbr - a waterfront city on the Planet of Portals. All of the portals here lead to random places.

Viiv - a family on Suus that feels they are entitled to rule. They attempted to assassinate Ciic before she could ascend to the throne.

VReoria - a species that attempts to enslave others, any species they cannot enslave they attempt to exterminate. Long ago they enslaved Dragona, but were eventually overthrown and thought to have been exterminated.

Wrexna - a planet with great technology and bad food.

Xinood 5 - a planet with humanoids. There is also a Xinood 1, 2, 3, and 4. But only 4 and 5 are inhabited. Xinoods are as black as obsidian with bright green eyes. Their eyes turn blazing red with they are angered. They are a highly intellectual species that values education and relies on trading for income. G'ist is a Xinood.

www.ingramcontent.com/pod-product-compliance
Lightning Source LLC
Chambersburg PA
CBHW061541170626
46811CB00001B/41